Titles by Kathy Hurley

Morrigan's Exile

Wyld Harmony Series

Song of Mirth and Mayhem

SONG

OF

MIRTH

AND

MAYHEM

KATHY HURLEY

RavenSidhe Publishing LLC
Meridian, Idaho

Published by RavenSidhe Publishing, LLC
Meridian, ID

Publisher's Cataloging-in-Publication Data:

Names: Hurley, Kathy A., author.
Title: Song of mirth and mayhem / Kathy A. Hurley.
Series: Wyld Harmony
Description: Meridian, ID: RavenSidhe Publishing, LLC, 2024.
Identifiers: LCCN: 2024922778 | ISBN: 978-0-9912113-8-8 (paperback) | 978-0-9912113-9-5 (ebook)
Subjects: LCSH Bards and bardism--Fiction. | Musicians--Fiction. | Elves--Fiction. | Fairies--Fiction. | Magic--Fiction. | Fantasy fiction. | BISAC FICTION / Fantasy / General | FICTION / Fantasy / Epic
Classification: LCC PS3608 .U75 S66 2024 | DDC 813.6--dc23

First printing: 2024
Printed in the United States of America
Copyright © 2024 by Kathy A Hurley
Interior Art and Cover Design by Kathy A Hurley
Editors: Val M Roberts, Alannah Keeton

Library of Congress Control Number: 2024922778

For Niall and all of my family on both sides of the Veil

Acknowledgments

The way this book came together was almost magical, but it would not have happened without the help of some amazing people. Thanks go to the Moxie Quartet both past and present, and the Boise Spec-Fic Writers' Group. Thanks also go to my family, for all your support in various capacities. Everyone who read, encouraged, suggested resources, or pointed out details that needed tweaking...all of you helped make the magic happen. And a nod to the Sidhe, whose influence runs through all of my work: I do not thank, but I nevertheless acknowledge the input. It was an illuminating journey, as always.

ONE

FIRESIDE TALES

The usually warm breeze from the south had grown chill, even for a night in the late autumn. It forced its way through the thin spots in Nymariel Morren's clothing, though she tried to ignore it and go on with the tale she'd begun by the caravan's small campfire. Her companions, merchants well-off enough to hire a bard to entertain in the evenings, shivered or pulled their cloaks closer in response, and a couple of the nearby horses snorted as though in protest.

Harvest this year had come late and sparse, but fortunately thus far most merchants were less affected than farmers. That didn't mean anyone's current employment would continue, however, so one had to make the most of it while it lasted.

Nym lightly plucked the strings of her battered old lute, using it as counterpoint to the cadence of her words. She wasn't highly skilled at this craft yet, but these merchants didn't seem to care. They hung on her words, one or two leaning forward eagerly. Or maybe they were just leaning closer to the fire. Either way,

Nym felt she'd caught their attention and now held it, drawing out the suspense of the tale just far enough, but not enough to frustrate her audience. That was how the last bard she'd heard in a larger town did it. It seemed to work well enough.

"Taking care not to dislodge himself from his hiding place, Pieter Woodcutter wiped the sweat from his eyes with his sleeve. Oh, why had he dared go closer to investigate the noise from the nearby grove? That was a foolish notion—one proven doubly foolish when he found the eyes of an angry tree spirit fixed on his. Of course he'd sprinted as fast as he could, away from the carnage. And of course, he had to hide. The tree spirit doubtless already blamed him for the destruction of the grove, and if they found him would take vengeance for a deed he hadn't done. Almost idly, he wondered who had.

"His legs trembled so much he feared he would fall, perched as he was on two narrow protrusions of stone in the inner walls of his own chimney. He could not hear anything but eerie silence. Anything could be waiting for him down below. Anything...or nothing."

Nym waited a moment, watching her audience. Their eyes were fixed on hers until one of the guards cleared his throat and made a show of looking around at the woods that surrounded the caravan. Doing his job, of course. Nym smiled.

"Pieter waited until he could wait no longer, then began to inch his way back down the chimney, toward the fireplace where he'd already laid the makings of tonight's fire. Perhaps none had seen him come in. Perhaps he'd emerge from the fireplace and all would be as quiet as it sounded, and he would be safe. It had all been nothing but a misunderstanding. *He* knew that he was not the one who had burned the tree spirit's grove. He was so careful; always so careful, and never took aught but deadfall or dead standing trees in the Murin Wood. But did the tree spirit know that he was innocent? Had they seen another man in the grove?"

One of the horses snorted again, which set some of Nym's audience to laughing, albeit a bit nervously, she thought.

"The woodcutter inched downward just a bit more, his foot stretching to reach the next protruding stone. It was then that he heard a sound, a harsh scraping, from directly below him. Frozen with terror, he peered downward. Then one more sound—the striking of a flint. He knew that sound, heard it every day, though usually the flint was in his own hand. From the firebox a spark flared to life, igniting the kindling that he'd trampled in his haste to climb into the chimney to hide."

Nym's fingers plucked at her lute strings with a musical *pop* here and there in counterpoint to the real popping and snapping from the caravan's campfire, doing her best to evoke the sense of danger from growing flames.

"Pieter's heart hammered in his chest, and his breath came in short gasps as he fought not to cough from the smoke that rose around him. Several wracking coughs escaped him anyway, despite his best efforts. Desperately, he hurried to climb the chimney, dragging himself ever upward on increasingly shaky limbs as the heat and flames rose beneath him. He had nearly given up hope of survival until his head popped out of the top, high up on the roof. Using all of his strength, the woodcutter managed to haul himself up and out over the lip of the chimney, his hands, face and clothes covered in black soot."

Someone from the audience gave an audible sigh of relief; Nym didn't see who.

"A desperate plan occurred to him, so outlandish that it might just work. The noise of the fire had likely obscured the noise of his climb, and if whoever was below indeed expected him to perish inside his own chimney, he would need to provide some sort of evidence of his demise. Before he could think too hard about what he was doing, he sucked air into his lungs, leaned back over the chimney and let loose several long, bloodcurdling screams, imagining himself burning alive the while. Then, casting about for something to use, his gaze fell on the thatch on the roof of his cottage. Stripping hastily out of his clothes, he rubbed as much soot upon himself as he possibly could, then stuffed the clothes full of straw from the thatch, until he had made a straw effigy of himself. This, he dumped back into the chimney, hoping and praying to his gods that the straw would catch and be engulfed in flames quickly."

"Did it work?" asked Deena, the wagoneer, her dark eyes flashing in the firelight. She seemed as eager as a child. Nym shot her a wide smile.

"Indeed, it should *not* have worked, for a straw man is, after all, only an effigy and not reality. But *someone* heard Pieter's prayer that night, and when whoever was waiting in his house by the fire saw the bundle of flaming cloth fall down into the fireplace, it was no straw figure they saw, but a man of flesh and blood, burning so bright and so hot that Pieter's enemy made haste to vacate the house before they themselves were set afire.

"Pieter himself remained on the roof, stark naked, for the balance of the night, huddled against the hot stones of the chimney for warmth, afraid to come down until daylight and his own extremity forced him to make his way off the roof as best he could. Fortunately, some vines that were growing on a trellis near the back side of the cottage gave him a ladder down to the ground, and he was able to escape the roof without injury. Venturing inside his house, he dressed, packed up his clothes and most essential belongings, and left that place as hastily as could be, eager to put as great a distance between himself and the tree spirit's grove as possible, lest his survival be discovered and his life be in danger again."

"But...did the tree spirit set the fire?" asked Dita, the caravan's cook. "I mean...that doesn't sound right. A tree spirit setting a *fire* for vengeance." She glanced toward her sister, Deena, and gave a sheepish but delighted grin. The women were twins—*double trouble*, the caravan master called them. But they were smart, competent, and very knowledgeable about their work. And they loved a good story, which Nym appreciated even more than their other qualifications. They'd been instrumental in recruiting her, after all.

"On his way out of the forest, the woodcutter had to pass near the tree spirit's grove—far closer than he would have liked," Nym said. "But he noticed something odd as he passed hurriedly by. A new tree that he had never seen before now stood near the road, and if one looked closely enough it seemed to have a face, that of a man frozen in anguish. It looked, Pieter thought, a little like one of his neighbors, a man whom he knew to be heedless of the spirits and hidden folk of the forest. At the tree's base were scattered some oddments—a flint and steel, a small hatchet, and a broken wreath of autumn leaves. Pieter eyed the items, took a shaky breath, and hastened away down the road as fast as his feet could carry him."

A pause, then laughter and a smattering of applause greeted Nym as she plucked the chords of a final ditty to end the tale, then put down her lute and reached for the bowl of food the cook dished up for her.

Nym lifted a hand to tuck a stray lock of autumn-leaf-red hair behind her ear, but stopped mid-motion and swept it over her shoulder instead. Everything had been going so well, there was no sense in calling attention to the fact that her ears were pointed, unlike the company she was currently keeping. Elves and humans had been mingling for centuries now, but even so, there was often a difference between what humans thought about elves in theory and what they thought when one group or the other was outnumbered.

Oh, there were plenty of both sorts in cities, sure, and a fair number of mixed-heritage folk as well, but out here with this caravan group, Nym was the sole representative of the elven species. Not that she had anything to fear from these folk, and they did actually know she was an elf; she hadn't been such a fool as to try to hide it altogether. But she saw no need to emphasize the difference, either.

People could often be odd about their perceptions of who was "us" and who was "them." And even back home in the mostly-elven village of Wimble where she was born, she was usually considered one of "them." Some of the more influential townsfolk muttered when they saw her busking for coin in the town square, armed with an old battered lute that an erstwhile teacher had gifted her before he left town to seek more lucrative environs. But it wasn't the busking that had caused all the talk and speculation. A bard could be respected. But an unacknowledged daughter might not be—not if one's peers saw something shameful in that lack.

Sighing, she tried to push the old hurt out of her mind and focus on what was right in front of her, here and now. Like the food. The stew was good and—more importantly—it was hot. It went a long way toward helping dispel the chill in the air, and by the time Nym had finished her meal and gratified the company's requests for a few simple tunes with voice and lute, she felt much warmer than she had earlier. This traveling life wasn't so bad, once one grew used to it.

When everyone retired for the night, she took her bedroll and made her bed near the fire between Dita and one of the guards—Massey, she thought his name was. The bedrolls surrounded the campfire like spokes around a hub. In larger caravans like this, two guards kept watch per shift. One couldn't be too careful nowadays, with rumors of war in the north and famine in the west to keep folk nervous and watchful.

Highwaymen also weren't unknown in this area of the human kingdom of Valterra, though they'd have to be especially bold or numerous to take on a caravan of this size. It was one reason Nym had chosen it as her means of transportation from the last small hamlet she'd been able to reach on foot to the larger city of Kalas, where the caravan was due in two days' time.

Just before she fell asleep, Nymariel breathed a short prayer to her people's gods, to watch over her mother. Not for the first time, she wondered whether she had done the right thing in leaving. But every time she went through the logic, she still found herself reaching the same conclusion. Back home, she was a burden to her mother, whose small income as a seamstress might just be enough for one but was nowhere near enough for two.

Nym's talents even when she reached adulthood had always run more to music and arts rather than the more practical things that might have helped earn a living. Her penchant for chatting up and begging lessons from every bard or musician who happened to pass through was well known and generally frowned upon. And her absence might help the snootier of her kinsmen to forget that her mother had had the temerity to give birth to a daughter whose father she refused to openly acknowledge. Without Nym's presence as a reminder, perhaps her mother could build herself a better life. Perhaps. And that was exactly the logic she'd used to try to convince her mother that her departure was for the best.

Nym still wasn't sure whether she'd actually been that convincing, but if she didn't start a new life for herself somewhere else, then she'd be forever trapped in the web of other people's judgment and perceptions. That somehow seemed worse than no life at all.

It was for the best; I know it was, Nym thought, letting her mind drift, reveling in the sound of autumn leaves rustling in the breeze, the scent of loam and moss from the forest around her, and the night music of crickets and distant owls calling to one another in the dark.

The sound of music woke Nym from an impossible dream filled with grand, opulent halls and dancing, laughing, beautiful people. She'd been lurking in a doorway, on the brink of discovering how to play the intoxicating music, of seeing who made it. But one step across the threshold and she jerked awake, trembling and disoriented.

Sparkling laughter echoed in her mind even as she sat up and blinked, allowing her eyes to adjust to the dim light from the low-burning campfire. It must be about the middle watch of the night, based on which guards' bedrolls were currently empty.

Then she heard it again—a faint and distant music, haunting and evocative. At first, she thought she must have a song from the dream stuck in her mind, repeating in an endless loop, as music was sometimes wont to do when the tune was catchy. But even as she decided that must be the source of what she heard, the tune changed to something unutterably lovely, poignant and lilting and almost sad. It called to her.

And it was real flute music, not the remnants of a

lovely dream. The tune beckoned from somewhere beyond the range of the campfire, out among the trees. *Fae music*, Nym realized suddenly, then wondered why that thought didn't frighten her. It should have, she knew. All her life she'd heard tales of the wylden, of what they did to errant stragglers in the deep woods, of comely young adults taken in the night, human children taken from cradles, all manner of dooms and harm done to the elf or human who failed to take proper precautions to ward off the *wyld*—the magic and enchantments fae used to trap the unwary.

She *should* be frightened. She couldn't just ignore all the cautions her mother had instilled into her while she was growing up; Nelise Morren was not one for telling idle tales—not like her daughter. But still...something about this music pulled at Nym in a way that nothing else ever had, and the urge to find out why was strong. Strong, yet not overwhelmingly so. Interesting. She could resist this if she wanted to.

Whoever was out there was crafting this music just for her. Nym could not have said how she knew, but she knew. They wanted something from her; they must. But what could that possibly be? No wylden would lure an elven woman to them for purposes of procreation, and no elven children were ever taken as changelings. The ongoing enmity between the fae and elven races on this continent was too great to allow such a thing. That left only two possibilities. One, that the unseen musician intended to lure her to her doom, so there would be one less elf in the world. Or two, that the wylden wanted something else from her. Something far out of the ordinary—something not covered in all the tales she'd heard.

Another look around the campfire showed Nym that none of her companions seemed to be hearing the music; all were asleep, with the exception of the two guards on duty. Nym could just make out the shapes of both guards, stationed on different sides of the camp. If the music had been audible to anyone else, there'd be more than one comely human stumbling off toward the woods right now. But the others slept on.

It was their peaceful faces that decided her. If this wylden was up to no good, then her resisting the lure was likely to only result in a tragedy for someone else. At any moment, the flautist could change their tune to lure a different victim, perhaps one of the innocent humans who'd listened so avidly to her tales by the fireside. But if she responded to the summons, then perhaps the wylden would focus solely on her and leave the humans alone, long enough for the caravan to reach the relative safety of the next village. The company would likely move on in the morning, regardless of whether Nym was there or not; they'd a schedule to keep. And that schedule, provided they did nothing else to tempt any wandering fae in these woods, would keep them safe. Probably, if fate were kind.

That left her with only one choice: get up, follow the music to its source, and find out what this unknown fae wanted with an aspiring elven bard with little to no means and no great talent.

TWO

A RISKY BARGAIN

Nym rose slowly, careful not to wake anyone sleeping next to her. She pulled on her cloak and boots; she'd slept in her clothing for added warmth, so there was little else to do except to strap on her hand crossbow and quiver of bolts, just in case she had either cause or opportunity to defend herself.

At the last moment and completely on impulse, she grabbed her lute and slung that over her shoulder as well; it wasn't any use at all in a fight, but she couldn't bear to just walk off and leave it behind; it was too dear and too irreplaceable to just abandon to the whims of fate. Taking anything else presented too much of a problem; if she paused to pack up any of her other belongings, she'd wake the others and they'd demand an explanation. And she dare not take too much time about complying with this strange musical summons, either; it wouldn't do to have the wylden become bored or impatient with her slowness to respond.

As she crept away from the fireside, she kept an eye out for the two guards. Both were alert, but currently faced outward toward the road and the forest, not inward toward the campfire. Nym used all her inborn talent for treading lightly to avoid making any noise that might alert them, and managed to sneak past the perimeter toward the western side of the campfire circle. When no calls of concern followed her, she knew she'd managed to slip out without notice.

Though perhaps I shouldn't be too pleased by that. She hesitated, suddenly uncertain.

The music changed again, and as she made her way toward the sound, Nym noticed a faint violet spark of light hovering about a foot above the ground in front of her. It bounced and flitted about in time to the music, which now sounded like a merry village dance tune. It evoked images of bonfires, harvest festivals and leafy wreaths hung on barn and house doors to signal hospitality available to errant travelers caught away from home during the nights of revelry that heralded the celebration of Wyldernight, or Soulhallow as the humans called it.

Fortunately, Nym's elven eyesight as well as the presence of the dancing mote of light helped her safely traverse the forest and avoid tripping over deadfall and tree roots. The night was dark otherwise—darker than typical, since tonight was the new moon. She couldn't tell how long it took to travel the distance between the caravan's small campfire and her unknown destination, but it felt as though she'd been walking for only a short while before she reached a small clearing that she was fairly sure hadn't been there when she and the others had made forays into the surrounding trees earlier to gather firewood.

There was another campfire here in the middle of the open space, blazing merrily enough that it should have been visible through the trees before she reached the clearing. But these flames glowed faintly violet, like the mote of light that had been her guide. A lone male figure sat next to the fire, and at her approach, he put down his flute and rose to greet her, nodding formally as though she were walking into his home or place of business rather than into his campsite in the middle of a hidden clearing in a forest that bordered human lands.

"I enjoyed your tale this evening," he said, smiling in a way that made Nym feel at once welcome and uncomfortable.

"You heard me? I had no idea you were listening," Nym said, carefully avoiding the forbidden words of thanks that everyone said were unsafe to offer the fae. For wylden he was. Nym could see the faint sharpness of his features in the firelight, the eyes of such a vivid hue that they reminded Nym of an impossibly blue lake she'd seen once in a painting at one of the more prosperous inns back in Wimble. His hair was the pale gold of wheat, and she noticed that his ear tips weren't pointed like her own, though that detail seemed less certain the longer she stared. Nym had the uncomfortable sense that his appearance was somehow less fixed, less...*permanent* than that of most beings— that it could change at whim. But he seemed solid enough as he smiled at her and turned away briefly to set a small copper kettle in the fire.

"I have been listening to your tales for many an

evening. They are all passable, as are your songs, however untutored they may be. All are worthy enough, and will be even better once improved upon with better tone and nuance. For instance, your tale tonight incorporated a delightful twist. It was clever of you to imply that the tree spirit only took vengeance on one who was actually guilty. It is almost as though you believe fae or elemental spirits have a sense of fair play." His voice startled her. It was resonant, magnetic, but with a hint of kindness she hadn't been expecting.

And had he reached through the flames to position the kettle, without being burned in the process? Nym blinked, unsure of what she'd seen. It was possible—even probable—that nothing she was seeing here was entirely real, except her host, who gestured to a nearby stump to indicate she should sit. He resumed his own seat and waited for her response, as though he had all the time in the world. Which perhaps he did. Still studying him, she took the seat he'd offered, calling to mind all that she'd read or heard about the fae. She would not address his comment about whether or not the wylden had a sense of fair play. Therein could lie a trap.

The fae, also known as wyldfolk, wylden, or wylderlost depending on which locale told the tales, were said to be nearly immortal, though it was possible to kill them. Elves were long-lived by any standards and usually outlived humans by several centuries, aging gracefully to upwards of a thousand years or more. But they were still mortal in the conventional sense of the word. Age caught up to them eventually. Fae, no matter the variety, seemed to have no readily determinate lifespan that anyone knew of. It was impossible for Nymariel to guess this one's age; he could be thirty, or three thousand.

"May I ask to whom I have the pleasure of speaking?" Nym gave him her most practiced smile and a respectful dip of the head, avoiding the subject of justice and fairness altogether.

"You may call me Erevan, if you must have a name. And you are Nymariel. Nym for short, to judge by the way your companions of the caravan refer to you. Be welcome at my fire."

"It is a pleasure to meet you, Erevan," Nym said carefully. Was that even his actual name? Probably not; no wylden would likely give her his true name, as it was said true names could give someone power over them. Erevan would be his use name, then. The name he used for random company, but not the name that truly defined him.

"Perhaps you will find it more of a pleasure when you hear my proposal. For that is why I have brought you here tonight; I have a proposal to offer you. A deal, of sorts. One that hopefully will profit and benefit us both." Erevan's smile flashed in his handsome face, and Nym found herself returning it before she thought.

She had to be more cautious. Handsome wylden were likely even more dangerous than those that were not. There was also the chance that this one was just taking whatever appearance she might find most pleasing, to lure her into dropping her guard.

"Is this form not to your liking? I can choose another, if you prefer," he said, as if he'd read her thought.

Oh, careful. Nym swallowed, mouth suddenly dry. She forced a smile again. "No, no, that form is fine. It will do well enough."

Erevan laughed. "Very well. Shall I tell you why you are here?" Without waiting for her to reply, he grinned at her in a way that made her toes curl and her heart begin to race, before launching into his *proposal.* "You are here because I need your help. You see, I too am a bard. My patrons, the King and Queen of Lyre, have an insatiable need for entertainment. Stories, songs, poetry. Those of us tasked with providing such entertainment are often hard-pressed to find anything new to offer. Those who are able to regale the court with new material are sure to rise quickly in the ranks. Clever bards have even managed to rise to the level of Counselor, on rare occasion. And I have need of such a trajectory and the influence it would bring."

Nym nodded, waiting, all her attention on this fae bard who seemed to have a knack for making a simple business proposal seem like a grand and epic tale.

Erevan continued. "You are a bard of no small talent. Even untaught as you are, your innate ability is formidable. You could even use your art to weave magic —magic such as has not been seen in the wider world in many a century. If you agree to travel the paths of men, elves, and whatever other races you may meet and gather their lore, music and poetry to bring back to me, I promise to become your mentor and muse. I will teach you how to wield the magic that is in your blood and to play *wyld* music that will entice and enchant your listeners. With this knowledge, you will never want for coin, sustenance and a roof over your head ever again. What say you to this?"

Nym regarded him, thinking. It sounded too good to be true, so of course it must be. "What is the catch?" she asked before she could stop the words from escaping. She hadn't meant to be so blunt, but then, she'd always tended toward bluntness, even when it cost her in some way. Why stop being true to herself now?

"You are forthright, and honest. I like that. The only *catch*, as you call it, is that you must never reveal the source of your skill to anyone. You must never tell anyone about me or about our bargain, unless I give you leave. And equally importantly, you must never perform more than a night or two in the same place at one visit, or your audience will become aware that they have been enchanted and will turn against you to try to recover that which they once gave so freely."

Nym stared into the flames, taking in all he'd said, but made no immediate reply. It was a lot to consider.

Erevan continued, "You will meet me in a place of my choosing each new moon, to pass on all that you have gleaned from your travels. Either of us may end this bargain at any time, but if *you* end it, I take back all of the knowledge and skill I imparted to you, and you will be again no better or worse than you are now. The memory of the music I teach you will remain, but you will not be able to recreate those chords again. If *I* end the bargain, however, you lose nothing, including skills you have learned from me. But you will still be bound never to reveal where you gained them, and you use them at your own peril, for I will no longer be able to assist you in any way."

Nym frowned, looking up and into his eyes. She saw nothing there but honesty, and in some dim corner of her memory, she seemed to remember hearing that fae could not lie...or at least *did* not, as a rule. Her own intuition insisted that he was telling the truth, though perhaps not all of it.

"I need not tell you the potential cost to us both if this bargain were to be found out," Erevan said, his tone the most solemn she'd yet heard from him. "Neither your people nor mine would be best pleased to find us working together. But there are magics we might yet unlock, forgotten and buried in the past, that may prove to be a great boon to both our peoples. This bargain is a start to eventually ending the enmity between them. But it must start small and remain hidden for a time, in order to grow with any safety."

Nym blinked, surprised at this more than anything he'd yet said. He was right. She'd never understood why the war between elf and wylden had ever happened, and she didn't know why any friendship, relationship or other collaboration between the two was forbidden. But one thing she believed to be true regardless was that no great good had ever come of ignorance or prejudice. Perhaps this was the moment to try something new. And if, as he'd said, she ended the bargain at some point, she would at least be no worse off than she was now, other than to retain a memory of music she could no longer play. Which, she had to admit, would be dismal. Determination swept through her.

Then I will not be the one to end the agreement.

"I accept your terms, Erevan of the Wylden," Nym said. "I, Nymariel Morren, accept your terms and agree to become your partner in this venture."

Erevan laughed. "Partner. Not student, nor yet mentee. You see yourself as an equal. Very well then, *partner*. Your agreement is heard and accepted. I also bind myself to this agreement, for the benefit of us both, until such time as either of us chooses to sunder it."

Two violet flames leapt from the fire and drifted toward Erevan and herself respectively. One spark landed on Erevan's outstretched left inner arm and sank into his skin, leaving only a faint violet mark that was invisible when he rolled down his sleeve. The other drifted to Nymariel and sank into her left arm in the same place, disappearing beneath the cloth of her garments without burning a hole or leaving any apparent trace. Hastily, she rolled up her sleeve and found a faint spiral mark on her inner arm, nearly invisible unless one was looking closely.

Nym swallowed, wishing she'd brought her canteen. Erevan noticed, and produced a cup from somewhere, adding herbs and water from the kettle he'd set to heat on the fire. "Here, it will warm you and ready your voice for singing. It is made only of plants from your world, so you need have no fear that drinking it will trap you here. That would not benefit either of us."

"Plants from...my world?" It wasn't a question. Not really. And she was in this bargain now, for good or ill. Nym accepted the cup from Erevan, trying to ignore the tingle that swept through her when their hands brushed. He was right about the tea; it was both warming and invigorating, and her mouth no longer felt so dry. She tried and failed to identify the plants to which he referred, but she had the feeling that if she ever tasted them again, she would recognize them.

Erevan reached for his lute, then eyed hers a little dubiously. "That must do for now, though we shall have to see about getting you a better instrument. For the present, however, let us begin."

Nym reached for the much-beloved old lute at her side, and then all her attention was taken up by the rush of information, sound and music that followed.

THREE

OUT OF THE WOODS

Nym woke to the clinging damp morning fog, which coated everything she was wearing in moisture and trailed cold fingers across her cheek. She lay on a strangely thick bed of fallen leaves beside the remains of a campfire. Coals still smoldered faintly, so the flames could not have been out for long, but of her wylden host, there was no sign. The lesson and musical training still stood out in her mind, shining and luminous and filled with wonder. She'd completely lost track of time while the lesson went on, barely noticing the changing cast of the sky as the night ran its course, full of warmth and music and...*life*. But a cold morning it was now, and she was utterly alone.

"No chance of breakfast, I assume?" she asked no one in particular. Then, groaning and stretching to limber up stiff and chilly muscles, she got to her feet, gathered her hand crossbow and lute, and prepared to make the trek back toward where the caravan had set up their camp. With any luck, they would not yet be finished packing up, and she'd be able to grab some toast and tea at least before they got underway.

And if they ask me where I've been, I'll just say I went off to find a bush where I could relieve myself, and got lost on my way back.

Wet as she was, her lute was surprisingly dry, and even with her rudimentary knowledge of magic, she could tell it had been spelled to repel the damp. Erevan must have done it. Pity he hadn't seen fit to do the same to *her*.

Well, I guess that'd be problematic when I eventually wanted a bath, so it makes sense, I suppose. She sighed, picking up the lute and slinging it over the opposite shoulder to the little crossbow. She should be grateful for small favors, and for the fact that he'd merely wanted to make a deal, not spirit her away to a life of servitude or worse.

Heading back the way she thought she'd come, Nym found that the way back was relatively straightforward, but it still took her more than an hour to make her way out of the thicker forest undergrowth and locate the thinner stands of trees that fronted the well-worn Forest Road leading toward the city of Kalas, the human city for which the caravan was bound.

She found the previous night's campsite, or what was left of it. But it was completely empty. Not even a trace of the caravan remained; in fact, the circle of stones and pit that they'd used for the fire was partially filled up with dead leaves and other debris. Even the tracks of the wagons were fainter than she'd have expected, especially given the perpetually damp and soggy ground in this part of the forest.

Something about the scene just didn't seem right.

How had her companions erased the traces of their passing so well? She didn't remember them being quite so thorough before, but maybe her disappearance had spooked them and they'd gone to extra trouble to disguise their erstwhile presence in this spot.

Whatever else they had or had not done, they'd clearly gone on without her. That in and of itself wasn't particularly surprising; she'd half expected they'd do so, especially when it had taken her longer to make her way back to the road than she'd planned.

One thing that did sting a little was the notion that they apparently hadn't even gone looking for her when they discovered her missing. She should have heard them calling, had they done so. If they had bothered to call out for her, she might have heard them this morning and found her way back to the road much sooner. And since they'd opted to move on so quickly after they'd found her gone, that meant she'd have no easy opportunity to try out her new performance skills during the final two-day journey to Kalas. The loss of the income she was supposed to have received from the caravan upon completion of the trip was a blow. And worse, they hadn't left any of her gear behind. They'd clearly assumed she wasn't going to return and had taken her bedroll and small pack of belongings with them.

Or perhaps I'm being extremely pessimistic. Perhaps they just got an early start and assumed I'd catch up? If that's what happened, then they can't be as far ahead or moving as quickly as I thought.

Heartened at the notion, Nymariel started off down

the track at a good pace, using effort and momentum to help her warm up as the wet clothes dried on her body. The horses pulling the wagons moved relatively slowly. Even on foot, if she moved quickly enough and they weren't too far ahead, she was sure to come upon them sooner or later, when they stopped for the midday meal, or at worst, by dusk when they stopped to make camp for the night.

By midday, though, Nym's cheerful optimism had dimmed considerably. Long past the time for luncheon, there was still no sign of the caravan. No sign of *any* caravan, for that matter, and no truly obvious sign that anyone had passed down this road recently.

The fall weather, ever capricious, was even more gloomy than it had been yesterday, the wind more biting and chill. Even the warmth generated by exercise began to leave her, and Nym found herself wondering what she'd do if she didn't find any sign of the caravan by nightfall. It would be a cold night if she had to bunk beneath a tree with not even the blankets from her bedroll for warmth. She didn't have the means to start a fire unless she tried to use magic, and the last time she'd tried that, it hadn't gone so well. Fire magic, it seemed, wasn't her forte, and when she did manage to ignite a blaze with it, it was usually either too small to last or too large to contain safely. Not like the steady, controlled violet blaze of Erevan's campfire last night.

Dispirited, she slowed her pace unconsciously until soon she was plodding along with all the enthusiasm of a tired draft horse. She'd had no breakfast, no lunch, and it was beginning to look as though she might have to leave the road at least briefly to look for some berries or something to sustain her—if there even *were* any berries to be found this late in the fall. If she risked losing a few small crossbow bolts, she might shoot a squirrel or a hare, but then she'd have fewer bolts to hand if she actually needed them for self-defense against a bigger threat than a couple of days without food. And she'd still have no fire to cook with, so hunting would be a waste anyway.

She was beginning to wonder whether she'd made such a good bargain after all when she heard the sound of a wagon behind her, and the jangle of harness. Confused, she whirled around to stare back down the road behind her. Had she passed the caravan somehow, and were they now behind her instead of ahead? But no. She'd been on this road all day; there had been no one. She could not have passed anyone without seeing them, unless they'd somehow become invisible. But that was preposterous; no one in the caravan had either magic or motive to pull such a trick.

A few moments later, a wagon appeared around a bend in the road behind her. Just one wagon, nondescript, piled high with hay and several bushel baskets of apples. A burly man sat atop the high seat, shoulders hunched against the breeze, a cap on his head and a knitted scarf wrapped around his thick neck to ward off the chill. When the wagon drew close to Nym he pulled on the reins, urging the big grey draft horse to a stop. The woman by his side peered suspiciously down at Nym, her eyes widening when she noted the pointed ears that Nym's mist-bedraggled hair couldn't quite hide.

"Oy there...what brings ye out here in the middle of nowhere with no horse or supplies, and the autumn so heavy on us? Ye'll catch a chill like that, or the wolves'll get ye. Are ye in trouble?" The man scowled at Nym, as though her presence on the road presented some problem that he wasn't sure how to deal with.

"I think I might be. I was lost and my caravan seems to have gone on without me. Is there any chance I might be able to catch a ride in the back of your wagon, at least as far as Kalas, if you're going that far? I can't pay; they took all my belongings but what I'm carrying, but I could earn my way with a song or several, if you're amenable?"

The woman's suspicious gaze softened further, and she lost her initial scowl as she peered at Nym's battered old lute. "Bard, are ye? Well, I suppose it can't hurt for ye to ride with the apples, up there on the hay. Burrow into it a little if yer cold. We're bound for Ramarth, but that isn't too far south of Kalas, no more'n a day's walk if you get a prompt start and don't dawdle on the road. We should be into Ramarth a bit after sundown if we keep a good clip."

"Your kindness is greatly appreciated, mum," Nym said, smiling and giving her a courtly nod, which seemed to make the woman puff up with pride.

"Ye look hungry, lass. Take ye some apples, too. We haven't enough fare for three, but for them apples. But of those, we can spare a few for a polite lass such as yerself. Especially for a lass as can play a lute."

Nym nodded to the woman again and went to the back of the wagon, using the spokes on a back wheel to clamber up and over the side. The hay on top of the pile was a bit damp, but underneath it was dry, and went a fair way toward dispelling the chill that had begun to creep into Nym's body. The food would help, too. A few small apples was far better than any withered berries she might have been able to find.

She snuggled into the hay, snagged a few apples from one of the baskets, and set about making up for her lost breakfast and lunch as best she could without overstretching her benefactors' hospitality. When she had finished, and carefully not using any of the *wyld* music in her presentation, Nym began a country song that she hoped would please her audience, picking out the chords on her lute with a skill she could have sworn she hadn't possessed the day before.

When the first song was met with exclamations of delight and even a bit of clapping from the woman in the high wagon seat, Nym began another. Then she offered a tale that kept her listeners entertained for much of the afternoon. By the time the little wagon creaked its way into the small village of Ramarth that evening, Nym's throat was tired from singing and talking, her body was sore from hours of jolting over uneven rutted roadway, and she was hungry again.

Bidding the wagon's owners goodbye, she headed for the only inn the little town could boast, a modest-sized affair with a clapboard exterior and bubbled glass windows. The sign outside named it The Fox and Hen, with a cleverly painted illustration of a hen riding upon a fox's back.

Nym searched her pockets and managed to scrape up just enough coin for a small bowl of stew, but not enough for a room for the night. Voice too tired to sing or tell tales, she opted to ask the innkeeper for sleeping room in an empty stall in the stable in exchange for a couple of hour's work washing dishes. She was no stranger to hard work, and if the innkeeper wondered why she asked to wash dishes rather than sing for her meal and board, he made no comment. Nym retired as early as she could and burrowed into the straw in the stall she'd rented, wrapping as much of her thin cloak around herself as she could manage and falling asleep nearly as soon as she lay down her head.

Her dreams were filled with music and food and revelry, much like the dream she'd had just before Erevan had summoned her to make a bargain with him, but unlike the first dream, the masks and costumes seemed to hide faces with sinister intent, and Nym woke in the middle of the night shivering, staring at shadows, unable to return to sleep for some time.

It wasn't that she had any doubts about the veracity of the bargain she'd made. Well, not many, anyway. It was the warnings Erevan had given her, vague though they were, about what would happen should this bargain ever be discovered. She realized that even when her subconscious was in charge—as when she slept— she was on high alert, ready to defend herself at a moment's notice whether an enemy proved to be elf, wylden, or human.

Once she did finally manage to sleep again, she slept fitfully until just before dawn, when she woke again, unsettled but determined. She used her last few coppers on a meager breakfast at the inn. Then, laden with her small crossbow, her lute, a couple of the gifted apples and a half-loaf of bread she'd saved from last night's dinner, she set out for Kalas, determined to reach the city as quickly as physically possible.

FOUR

THE RING AND DAGGER

By the time Nym neared the city of Kalas, it was past dusk and she was covered with mud. Her feet ached not just from the long walk but from the uneven purchase her thin-soled boots made on the road, slipping and sliding as she walked on the rain-washed, rutted surface. Passersby barely spared her a glance, which was probably just as well. As mud-caked as she was, nothing about her outfit marked her as a bard of any caliber, though the presence of the old lute helped somewhat. Still, what inn's patrons wanted to be entertained by a road-weary bard who wore part of the road on her garments?

Nym headed for the Ring and Dagger, the inn where the caravan had planned to stop when they reached the city. If they were there now, she might be able to get her belongings back, and that would include a change of clothes. She'd never been in a city this large before, much less this specific one, but it wasn't too hard to get directions to the inn; it was frequented by quite a few of the caravans that traveled the Forest Road.

The inn itself was impressive, at least to Nym's small-town eyes. It had two floors and multiple chimneys, which meant that at least some of the rooms had fireplaces. The glass windows were of higher quality than the typical bubbled glass most villages used, and the roof wasn't thatched, but finished with clay tiles of white and red. The white tiles were more grey than white from the smoke and dirt they'd accumulated over the years, but it was still a fancier roof than any back home in Wimble.

I've got to stop thinking of it as home, now, Nym thought. *I won't be going back there for a very long time, if ever.* It was an odd feeling, comprised of equal parts nostalgia and excitement, and Nym didn't want to dwell on it too long nor analyze it too closely.

She wiped her boots as well as she could on the mat by the inn's front door, then went inside, heading for the bar area. A man in the requisite brown apron was pouring drinks for customers, but at the sight of Nym he handed the task off to one of the servers and came around the bar to where she stood.

"Welcome to the Ring and Dagger. If it's a room you want, you'll need to pay up front. There's a fair crowd tonight, and not many rooms left. Eight silver, and I'll throw in a bath as well." Expression dubious, he eyed the mud on Nym's clothes.

"I can't pay much. I was supposed to be with the Nebron caravan, but I got lost on our way through the woods and they went on without me. If they're here, I can get them to settle any bills I incur. I was working for them as a bard, and they still owe me money. Maylor Nebron is the caravan boss."

"Nebron. Nebron..." The innkeeper scratched his chin, as if that somehow helped his brain work better. "That name sounds familiar. Wait...I have it. Yes, there was a caravan with a master of that name here some while back. But that's been, oh...nearly three weeks ago, now. They've already gone. I remember them talking about a lost crew member, though. Took you quite a while to get yourself un-lost, didn't it?"

"I...guess so. I must have been wandering for a lot longer than I realized. You know how fast the days can pass by in cloudy weather," Nym mumbled, a sinking feeling stealing over her. *Three weeks* gone? She vaguely remembered hearing somewhere that time could pass differently in the fae realms, but she'd only been with Erevan for one night.

One night that taught me three weeks' worth of music lessons. Gods preserve me.

"Is there a way I might earn my keep, since my caravan has moved on?" she asked the innkeeper, giving him a wan smile that she hoped would arouse mercy or generosity. "Or if there is not a room for me, could I trouble you for a bath and a meal at least, in return for me playing for your patrons for an evening?

Nym wasn't sure whether it was the wan smile or the lute strapped to her back that convinced the man, but the innkeeper studied her hard for several long moments, then nodded.

"Tell you what. Since I do remember the caravan you spoke of, since they did mention a missing employee and it's obvious you've been through something, I'll give you a chance. You go down that hall there," he indicated the direction with a wave of one hand. "There's tubs in the bathroom, and I'll send down some hot water. You clean yourself up, clean your clothes, come back and eat a bowl of stew, and we'll let you try your hand with that lute of yours. If things go well this evening, there's a small garret room I could let you have for a night or two. No fireplace, but the bed's clean, and you don't seem to have many belongings to speak of anyway. You play for us tonight, and it pays for the bed, bath and meal. You play two nights, and you get to keep any coin you make, minus the cost of room and board for the second night. That suit you?"

"Done," Nym said quickly, before he could change his mind. "You're a generous man, sir."

"Ahh, it's nothing." The innkeeper brushed off her gratitude. "It's the least I can do for someone who's fallen on bad luck, what with all the troubles people speak of these days. Wolf attacks, murders in back alleys, stalkers in the shadows, bad crops and bad weather...you mark my words, friend--?"

"Nym."

"Nym. You mark my words, this is an evil year, and an evil season. And the winter's like to be even worse. Decent folk need to watch out for one another, is all. Can't be too careful; the person you help might be the one as saves your life. That's what my mam always said, and I believe it, because it's true. You just never know."

"You never know," Nym said, nodding. She hitched at the strap of her lute. "I'll go get that bath now, then."

"You do that. I'll have the girl leave you a spare maid's outfit you can wear, until your clothes have a chance to dry. Unless you'd prefer a boy's clothes? You know what—I'll just send the whole lost-and-found box down. You can pick and keep whatever fits from there. No one's coming back for them."

"That would be very helpful, and very welcome. Anything will do, I'm sure," Nym said, smiling her gratitude.

She found the bathing chamber easily enough, and before long she was waist-deep in a tub of hot water, scrubbing away the mud with a course cloth and a bar of tallow soap. It wasn't sweet-smelling or lovely, but it would get her clean, and that was all that mattered. And to be able to soak in hot water after miles of muddy road seemed like the most decadent of luxuries.

Nym scrubbed her body and then her clothes, grimacing over how worn and thin they were. She'd made up for their poor state by using multiple layers, but it had been a long time since she'd had anything truly fine. Her mother's dressmaking and laundering had made overly-worn clothes stay serviceable for far longer than they would have otherwise, but Nym didn't have that level of skill. She could darn a sock or mend a rip in cloth with needle and thread, and she could even make a garment if she ever came by the cloth to do so. But there wasn't much one could do with patches upon patches, even if that did lend a certain rakish mystique to a traveling bard's ensemble. Or so she had always told herself, just to make it all seem more of a deliberate choice than it actually was.

By the time she'd finished bathing, rinsed out her clothes and hung them to dry on a drying rack, one of the housekeepers had brought in a small crate of miscellaneous clothing that had been left behind in the past by various of the inn's guests. Wrapped in a towel, Nym sorted through the random, motley collection of garments.

She found a medium-sized man's shirt with a ruffle around the collar and partway down the front that would do well enough if she rolled up the sleeves, and a pair of grey woolen breeches that bloused out too loosely around the waist. She could make them work with a belt she found in the bottom of the crate, at least until she had a chance to obtain needle, thread and scissors and take them in properly, but they would look odd until alterations could be made. There was also a dull red page's coat that had no doubt seen brighter days but was still in good repair and fit her surprisingly well. All in all, it was a better bard's outfit than what she'd been wearing, and in much better condition. The clothes mightn't be as flamboyant as a bard's clothes could be, but they would do for now, until she could obtain better.

Her undergarments were still wet, of course, but they were thin enough they could dry on her body. Nym put those back on, then donned the newer clothing, using some of her mother's tricks with an artful drape here and a fold there to make it look as though these were in fact her own clothes and she wasn't dressed in random strangers' lost garments.

Then she finger-combed her long hair as smoothly as she could and made a thin triad of plaits on both sides. Joining the six plaits together behind her head, she let the resulting thicker braid hang down over the fall of the remaining unplaited hair at the back. It was practical, but nice enough for performing, or so she'd been told by one of her erstwhile passing mentors back in Wimble. In any case, it would look more respectable than simply leaving the wet mass of hair hanging loose.

Erevan had taught only music, not appearances, and indeed Nym had the feeling that he wasn't particularly attached to any single appearance anyone might have. On a personal level, he seemed too changeable in nature for that, though he had also seemed to take delight in teasing her with an appearance she would find pleasing to the eye if she were to encounter him on the street. The idea unsettled her more than she cared to admit, but now was not the time to entertain such thoughts. She had a show to perform.

Nym grabbed the lute she'd leaned safely against the wall out of harm's way, and made her way out of the bathing chamber and back into the common room, where a fair-sized crowd had already gathered. Apparently, the innkeeper had done a little advertising while she'd been bathing. He came toward her as soon as he saw her, motioning her to a small table in a corner near the bar.

"Eat quickly, now; the customers are waiting. Stew's hot, and there's plenty of it. If you're still hungry after you perform, you can ask the kitchen staff for another bowl. You play your set, and then we'll see about tomorrow. The girls will take your other clothes to your room, and you can leave your crossbow behind the bar. No one will bother it there, and you can get it when you're done."

Nym nodded, already digging into her meal, the best she'd had in the past two days. The innkeeper had left her half a loaf of bread, which she tore into chunks and used to sop up the stew, which tasted of goat meat and root vegetables. It seemed like a feast after her previous fare of apples and foraged berries, water dipped from the occasional roadside well, and little else.

The innkeeper needn't have told her to hurry in finishing her food; she was too hungry to dawdle in any event. But there were also all those eyes on her, curious stares she felt more than saw, from the crowd of people gathered to hear her play. Fortunately, she was also too hungry for the nerves she felt to make her lose her appetite.

She *was* nervous, she realized, the more so as she went to sit atop the small square wooden platform at the back of the common room, clearly meant for the use of musicians and other entertainers. Unlike some of the places she'd visited in the past, this was a proper inn; by far the largest she'd yet seen, and she was sure it wasn't all that large by the greater standards of the city in which it stood. Nym had never been much prone to stage fright, but she felt it now, with all those eyes on her, waiting, expectant.

Slowly, taking time to guage her audience, Nym tuned her instrument and made a show of the preparation. Then on impulse she began a ballad, one of the ones Erevan had taught her, with just a hint of the *wyld* he had shown her woven through the notes.

Hesitantly at first, then gradually with more confidence, she made her way through the song, sweet and haunting, using her voice and her lute to weave together a tapestry of music and story.

Her audience listened, rapt, and other than the music, it was so quiet that Nym wasn't quite sure her listeners hadn't forgotten how to breathe. She finished the first song, dropping the last few notes into that silence. It continued for a long moment, then several. So long, in fact, that Nym began to tremble.

They hated it, she thought. *Erevan tricked me.*

Then a faint sound of hands clapping began, and more pairs of hands joined with the first, until the entire room had erupted in clapping, punctuated with cheers and whistles and requests for more, old favorites that Nym had known from before she met Erevan.

For life had taken a sharp turn, she realized now, watching a hat being passed around and coins dropping into it, while other coins spun through the air toward the platform and dropped onto the soft leather bag that normally held her lute. She could now see her life as divided into two separate eras—the time before she'd met Erevan, and the time from that night forward. The past, and the now.

The *now* was immensely profitable, she saw, if the number of coins coming her way were anything to judge by. Of course, those coins were the rightful property of the innkeeper, in accordance with their agreement. But if this was any indication of what she could expect in the future, then she would indeed soon be in a much different situation than she had been in before.

Nym had just begun one of the common tunes in response to a called-out request from the now-enthusiastic audience when she happened to catch the gaze of a man seated across the room from her at one of the tables near the door. He was tall and muscled, clad in leather and a dark brown travelling cloak, and his deep brown eyes met hers with a gaze she found a little unsettling. His light skin was tanned from sun exposure and he had short dark hair and a thick beard with a hint of grey. The way he carried himself made Nym think of the caravan guards she'd so recently been traveling with. But she'd never seen him before, so why was he looking at her with that piercing gaze, as though he intended to find and expose all of her secrets? It was unnerving, but then maybe he was just that suspicious of everyone.

She didn't have any more time to worry about it, though, as more requests for favorite songs were pouring in. She finished the first request and launched into another, and before long an impromptu party was in full swing, with guests clearing room for dancing as best they could in the crowded room.

Everyone seemed in high spirits, and by the time Nym finished her set and could reasonably stop for the evening, she was inundated with well-wishers and delighted compliments. So many people crowded around her that she lost sight of the burly man in the crush of bodies.

When at last most of the inn's patrons had cleared out and either left for their homes or gone to their rented rooms, the man had gone, much to Nym's relief. The last thing she needed was for someone to take too deep an interest in what she was doing. Fame as a bard was one thing, but undue scrutiny from an intense stranger was entirely another.

The soft leather lute bag now held a fair pile of coins, but Nym poured those off onto the surface of the platform. The innkeeper came up to Nym as she eased her lute into the bag, gathering the coins into a bowl he held, already half filled with more coins—probably those that had been in the hat the patrons were passing around.

"Well, I'd say this was quite a success tonight, wouldn't you? They were hanging on your every note! Needless to say, you've a job here just as long as you want it. If you want to stay, we can strike a new agreement after tomorrow. I'll let you stay here in a better room, board included, minus a small share of your take every night. Shall we say, thirty percent? That should more than cover your lodgings and food while also netting me a small profit, while you get most of your earnings free and clear."

Nym smiled, but shook her head. "That's a very nice offer, but I have other places I need to be, so I'm afraid I won't be staying beyond tomorrow night."

The innkeeper's face fell, but he nodded. "Ah, well, I figured it couldn't hurt to try. Now since your earnings tonight went over and above what would pay me for your room and board for tomorrow, I'm giving you some of the balance. Maybe you can use it at the shops, to replace some of the supplies you lost when your caravan moved on without you."

As she watched the innkeeper count out the bowlful of coins, she had to fight not to stare at the amount.

How could those patrons afford to give so generously to a bard? Wasn't everyone hurting for coin at least a little these days? She felt a little guilty, but the innkeeper looked so pleased that she allowed his enthusiasm to assuage the guilt somewhat. After all, she had earned the coin, hadn't she? And she'd only used just a small hint of the *wyld* in her music. Just enough to titillate, but not enough to compel. Hadn't she?

"Here's your share, now," the innkeeper was saying. "You keep that close, and bolt the door on your room tonight, just in case some nosy sot was watching the hat. You can't be too careful around here these days." He took the coins he'd counted out for himself and put them into his cashbox, locking the box with a key he pulled from his apron, leaving the rest in the bowl, which he shoved closer to Nym.

Trying not to seem too eager, she gathered up the coins from the bowl and hastily tucked them into the pockets of the page coat she was wearing. Tomorrow she would need to go out and obtain some necessities, such as a leather coin purse now that she had enough coin to put *into* a purse.

When Nym had retrieved her crossbow from behind the bar and slung the strap of the lute bag over her shoulder, the innkeeper led the way up to the small garret room he'd promised and let her in, handing her the key before heading back down the stairs. Nym took his advice and bolted the door as soon as she'd closed it, then turned to survey the room that would be her home for this night and the next.

As promised, it was small; there was just enough

room for the narrow bed and a tiny washstand with a pottery bowl and pitcher of water. Nym's wet clothes were now just barely damp, and had been draped over the curtain that covered the dormer window, where they could finish drying overnight. Nym slid the crossbow underneath the bed, then removed her boots and the clothing she'd found in the lost belongings crate.

She was bone weary and long past ready to drop into an actual bed for the first time since she'd left home. Even the slightly lumpy mattress and thin pillow couldn't keep her awake, and for a wonder, no dancing people, sinister or otherwise, appeared in her dreams. She had a lot to do on the morrow, and for the first time in her life, enough coin in her pockets to make at least some of it possible.

FIVE

KALAS

Nym woke just before first light to the noise of horses, carts and stable attendants calling to one another. The sound was close enough that she could not have slept through it even if she'd wanted to. A quick glance out the dormer window told her that her room was situated not far above the stable; in fact, the roof planes came together just to the left of the window, making a steepish groove nearly all the way down to the stableyard. A poor design, she thought, considering that rain would run down that groove and into the yard below, making more mud for the horses' hooves to churn up.

At least for now, the rain that had been on-and-off for the last couple of days had stopped. Perhaps it would be a good day for shopping. Nym surveyed her two outfits, frowning. Even with the addition of the clothes she'd been given by the innkeeper, they left much to be desired.

She reached for the pair of breeches she'd washed yesterday. At least they fit her properly, threadbare or not, and they wouldn't attract undue attention. In the end, she decided to wear her own tunic as well, and her old coat and boots. If she brought the clothes she'd taken from the lost-and-found box with her, it was possible that she might find a seamstress who could alter the too-large wool pants and ruffled man's shirt to fit her properly. And surely there must be some way to make the muted red coat look less like a page's uniform and more like something a bard would wear.

She ended up bundling them all into the pillowcase, sans pillow. Her crossbow and lute bag she slung over her back; there was no way she'd leave the lute in her room, old and scuffed though it was. She pocketed the key the innkeeper had given her after locking the room door behind her. Now all that remained was to find some breakfast and directions to the shops.

Downstairs, the kitchen already bustled with activity as the staff went about the business of baking the day's bread and preparing to serve breakfast. Eager to be off about her errands, Nym obtained a mug of hot tea, some toasted and buttered bread, and a wedge of cheese from a busy server. She took it to the small table in the corner nearest the bar where she'd eaten her meal the previous night, and ate, watching as the inn's guests began straggling downstairs, one or two at a time, yawning and stretching as though waking up were a chore they'd rather not be bothered with. But then, she'd had plenty of days like that herself, Nym mentally acknowledged. Some days were just harder to begin than others.

Fortunately for her, today was a day like no other, and she had more to look forward to than she'd had on any day previously, or so it seemed. Or maybe it was just the sight of the rays of sunlight finally slanting through the windows, proclaiming that today was going to be fair and fine and full of promise. Amused at her own fancy, she finished her breakfast and headed out, ignoring the curious and bleary-eyed stares of the few patrons who saw her leave.

One of the hostlers at the stable kindly gave her directions to the closest market. Kalas boasted three. One was in the noble quarter, farther toward the city center, and undoubtedly out of Nym's current price range. The hostlers called it the "Roses Market" as though the name somehow implied something higher quality or at least sweeter-smelling. The second, the Drover's Market, was on the opposite side of the city, near the Oxen Gate, mostly used by drovers down from the north and the surrounding villages, and apparently sold live animals as well as sundry goods.

The third market was closest to Nym's current location. This one was called the Woodgate Market, though Nym wasn't sure whether the name had more to do with the fact that the Forest Road curved past this side of the city before it became the West Road, or whether the main gate that now consisted of stone arches and a metal portcullis had once long ago been constructed of wood.

Either way, the name didn't do justice to the content of the market in any way. Had she been tasked with naming it, Nym would have called it the Hodgepodge Market. Stalls and shops of every description lined a three-block area of the district. Just off the first street was a broad public square paved with cobblestones interspersed with brick in some mason's attempt at an artistic pattern, perimeter lined with deciduous trees of middling size. All across the resulting open space, traveling peddler's carts had been pulled up helter-skelter, as well as carts that seemed to sell nothing but drinks and food, some of it cooked on-site on portable braziers.

After buying a small puffed pastry from one of the food carts in the square, Nym made her way down the several streets of the market district proper, gazing at all the colorful signs and awnings while she munched her pastry and got her bearings.

She found two or three tailor shops easily enough. After perusing their goods through the window, she decided on one that appeared to sell good durable clothing as well as a few fripperies. Rolls of wool and fustian seemed to make up most of the fabric on offer, but here and there she caught a glimpse of linen so thin as to be nearly see-through, and even the occasional bolt of silk.

"Morning! I'll be right with you." A slender, dark-skinned woman with multiple rows of tiny beads braided into her hair was bustling about the shop, and after stowing several bolts of cloth back on the high shelves at the side of the room, she came over to Nym and looked her up and down. "I see you are in need of some new clothes. What can I help you with today?"

"Do you do alterations?" Nym hefted the pillowcase with her recently-acquired garments.

"Yes, indeed we do. What do you have there?" The seamstress gestured to the wide counter, and Nym took out the garments she'd been given at the inn.

"I'll need the breeches made over to fit me, and if we can make anything extra of any leftover wool bits, so much the better. The shirt is closer to fitting, but still too large, so I'll need the same done for it, and perhaps a more feminine neckline? I like the ruffle, but the sleeves are too long and the whole thing fits more like a tunic than a proper shirt."

The seamstress nodded, smiling. "Yes, this will make up quite nicely. They are still of good quality, and not too worn. What of the red coat?"

"It's a page's castoff, and while it fits quite well, I'd like it to look a lot less like a uniform and a lot more like...well..."

"Like a bard's coat? With the collar removed and some embroidery or appliques on the arms and at the neck in contrasting colors, this would make a lovely garment for a bard. It's a nice red, if just a bit muted." The woman's eyes were shining. "You were right to bring these to me bright and early. I like a challenge, and this shouldn't take a terribly long time to alter. I will just need to take your measurements, and if you have the time, perhaps you will return this afternoon for a preliminary fitting? My assistants and I can do quite a lot in a short time, I assure you."

"That sounds perfect," Nym said, returning the friendly smile. "I will also need to see whatever you might have in the way of ready-made everyday clothing —some new undergarments and perhaps a dress and a heavy cloak? I don't know how much that will all cost, so I'll need an estimate before I decide for certain on anything but the alterations."

"That is no trouble at all. I am certain we have things that will be adequate for your needs, friend...?"

"Nym. And that's perfect. Just what I was hoping for."

Nymariel allowed herself to be measured, and then took great pleasure in choosing from among the ready-made garments for sale to replace what she'd lost. Wearing new linen undergarments and new woolen socks seemed like a rich woman's luxury, especially when she added not one but two pairs of socks to the pile. But when she'd paid for the underthings and other personal necessities, the socks and one new plain tunic-dress of fustian, then added the cost of the alterations, she found she still had coin left over. Not a great amount, but perhaps enough for the other items she needed to find elsewhere.

The seamstress, whose name Nym now knew to be Chalia, wrapped up her premade clothing purchases and stowed them under the counter to be picked up later along with the altered garments. After hearing her recommendation for a good but affordable cobbler, Nym set off again, wending her way through the streets with a sense of confidence and security that she had never before known. Maybe this wouldn't last. Maybe she was living in a dream right now. But if it was, it was a good dream, and she refused to allow herself to wake up before she experienced it to the fullest.

After a visit to the cobbler, who sold her a pair of plain but serviceable boots with good soles, Nym paused under the eaves of a bookshop to count her remaining coins. There weren't many left, but that wasn't surprising. It was as well that she was performing again tonight, because she still needed other items for travel. At the moment, all she had to sleep in was the heavy cloak she'd purchased earlier that day from Chalia, though gods knew that was far better than nothing at all.

The bookshop was a temptation she dared not enter, especially when she still wasn't fully outfitted. *Never take coin for granted*, she reminded herself. It was possible that the first night's success would prove to be a fluke. Even with a little fae enchantment, folk had only so much coin, and she doubted the crowd from last night had much left to spare. Briefly, she debated performing openly in the market square to drum up a new audience for the evening, but it was nearly dusk and she still had errands to complete.

She stopped at Chalia's shop for her afternoon fitting, amazed at how well the whole alteration process was coming along. Then she went back out and located a peddler of sundries, where she purchased a flint and steel, two small leather pouches, and a sturdy knife with a leather sheath. There wasn't enough coin left for more, and if tonight didn't go well, she'd need all she had left until she could find a different venue. The few coins that remained nonetheless made a pleasant jingle inside their pouch, which she hung on a long cord around her neck and tucked under her shirt next to her body. There was no way she wouldn't notice the attempts of any would-be pickpocket or cutpurse with the pouch stowed next to her skin rather than in a pocket or tied at her waist.

Pondering the possibilities of where and how to earn more, she spent a couple of hours drinking tea at a small teahouse just off the market square. Surely, she was better off today than she'd been at this time two days prior, but it was funny how the notion of "better off" changed depending on one's perspective.

Nicer clothes and boots didn't feed a person. They could, however, help her give potential audiences a better illusion of her bardic expertise. To the average citizen, if she *looked* like a bard, she therefore must *be* a bard, and it wasn't just a lute strapped to her back that made that impression. Better-dressed bards must by default be better at their craft, or so people tended to think, according to the few bards that Nym had met. So, the clothes were necessary even if pricey, and she could do without a bedroll for a while if she had to.

She made her way back to Chalia's shop just before closing. As the door swung shut with the chime of small bells, the seamstress looked up from where she sat behind the counter. Smiling, she put down the sewing that she held and stood, beckoning.

"Mistress Nym, you're back just in time! Come into the back room, and we'll see how everything fits. We've just finished, thanks to some hard work today from my apprentice, Lena, and my wife, Yarene."

"This is amazing," Nym breathed, looking at the clothes laid out on the workroom table. The pair of too-large woolen pants were now a form-fitting pair of women's breeches, with clever hidden pockets in the sides made from the extra material left from the makeover. The ruffled shirt was now collarless and cut to accentuate Nym's female figure. It laced up the front while allowing a modest but attractive decolletage, and the sleeves could either be worn over the shoulder or off the shoulder according to Nym's preference. A tiny bit of delicate flower and leaf embroidery ran around the border of the neckline next to the ruffle, simple and subtle, but lovely.

The red page's coat was the showstopper, though. It no longer looked like a garment that a young person might have once worn to serve a noble family. Its high collar with lapels had been removed altogether, and darts had been taken at the sides to make it more form-fitting. A combination of embroidery and applique now lined the entire hem, up the front sides and around the neck, trailing off onto the bodice in multiple places like a creeper vine gone wild. And that vine was a riot of rich amber, brown and other autumn-colored hues in different weights of thread and fabric pieces, with just a hint here and there of sky blue and purple. It made Nym stare in combined amazement and delight, and if it made *her* stare, then it would draw the eye of an audience as well. It was a bard's coat such as she'd never hoped to own, though at the core of it, it was still just a secondhand, castoff garment.

"This is amazing! I don't know how you did it in such a short time, but it is more beautiful than I dared hope. I'm so pleased." Nym refrained from clapping her hands like a child, but the beaming smiles on the faces of Chalia and her assistants told her that her reaction had made all their hard work worthwhile.

She understood people like these—people who loved to make art just for the joy of it. And if they could be *paid* to make art, so much the better. She refrained from commenting that in order to pull off such a feat as they'd done today, they must have had to use magic of some kind. They didn't ask how she did her business, and she wasn't about to ask how they handled theirs.

Still beaming, Nym took the clothes behind the changing screen to put them on, as well as a set of the new undergarments she'd purchased earlier in the day. When she emerged in the made-over bard's ensemble, the three women clapped their hands delightedly, wide grins on all their faces.

"Oh, lovely!"

"Wonderful; it's simply stunning on you!" Chalia looked so delighted and energized that it was hard to tell she was a tired woman who had worked double-time all day long to pull off a sewing miracle.

Nym didn't try to keep the grin off her own face. She'd never felt more beautiful, whether she was actually beautiful or not; that was the allure of clothing that fit perfectly. And she now knew what a good seamstress—or three—could do. They were worth their weight in gold, and if she ever had the chance to do them all a good turn and recommend them to someone rich and important, she intended to do exactly that.

SIX

A LITTLE GOES A LONG WAY

It seemed Nym needn't have worried about the size of her audience on this second night of performance at the Ring and Dagger. If anything, the crowd gathered to hear her had grown by a large enough factor that there was no room for inn patrons and servers to move freely about, much less dance. Master Ogellem, the innkeeper, had clearly done some advertising, other people had obviously told their neighbors, and now the crowd that filled the common room held far more than just the current guests of the inn proper.

Servers had to pass mugs of drink from one patron to another in order to reach customers in the middle of the seating area, and everyone seemed to take this as good-natured fun, even when someone jostled the person sitting next to them or spilled a drink on a fellow patron's clothes.

A quick glance around the crowd showed Nym that the man whom she'd noticed watching her the previous night had taken the same seat as before, and this time he had a woman with him who seemed to share his penchant for staring.

Nym's first song was a wylden jig that she could remember repeating for Erevan over and over until she got the nuance and rhythm just right. It left people bouncing in their seats, pointing and exclaiming in delight, and Nym found herself somewhat grateful that there really wasn't room for anyone to cavort about. She tried once again to use only a small amount of *wyld* in the music, and could only hope she'd succeeded. People murmured to one another, and a couple of them were pointing at her, talking excitedly to whomever was seated next to them. That had to be a good thing, surely. Of course it was.

Nym made sure to keep her other music free of *wyld*, but once again a hat was making its way around the room, and people were digging into their pockets for coins, which they tossed into the hat without seeming to look too closely at what they were doing. The ale flowed freely, but Nym had the feeling that even a hint of fae music might be more intoxicating than the drink.

She worked to keep her audience entertained with more than one style of performance, putting a story into the middle segment of the evening that she'd heard snatches of in the marketplace and then embellished to suit her own imagination. It was something to do with a magical horse and a stableboy, and the grins of delight from her listeners made it all the more gratifying.

This was the life she'd always wanted. This was how it should be—was in fact how it *would* be as long as she kept to her bargain with Erevan. She made a mental note to buy a journal and writing materials so that she could write down the stories she encountered and record them for future reference. She had a good memory for such things, but it never hurt to have a little something to refer to now and then. Nym knew next to nothing about her mother's past prior to her life in Wimble, but Jarinda Morren had seen to her daughter's education even though they didn't have much money. The ability to read and write would stand her in good stead now that she needed to be able to recall as many stories and songs as she could learn or devise.

Halfway through the last segment of the evening, one of the patrons began to weave about in his seat as though he were having trouble with his balance.

"You in front of me. You're too tall, and you're gettin' taller. I can't see the bard prop...prop'ly. Shove over so's I can see." He poked at the pair of shoulders in the seat in front of him, pushing at the other man.

The man who'd been prodded glanced over his shoulder with a scowl, and Nym could feel the mood of the crowd subtly change from fun and engaged to concern and something verging on annoyance. The serving maids looked openly alarmed, no doubt having dealt with drunk and unruly customers before. One of the men who worked as security for the inn began to inch his way toward the drunken man, though he had a hard time making any headway through the crush of bodies.

Nym changed her tune to a slow, peaceful lullaby, infused with just a hint of the *wyld*. It might not be wise to use it too liberally during the course of one performance, but surely that was better than having a fight break out in the middle of the crowded common room.

She could see it take effect; people began to calm a little and even the belligerent man seemed to back down a bit. But the mood of the crowd had changed nonetheless, and Nym had the feeling that she'd better wrap up the evening before something worse happened.

She made the lullaby her last song of the night. It seemed the most likely place to end, but it also seemed to have the result of making people reluctant to leave, even after the innkeeper took the subtle cue and announced the last call.

Nym had trouble disentangling herself from the patrons who begged her for "just one more, please, just one more." They plucked at her sleeves or made any excuse to touch her, one even tugging on her braid to get her attention. They didn't seem pleased when she told them that the inn was closing and that both she and they had to go. But go they did, eventually, albeit with dissatisfied looks, whereas last night upon leaving, the majority of the faces had been wreathed in happy smiles.

This must be at least part of what Erevan had warned her about, Nym realized. She had to learn to parcel out the *wyld* even more carefully, so that it didn't intoxicate or ensnare people too much. The last thing she needed was to incite a riot or pick up stalkers. It seemed that a little magic went a long way.

She noticed when most of the non-resident patrons had reluctantly gone out the door to head for their homes that her observer of last night, as well as the woman he'd brought this evening, were still seated at their table by the door. The intense looks they were both giving her sent a chill up Nym's spine. There were a handful of other patrons hanging back as well, but most were being firmly herded toward the door by the guard. One of those stragglers met Nym's eye as he let himself be chivvied, but instead of scowling, he grinned at her— a gap-toothed grin below intense, sparkling eyes. His demeanor seemed not so much friendly as disturbed. The guard had to prod him a bit more strongly to get him moving again, but even after he'd turned to face the door and gone through it, Nym couldn't shake the feeling of those madcap eyes on her. It made the back of her neck prickle.

Had she overdone it with the *wyld*? But she'd been so careful. She'd tried so hard to open up to the *wyld* just enough, but not too much. Erevan had said it could be a delicate balance, but surely she'd managed it after all the practice he'd urged upon her during the three-week-long night of training in the forest. Nym tried her best to ignore the pair by the door as the innkeeper took her aside to settle up.

"As promised, Mistress Nym—your share of the profits," he said, handing her a bowl of coins.

Nym poured the coins into the pouch she'd bought that day. "This is much needed and appreciated. And it has been a pleasure working with you." She smiled at him, but there was no way she was going to count those coins out here in the common room, in front of the two strangers who seemed to be lingering over their last mugs of ale.

"Have you given any thought to my offer? Will you be joining us here for a while longer?" he asked, sounding vaguely hopeful.

"I won't be, Master Ogellem, though of course I did consider the offer. I must be on my way; I have business elsewhere. I'm afraid that's the lot of a traveling bard," she said, earning a smile from him as he realized that she'd taken the time to find out his name from the serving staff. She thought there was a bit of relief in that smile, though—albeit tinged with regret for the extra profit her presence might have garnered for him.

After the way people had been acting toward the end of this night's performance, it was as well that she would be on her way tomorrow. After all, inspiring generous tipping was one thing, but inciting trouble was entirely another, and any reasonable person would prefer to avoid the latter. She had no desire to make trouble for either Master Ogellem or herself.

"Ah, that's a shame. But a businessman has to try, doesn't he? Ah, well." Ogellem nodded to her briskly

The two at the table by the door finally rose and made their way out, but not before the man had deliberately met her eyes and gave her another of his intense, searching looks that left her nearly as uncomfortable as the openly disturbed stare from the scruffy little man of a few moments prior. The amber eyes of the woman who'd accompanied the burly stranger were no less inscrutable, and they made Nym feel a bit like a cornered mouse, just for a moment.

What was wrong with all of these people? Did the *wyld* really affect them that strongly, or had the crowd tonight just attracted some people with less than stable personalities? Either one was a strong possibility, and either one was enough to make Nym hurry up the stairs to her room and lock the door. Somehow that just didn't feel like enough security, but it was at least a start.

She removed the red coat, folded it and put it into the bag the seamstress had given her to hold her purchases and other clothing. Then she changed out her ruffled shirt for the plainer shirt and tunic she'd bought. Regret tinged her gaze as she looked at the bed, freshly made and looking so comfortable. She'd fully intended to sleep here this one last night, then get an early start in the morning. But with what she'd felt of the mood from the crowd at the end of her session just now, intuition told her she couldn't chance it.

What if some of the inn's guests took it into their heads to try to get into her room during the night? Even if she defended herself successfully, she wouldn't just be guilty of having magically inspired many of them to part with more of their money than they'd perhaps intended to; she'd also likely have had to kill one or more of the attackers. And that would not be good for her or for Master Ogellem. Self defense might not be murder, but if the true circumstances of her performance were to come out, things would not go well for her.

Gathering the last of her belongings and consolidating them as well as she could, Nym considered. She still had no means of transportation; she'd had no time to arrange employment with another caravan. The direction they were heading wouldn't matter; any place but here would do. Perhaps instead of taking in the sights and shopping, she ought to have been setting up her next traveling situation. But the time was already spent, and she'd very much needed both the money earned and all of the items purchased, since the caravan hadn't seen fit to leave behind either her pay or her other belongings.

It was also hard to regret spending such a delightful afternoon shopping, when she'd never had the privilege to do so before. But now it seemed she'd be paying for that privilege with the coin of uncertainty. She would have to get better at this if she meant to continue to honor her bargain with Erevan. She put on her new cloak and fastened it, then surveyed her small pile of belongings, wrapping up the newer clothes in the oldest tunic and tying the bundle shut with the tunic's arms. She left behind the pillowcase she'd borrowed, but the bag Chalia had given her would do until she could purchase a real leather travel pack.

At least Chalia's bag had long strings that she could use to fashion a makeshift harness to help her carry her dearly-won possessions. What with the small clothing sack, hand crossbow, lute bag and waterskin, Nym was beginning to understand how a packhorse must feel—and this was traveling light.

Nym laid her room key atop the pillow on the bed, where the innkeeper could find it tomorrow when she didn't appear for breakfast and he had to unlock the room with his master key. Then she went to the dormer window and unlatched it, pushing it fully open. There was enough room for her to climb out if she pushed her belongings out onto the roof ahead of her. From there, all she had to do was move slowly down the groove in the roof until she reached the low eaves just above the stableyard. They reached down low enough that she could probably jump from there, and as long as she didn't land on her lute or the crossbow, she could leave the area of the inn through the stableyard, with no one the wiser.

Following this plan was harder in practice than in theory. She was able to get herself and her belongings out through the window and push it shut behind her, but the tiles were a bit slicker than she'd anticipated and she ended up sliding partway down them before she was able to catch herself.

Fortunately, she managed to grab her makeshift clothing pack and pull it down after her, and also fortunately, the lute and crossbow she wore slung over her shoulders were the heaviest items she had to contend with. Traveling lightly had its benefits. She'd strapped the new knife in its sheath to her belt, and her new boots had far better purchase on the roof tiles than her old ones would have with their thin, slick soles. Moving as quietly as possible, she made it to just above the eaves in relative safety, but then she froze, listening. There had been the sound of voices from somewhere below—or was that her imagination, envisioning attackers behind every barrel and post?

"She'll be in the inn somewhere," a gruff voice said then, from not far below her in the stableyard. "And I know a way in through the wine cellar. But we have to go *now*."

A low *tsk* sound came from nearby. "And what if she's not alone when you tap on her door? What then?

Assuming she opens the door and you don't have to break it down, you gonna knock her senseless and drag her off down the stairs and outta the inn with the guards watching? I say we do *my* plan; rouse the innkeeper and say we have an important message for the bard. Then when she comes down, we dose her with the Bewilder Mint, and she'll come with us willingly. No need to roust out the whole inn and get into it with the guards. Subtle is better than whatever it is you were planning." The second voice sounded higher-pitched— possibly female, but something about it hinted that it might not be a human voice.

Nym remained still, barely breathing. Whoever these people were, they were right below her; no chance she might sneak past them unless they moved. They might have been arguing too much to notice her descent down the roof, but if she moved a muscle now, they'd probably hear her. And Nym had little doubt as to which *she* they were arguing over.

"Ah, all right. We'll try it your way. If that doesn't work, we can always follow her when she leaves tomorrow and nab her when she's alone. Even as impatient as Himself is, he has to know these things take subtlety." Gruff Voice sounded perversely pleased for someone who'd been convinced of someone else's plan. When he moved further out from under the eaves, Nym recognized him as the man who'd been grinning maniacally at her before being hustled out of the inn. She'd known he was trouble; she just hadn't guessed how much.

"You wouldn't know *subtle* if it came and bit you in

the arse," said the lighter voice. When that person came out into the open, Nym made out a short profile with long pointed ears. Goblin, by the looks of her. They weren't common in most human cities, but they weren't entirely unheard of. She hadn't been in the crowd at the performance, so this little weasel of a man had probably sought her assistance after he'd been removed by the guards. That, or she had some sort of illusion spell to disguise her true nature from the humans. And wasn't *that* a disturbing thought?

The two moved off toward the front side of the inn. Nym, plastered against the roof tiles, didn't dare continue her descent until she was sure they'd gone. As soon as she was sure they'd moved out of sight and earshot, she inched her way down to the bottom of the groove, then looked for a landing spot.

Luckily, there was a rain barrel below the groove that she hadn't been able to see when she'd looked out the window earlier. The barrel had a lid of sorts, with a small hole in the middle to allow rain in but to keep horses and other animals from drinking the water, which was likely to contain ash and soot from the various chimneys. Carefully, so as not to dislodge the cover, Nym balanced on the edges of the barrel for a moment before jumping down to the ground.

Keeping to the shadows whenever possible, Nym crept across the now-quiet stableyard. She paused near the stable itself, eyeing the door. It would be much safer and easier to avoid pursuers if she had a horse, but the day when she'd made enough coin to afford that was quite some while off yet, and she had no wish to add "horse thief" to the list of things people would insist she account for.

Only two nights' performance at a larger inn, and already she was in danger from disgruntled listeners. Mentally, she cast back over her latest performance, but she couldn't bring to mind anyone in the audience who seemed well enough to do that his minions referred to him as "Himself."

A horse snorted from somewhere close at hand, and Nym jumped, biting back a yelp of startlement. Honestly, if she didn't get her act together quickly, she wouldn't last long. Not if the faintest peppering of *wyld* into her music was enough to get her marked for... whatever it was she'd been marked for.

Nym crept farther around the side of the stable, heading for the alley leading to the street behind. She hadn't gone five paces when something hissed. The hiss was followed by a guttural chattering sound, off to her left but too close for comfort. It wasn't a sound Nym had ever heard before, and it raised the hairs on the back of her neck.

The small crossbow was a better weapon than the belt knife. Backing away from the sound, Nym grabbed for the crossbow slung over her left shoulder, aiming toward the source of the sound.

Her elven eyesight helped immensely in the darkened stableyard, but when the creature stalked toward her out of the shadows, Nym almost wished she couldn't see it. It was something out of a nightmare. No wonder the people telling tales in the market had seemed so genuinely frightened.

On first glance, it looked like a large rodent, but it

had too many limbs, and some of the limbs were more insect than animal. It was as mottled blue-black as the night itself, making it hard to focus on even with good night vision, except for the lurid yellow-green of its several eyes, shining in the dark with some inner light of their own.

It moved toward her with fluid grace that its misshapen form didn't suggest. Just as Nym had her crossbow leveled and ready to fire, it leapt. She dodged, then promptly slipped in the mud and fell heavily onto her back. Something gave a crunch beneath her when she landed, but she had no time to worry about the lute as she flung herself to one side, scrambling to her feet as nimbly as she could. Somehow, she'd managed to hang onto her crossbow, but all the bolts were scattered in the mud where they'd slipped out of the quiver. Frantic, she scrabbled for them, finally finding one and fitting it to the flight rail with trembling fingers.

The creature recovered from its surprise quickly and now it stalked her, still making the raspy chattering noise that grated on Nym's ears and sent chills down her spine. Desperate, Nym nocked the bolt and pulled the trigger, catching the beast in its shoulder instead of what passed for a face, as she'd intended. Grimly, she tossed the crossbow to the side and pulled out her belt knife. She wouldn't get a second shot; she already knew that, and running from this thing was clearly out of the question.

She'd backed up so far that she was fully in the middle of the stableyard again, but just now the possibility of being seen by angry villagers seemed far preferable to whatever fate this creature had planned for her. The idea of using the *wyld* for defense struck her, but she had no idea how to do so.

A muffled exclamation came from the stableyard entrance, and suddenly a long arrow embedded itself in the creature's eye, making it stagger and shake its head violently. Heartened at the unexpected intervention, Nym was about to dive for the crossbow she'd tossed aside when a large male form rushed past her, toward the creature. A sword flashed, and the creature's head landed on the ground, rolling. It came to a stop at Nym's feet, all eyes but the ruined one still open and glaring at nothing.

Nym shuddered and backed away, wanting to kick the head farther from her but also unwilling to touch it even with a boot. The burly man she'd seen in the inn strode calmly up to the head, lifted it by the long fur on the back, and dumped it into a canvas sack tossed to him by the woman he'd been sitting with earlier.

The woman tossed a lock of raven-colored hair over her shoulder, then gave Nym a brusque nod. "All right?"

"Yes, I...I think so. Though I'm pretty sure the same can't be said for my lute," Nym said, still trying to gather her wits. "I'm glad you came along when you did. It nearly had me—whatever it was."

"It's a tarinx, a nasty piece of business. They're magic-spliced, originally created by an insane mage locked up in a cell with lots of rats and spiders. Seems whoever had the chore of eradicating his experiments missed a few, and somehow they reproduced and got... large," said the man, stooping to pick up Nym's lute bag and hand it to her before heading into the stable. "Or maybe someone decided they were useful."

She took the lute, not bothering to inspect it further until she was sure she wasn't still in danger. The leather bag wasn't stiff enough to have protected it from the damage of her weight falling on it, so she had a pretty good idea of what she'd find.

"What was the tarinx doing in a city, much less one as large as Kalas?" Nym asked.

The woman grimaced in obvious distaste at the headless corpse. "That is part of what we hope to find out. And now that we know you aren't in league with whoever's sending them, I suggest you come along with us. From the argument the two fools who were planning to abduct you were having, it sounds like you've gotten yourself on someone's hit list. You can't stay here. And if the two incidents are related, then we have an even bigger puzzle to solve."

"In league with...whoever's sending them? So, more unknown enemies skulking in the shadows. Great." Nym shook her head. "Normally I'd tell you to be about your own business, but seeing as you just saved my life and I really do need to get out of here, I'll go with you for now. I don't have a horse, though."

"That's all right. You can ride double with one of us until we can manage to get you a mount." The woman was gathering up Nym's scattered crossbow bolts, and Nym noticed that as she did so, her amber eyes glowed, as though she were using some sort of spell to enhance her vision. Those eyes made a striking contrast with her teak-colored skin, and she held herself with a lithe confidence that Nym envied.

"Fair enough offer. I'll take it. My name is Nymariel Morren. Nym for short."

"Faraine Iarberos. And the big fellow is Aeson. He doesn't use a surname." Faraine gestured to the man, who was just emerging from the stable leading two saddled horses behind him.

Nym accepted the quiver of muddy crossbow bolts Faraine handed her and paused to pull the one she'd used out of the dead tarinx's shoulder, cleansing it in the mud just in case being embedded in the body had somehow poisoned it. She noted that Aeson had promptly cleaned his sword after cutting off the head, so the caution was probably warranted.

Nym's bundle of clothing was still intact, even if the outside of the bag was muddy, so other than the likely damage to her lute, she seemed to have all her belongings, for all the good they might do her with creatures such as the tarinx stalking the back alleys and other dark places of the world.

Faraine mounted her dark bay gelding and sat waiting as Aeson extended a hand to help Nym up behind him. Aeson's mount was a big dun stallion with larger hooves than any Nym had ever seen, and long hair on the lower legs that she knew was called "feathers" by horse experts. She'd hung out in stables often enough to pick up some of the terms, and she'd even ridden a bit when working with the caravan. This was the type of horse that knights often used, as they could handle the greater weight of full metal armor, plus the rider and weapons.

Regardless, the absence of a horse of her own was going to be a problem if she was going to be traveling with these two strangers instead of in the relative safety of a caravan with wagons and multiple guards, though how long she'd be with them remained to be seen. Whether or not she could trust them also remained to be seen, but until they proved to be a threat, she'd bide her time. It wasn't as though she had any better options at the moment.

Aeson turned his horse down the street that led toward the Drovers' Gate, and Faraine's horse followed. Perched on top of what was probably Aeson's bedroll behind the saddle, Nym held on as best she could without getting too familiar. She'd been in more awkward situations, hadn't she?

Well, maybe not. But at least she'd found transportation, and that was a start to getting herself out of the predicament she'd somehow gotten herself into with her performance at the inn. The big question now was whether she'd leapt out of the frying pan straight into the fire.

SEVEN

IN THE COMPANY OF STRANGERS

The streets of Kalas were still dark, the night only about half over as Nym's small party rode out of the Drover's Gate, which was opened for them by a bleary-eyed gate guard. If he wondered at the strange hour of departure, he didn't show it, but then maybe he'd been sleeping on the job and was in no mood to question the business of strangers.

On the way out of the city, they'd stopped only briefly. Aeson had turned aside to pitch the bagged head of the creature into a smoldering outdoor furnace that looked to be part of a large smithy. No one seemed to be about, but by the way the fire blazed up immediately, it was apparent that someone maintained and fed it at regular intervals even during the night. Nym felt sorry for the poor apprentice who had to make the next rounds; the stench from the burning head was atrocious, and finding such a thing would be alarming in the extreme. Even the flames Nym could see through the grate were tinged with a sickly green as the bagged head caught fire.

"It will be ash by morning, with nothing left to alarm anyone," Aeson said quietly, as if in answer to Nym's thoughts.

The short city access track quickly joined back with what had formerly been the Forest Road, but which from this point on was called the West Road as it headed across open country. Aeson urged his stallion to a brisk walk, with Faraine's horse close behind. Nym noticed that he had a sword scabbard on the saddle at the front left, which meant that if he needed to draw it suddenly, he wouldn't be reaching over his shoulder to do it. That was a relief. Big as this horse was, there was really nowhere else on it that Nym could go to be out of the way if something attacked, and dropping to the ground when they might need to run was not an option she wanted to consider.

The terrain from here consisted of mostly open fields, some of which were farmed, interspersed by the occasional copse fed by a narrow creek here and there. As the sun rose, songbirds began to make their presence known, which Nym found comforting despite the fear of pursuit and the threat of danger that she'd been entirely unaware of yesterday.

They rode in silence until dawn, when Aeson led them off the road into a small copse with a depressed area in the center, which would make them less visible to anyone passing.

"We'll stop here for a bit to rest the horses and eat some breakfast. There isn't much, but you're welcome to a share of what we have," Aeson said, offering Nym a hand to get down from the horse. "We can resupply our rations in Tilsk, the village a few hours' ride farther along this road. It's the best-sized village for another couple of days, and it has a reasonable market. But after we buy food we have to keep moving, put more distance between us and whomever was after you in Kalas."

He took a loaf of trail bread from one of his saddlebags, slicing it neatly onto a cloth with even strokes of the sharp knife he wore at his belt. Faraine produced a wheel of cheese from her own saddlebags and handed it to Aeson, who cut off a portion that he then proceeded to slice in the same way he'd sliced the bread.

They ate, sitting on a fallen log and making short work of the bread and cheese, washed down with water from the waterskins. Nym was grateful that she'd filled hers up the day before while she'd still been at the inn. It was bad enough that she'd had no chance to purchase more food, but aside from a packet of dried meat that she'd bought from a food cart in the square, she had no other rations to speak of. Up until the unexpected issues at last night's bardic session, she'd assumed she'd have the ability to buy food for the road on her way out of town. Then by the time she'd realized she had to leave the inn in the night, it had been too late to worry about provisions.

But I won't be caught off guard like that again.

Determined, Nym ate her share of the bread and cheese as quickly as possible, a sense of urgency driving her. It wasn't just that someone had sent a monster to attack and probably kill her, alarming as that was to think about. It was that she'd underestimated how dangerous using the *wyld* could be, and the scope of the possible consequences. She wasn't ready to opt out of her bargain with Erevan, but if she was going to wield this magic, she had to learn how to use it with a deft and fine touch, and that meant she needed practice and more opportunities to perform in that way. And more performing with the *wyld* meant more risk.

She also had to be careful not to reveal too much to her new traveling companions, however temporary the association might be. The whole situation was fraught with risk, and it wasn't truly fair to them for her to put them at risk without their knowledge. But on the other hand, they'd involved themselves in her situation for reasons of their own, so perhaps any risk to them was on their heads. It was a quandary.

If only she knew whether or not they could be trusted, and what their motivations in helping her actually were. There was one topic that could be broached, at least. It was a start. But how best to do so?

After they'd finished the brief respite and were back on the road, Nym lightly tapped Aeson on the shoulder.

"Eh?" he grunted, turning slightly in the saddle to give her a quizzical look over his shoulder. When she didn't speak immediately, he raised an eyebrow and faced forward again. "Ask what you want to ask," he said, with a short huff of what sounded like amusement.

So she amused him, did she? "I'd like to know why you two decided to help me. What's in it for you? If we're going to travel together at least for now, I'd like to know a bit more about the people I've thrown in my lot with."

"That's a fair enough ask, as long as you're willing to reciprocate," Faraine commented, pulling her horse up to walk beside Aeson's. Her amber gaze met Nym's, searching and intense. "In fact, maybe you should go first, and tell us why those bumbling kidnappers, or the tarinx, for that matter—were after you."

"I don't know why. I've never met either of those people before, although I think one of them was in the room when I was performing last night. Maybe something in my songs insulted someone they work for. Maybe they dumped too much coin into the hat and wanted it back. Or maybe there's a crime lord somewhere who is in desperate need of a bard. I don't know. I saw the man staring at me during the evening, and something about him looked a bit *off*. Like he was feeling especially reckless, or was, I don't know... insane."

Faraine nodded. "I think I know what you mean. And the woman with him—she wasn't entirely right either. I'm not sure she was even human."

Goblin, Nym wanted to say, but decided to wait and learn more before she revealed that little bit of insight.

She continued. "As for the tarinx...I've never even heard of such a thing, much less seen one or been educated as to its possible motives, other than to kill and eat me. I did, however, hear a lot of rumors in the marketplace about strange things people have seen creeping around in the shadows and people who've disappeared, never to be heard from again. Maybe they've been seeing these creatures. I'm pretty sure that the one at the Ring and Dagger was about to make *me* disappear, whatever its motive, though probably just because I was there and looked like a snack."

Faraine nodded. "That all makes sense. What doesn't make sense is that you haven't said anything about the fact that you were using magic during your performance. Aeson and I both have the ability to sense it, to some degree or other. So let's just assume you were using a spell of some kind to encourage your listeners to drop a bit of extra coin into the hat."

Nym tried to keep her expression neutral. "That's a big assumption."

Faraine snorted, a sound that was echoed by her horse, which would have been funny if Nym's heart hadn't been trying to beat itself out of her chest.

"Look, I don't care if you were using a spell or a charm to influence the flow of tips. I'm not going to judge you for that. In fact, it might explain the occasional disgruntled patron if they got wise to what was happening. But what doesn't make sense is why that would move someone to try for an abduction instead of just picking your pocket or mugging you in an alley to take your purse. The fact that they were talking about abduction says that this wasn't about money. And *that* is what concerns us."

"Why?" Nym was startled into asking.

"Because if they'd succeeded, you wouldn't have been the first person to have gone missing in recent days. And now that I think of it...you wouldn't have been the first person gone missing who could also use some form of magic. Someone in that crowd besides myself or Aeson might have sensed you using whatever magic charm or trinket it was you used to enhance your performance and marked you as a target for that, not for bilking them out of a few extra silvers."

Nym stared at her, that same sense of foreboding stealing over her again. "I think it's time for you to tell me more of what you know about all of this, and why you decided to help me."

In front of her, Aeson nodded. "That's fair. But where to begin?"

"Well, for a start, are you a mage? Either of you? I won't judge you, if you are." Nymariel knew she was treading on dangerous ground here, but one had to give a little to get a little. She hadn't *quite* admitted to using magic on her audience. Not quite. But if she allowed these two to assume that she'd used some kind of common mage spell to tweak things in her favor rather than pure unfiltered fae magic, then maybe they'd leave off this line of questioning. And maybe they'd be more inclined to reveal something of their own—anything about themselves that might give her a better idea of what they wanted from her, and why.

"I am a mage," Aeson said, surprising Nym. "I've been a scholar of magic for the past thirty years."

She'd taken him for a typical soldier or guard. She nodded in response to his admission, even though he wouldn't be able to see it. Then she called to mind all the descriptions of mages she'd ever heard, trying to make them fit the man in the saddle in front of her, but she couldn't. Aeson seemed like no type of mage she'd ever heard of, though admittedly her sources of information hadn't been vast. He seemed much more like a battle-hardened warrior than a scholar of arcane arts. Hastily rearranging her paradigms, Nym waited for him to say more.

"I'm a member of the Order of Hawksfire," he said, as if that explained everything. When Nym stayed silent, he tried again. "You haven't heard of it? We're a mage order that seeks out all manner of magical aberrations and corruptions, and deals with them if they begin causing problems for any of the common folk. Nobles often hire our services if they have a magic-related problem that their own spellslingers can't handle."

"So, you're mercenaries?" Nym asked, trying to decide what she thought of the concept.

"In a manner of speaking, yes. But we're all bound by a set of tenets and laws, enforced with spells that prevent any of us from having unlimited access to power. We can do only so much magic in a set period of time and no more, power levels are equalized, and we hold one another accountable for the ethics involved in using magic. That way no one member of the order can gain more power than their fellows and use it to further their personal agenda. We leash our power so we can't abuse it, and to keep us all on an equal footing."

"That sounds like a good thing, in theory," Nym said. "But I'm not sure how well something like that would prove out in actual practice. Most people wouldn't want to limit themselves like that."

"Nevertheless, it is our code, and we all live by it. We believe that those who have magic should use it responsibly and mindfully, preferably for the benefit of others. Ensuring equality in our ranks is a part of that. Order policy also includes magically blocking the memories of our lives prior to the Order, so that we aren't haunted by our past and it cannot influence what we do going forward. It gives us a true second chance. It is our onus to make the most of that chance.”

“I see. I appreciate your explanation, whether or not I fully understand it.” Nym *didn't* see, but she refrained from saying more; she didn't want to alienate the man. At least, not so soon after he'd saved her life.

The big horse tossed his head and snorted, and Aeson reached down to pat the glossy neck. If he minded what Nym had said, he gave no sign.

Faraine laughed. “I don't fully understand it either, and I've been riding with the man for almost a year. But his sword arm is as steady as his magic, and he's a good friend to have in a fight.”

“Yes, I could see that,” Nym said, remembering that sword lopping off the tarinx's head in one stroke. A good friend in a fight indeed. And not someone you wanted as an enemy.

“I met Aeson in an alley in Somber, farther north. My brother's been missing since early last year, and I've been trying to track him down ever since. Aeson and I sort of bumped into one another while I was—or I guess we both were—following a lead on a gang known for kidnappings and clandestine assassinations. At first, he thought I was one of the group he was there to investigate, and before I knew it, he'd disarmed me, tied me up, and thrown me across his saddlebow.”

Nym laughed. “That must have inspired a great deal of trust.”

“Oh, loads of it.” Faraine was grinning. “But after he'd taken me to a more secure location, as he called it, and we had a little talk, he realized that I wasn't affiliated with the gang in question.”

"Of course, the truth spell helped," Aeson commented, still facing forward.

"Right. Because apparently, I wasn't very convincing of my sincerity while I was sitting there snarling at him like a cornered kitty cat." Faraine eyed Aeson with a tolerant look that told Nym the two had become considerably more trusting of one another in the months since their meeting.

"So, you're looking for your brother and you think he may have been taken by this organized group of thugs and kidnappers. And Aeson is after them too, so that gives you a common goal. That makes sense." Nym thought for a moment. "You know, I'll probably just slow you down if I stay with you, especially without a horse of my own. You could just drop me off in this village we're heading for and I can arrange my own transportation going forward. You don't have to feel responsible for me just because you saved my life back there."

"We don't," Aeson said, so quickly that it took Nym aback. "But think about this before you're in such a hurry to part company. Last night—for whatever reason—you were nearly abducted, which might easily have put you in the ranks of all those other folks who have disappeared. The creature in the stableyard was just an added complication, and the two things may or may not be related. Pray they're *not* related, because none of us are going to like where this is leading if they are. But if your would-be abductors are affiliated with the same group that may have taken Faraine's brother and quite a list of other people, then your presence with us may just give us all an advantage against them, because we'll be ready. You could use our help, and we could use you."

"As *bait*, you mean," Nym said. "I already don't like where this is leading. But you do have a point. I probably stand a better chance with you, especially if you're hunting the people who are hunting me. But if I continue with you, then we need to set some ground rules."

"Fair enough. What rules do you suggest?" Faraine was grinning again as she turned to Nym, but not in a mocking way.

"I still need to be able to perform in order to make a living. And I'd prefer not to be judged on how I choose to do that. So, I need you to stay out of my business where the performances are concerned, and that's non-negotiable."

"All right. But for your part, we need you to at least try not to inspire your audiences to come after all of us with torches and pitchforks. Or anything else, for that matter." Faraine seemed to ignore Aeson's raised eyebrow. "Attracting undue attention is not something we want right now."

"Oh, believe me, that's not something I want right now either. I want an audience for the music and tales, not an angry mob," Nym said emphatically.

"Good, then we understand one another." Aeson nodded, though his back was to her.

"Well, no, not yet...but we're working on it," said Nym dryly, earning a chuckle from the warrior mage.

"Any other rules from our new bard companion?" Faraine asked.

"Well, naturally I keep whatever coin I make from

my performances, but I will contribute a fair share toward our traveling expenses, like food and such."

"I like this rule." Faraine's eyes were sparkling with humor—the kind of humor that drew Nym in and made her feel party to some sort of friendly conspiracy.

She'd never had many close friends back home, so if they got on well, this could become a whole new experience. Faraine's apparent willingness to extend a hand in friendship was somewhat different from the sort of casual comradery Nym had experienced with the merchant caravan folk. She had a feeling that the more she got to know her new companions, the closer she'd get to them, and the more apt they might be to discover the secrets she could not afford to let slip. She'd have to let them in just so far, and no further.

"Other than what I'm telling you now, I don't like to talk much about my personal life," she continued. "I hail from a small elven village, and I decided to become a traveling bard to spare my mother the expense and worry of having to try to support us both. Not much call for bards, back home." She smiled, and her attempt at humor earned her an approving nod from Faraine.

"I'm sorry. But I can see why you'd make that decision, and I admire you for it."

Words of thanks nearly escaped Nym, but she bit them back just in time and merely nodded. She made it a policy never to openly thank anyone, just in case, but the urge was still strong when thanks seemed truly warranted.

"I'm glad you feel that way. Part of me feels like I abandoned my mother," Nym admitted, before she realized she was going to.

"We all make the choices that seem the most right to us in the moment we're faced with them," Faraine said quietly. "I did something not entirely dissimilar when I left my village to search for my brother, even knowing it would hurt my parents to feel like they'd effectively lost a second child. But I felt I *had* to look for him, not just because I miss him, but in case if I found him, then maybe I could somehow bring to justice whoever had taken him, and prevent others from becoming victims."

"Are you sure he was abducted? Could he have just wandered off and been killed by an animal or something?" Nym asked, wincing a little at her own bluntness. But she felt it had to be asked.

Faraine frowned as though she'd had to answer this question before. "He was abducted. I'm sure of it. I found his bow and his favorite book lying on the ground not far from the village stables, and the only tracks leading away from the area were from horses. Aside from the fact that I knew he'd been talking to some newcomers in the pub prior to his disappearance, we had several trackers from the village search in all directions, but there was no sign of blood or animal tracks except for horses. And last I checked, horses don't eat people."

"You might be surprised," Nym mumbled under her breath, but refrained from repeating herself when Faraine gave her a quizzical look. "I'm sorry, Faraine. It's been a long few days, and stress makes me more blunt than I mean to be. I hope we find your brother. He's got a loyal sister, so he's luckier than many."

"We're here," Aeson announced before Faraine could reply, pointing to where the rooftops and chimneys of a village could be seen just beyond a small rise in the road. "The village of Tilsk in all its glory."

"All right; if we need any additional ground rules, we can discuss them later," Faraine said, letting her horse drop back behind Aeson's. "For now, let's just get what we need and be on our way again as soon as we can. We're still too close to Kalas for my peace of mind."

"Mine, too." Nym peered around Aeson's broad shoulders at the village as they grew nearer. It seemed as unassuming as any, but if unnatural horrors like the tarinx could lurk even in the dark alleys of a city, Nym wasn't prepared to take even the most peaceful-looking village for a place of safety—if such a place even existed.

EIGHT

A SEMBLANCE OF A PLAN

Tilsk was small, but Faraine and Aeson were correct; the market was adequate for restocking their food supplies. Nym counted a few coins out into Faraine's hand for her share and left it to her companions to decide what food they'd purchase. She had another urgent matter to deal with.

The town had a carpenter. It was likely too small to have a luthier in residence, or so Aeson had gruffly told Nym when she inquired. But she'd held off too long already on surveying the damage to her lute, and if there was anything to be done, then this carpenter was her only possible chance for even a temporary repair— at least until they reached a larger city that actually had an instrument maker. Barring anything else, he might be able to make a recommendation for a luthier elsewhere, if he happened to know of any. It was a shot in the dark, but the lute was too important for her not to try.

She found the carpenter soon enough. He was working on some cabinetry, from what Nym could tell, smoothing a piece of wood with long strokes of a hand plane. She saw some other pieces of the cabinet-to-be, already smooth as glass and ready to be assembled, as well as some fancy carved wood pieces that she assumed would be affixed for decoration. The obvious craftsmanship was a good sign that he might be able to help somehow.

Loosening the fastenings of the soft lute case, Nym drew out the instrument. As soon as she'd felt it crunch beneath her, the probable outcome was obvious, but she'd been unable to bring herself to look at the damage properly until now, not least because of their haste in leaving Kalas. Now she examined the lute from every angle, sorrow for the loss of the one precious thing she owned making her throat tight and tears sting her eyes. The lute hadn't been much to look at, but it was hers, and its giver had been kind to her.

It was just as bad as she had feared. If the neck had broken, they might have been able to splint it until it could be replaced, but a part of the soundboard had cracked and caved in, and short of having a skilled instrument maker replace the whole thing, Nym saw no way to mitigate the damage. She shook her head at her own foolishness. She shouldn't have come here. It had been wishful, desperate thinking anyway. Squaring her shoulders, she turned to go.

The carpenter noticed her expression and the instrument in her hands. He put down the plane and walked around the stacked wood to join Nym where she stood near the front of the shop.

"Had an accident with your lute, I see," he commented. "Pity you didn't bring this in just a couple of days sooner. My brother does a bit of instrument work; he might have been able to help. Would have taken several days, though, and he's already en route to Cambermere for one last supply run before winter."

"Is there a luthier in Cambermere?" she asked, sighing and replacing the lute in its bag. At least she'd tried. She owed her former teacher that much. It was hard to imagine going without her lute for as long as it would take to first reach the city and then obtain the necessary repairs, but somehow, she'd have to manage. That was part of being a bard after all, wasn't it? Thinking on one's feet and being adaptable was part of a bard's stock-in-trade.

"Aye, there is. If you're going to Cambermere, look for Davic Mercery. He's as good an instrument maker as I've heard of, at least according to my brother. I'm sorry I wasn't able to help you myself."

"It's all right. I knew this was a long shot, but I had to try, just in case there was any chance at all that the damage wasn't as extensive as I feared, or that someone here would be able to make at least a temporary repair. And you have still helped me, in any case. With a name and recommendation for a luthier, I'd say my lute's got more of a future now than it did before I walked in here."

"All right then, friend. I hope you find what you're looking for, and that better days are ahead. I've got nothing but respect for those as are able to make their way with just their music. It's the life some of us dream about, before we turn our hands to more commonplace work."

Nym nodded to him and left the shop, turning his

words over and over in her head as she headed back to the small market square. He had respect for people who made their way with just their music. Well, now she had no instrument—at least for the foreseeable future—but it was the lute that was out of the picture, not the music itself.

She was a bard, after all. Any bard worth their salt could perform without an instrument. She'd always had a good singing voice, and she could still tell tales for an audience. All of it came under the aegis of Erevan's bargain. Until she could have the lute repaired, she'd perform where she could and when she could, using whatever means necessary, and she'd still have something to offer Erevan when he called her next.

And that would be soon, Nym realized with a start. Tomorrow night was the new moon. It seemed far too soon, but since she'd been with Erevan in the fae realm for a night that had spanned three weeks in the mortal world, that meant a month of mortal time had nearly passed already. She wondered how Erevan would manage to spirit her off to convey the few stories and songs she'd heard since she'd seen him last without alerting either of her new traveling companions. A small, perverse part of her was excited to find out. As long as weeks did not pass each time she had to speak to Erevan, she'd no doubt he could somehow communicate with her and leave no one the wiser.

"We'll have to make a cold camp tonight, at least after dark," Aeson said when they'd resumed their journey, Nym once again riding behind him on the big dun, whose name she had learned was Seralo. The saddlebags bulged with supplies Aeson had purchased in Tilsk, and Nym found herself hoping that at least one item had been a packet of tea, assuming they had something in which to heat it.

The long hours on horseback—especially a horse as broad as Seralo—were beginning to take their toll on Nym, but she didn't dare complain. There was far more at stake than her personal comfort or dignity, and no matter how sore she became, she was not going to let on if she could possibly help it.

"What is our plan going forward?" Faraine asked, presumably directing her question toward Aeson, who seemed to have taken on the role of leader. Nym wasn't sure how she felt about that, but seeing that she had no horse of her own and had just joined them, she'd let it go for now.

"Well, what have we been able to determine thus far about our opponents?" Aeson asked.

Nym didn't reply; she could tell he was about to answer his own question. It was a habit she'd noticed in some people, men in particular. She had no doubt that if he actually wanted her opinion, he'd ask for it.

As she'd predicted, Aeson barely paused before continuing. "We know that multiple people have gone missing, presumed abducted. We know that Nym was very nearly among that number. As far as I can determine, most of the missing people were known to be able to use magic of some kind—or at least, they had access to magical energy of some kind. Except your brother, Faraine, so perhaps I'm going in the entirely wrong direction with this."

"No, you're not."

Aeson glanced over his shoulder at Faraine's low reply. "Eh?"

Faraine guided her dark bay, Caeros, to walk beside Seralo, then began again. "There's nothing wrong with your assumptions, Aeson. I haven't mentioned this before, but...my brother had begun to study magic, before he disappeared. It wasn't anything much. He had a book he always kept near him; one he'd bought off a traveling peddler. It was a compilation of magical theory or the like. He was always practicing spells out in the barn where he thought he'd be undisturbed. But he always wanted a tutor, always stayed on the lookout for anyone passing through town who might be able to teach more than the basic spells in the book."

Nym could see where this was going. "Perhaps he finally found one. The men he was talking to in the tavern—they could have been mages. Maybe they just took him with them."

"Maybe, but he'd never have left home without saying goodbye, and without his clothes and other belongings. So, if they were mages and he did go with them, he didn't go willingly."

"Why didn't you tell me this sooner?" Aeson asked, sounding annoyed.

"I...until we reached Kalas and then someone tried to abduct Nym, I wasn't seeing an actual pattern in all of this. All of the people missing seemed so dissimilar. A cook, a noble, a weaver, a fisherman, my brother...none of it made any sense, until we found out more about all of their histories. It was only then that I realized the *magic* was the common thread in all of this."

"You have a point," Aeson admitted. "We'd only just begun to put it together when we met you, Nym, and you inadvertently confirmed it by using your little charm or whatever it was in your performance and then being targeted. But one thing we haven't been able to confirm is whether all of those people had an equal talent for magic or whether they just had access to it somehow, via some charmed object they were carrying on their persons, for example. If someone *is* targeting magic-users, then how strong does one have to be and how much magic does one have to use before one becomes a target? There are too many variables as yet. We need access to more knowledge and expertise than we currently have at our disposal."

"What do you propose we do, then?" Nym asked.

Aeson's shoulders straightened. "I think we must do the only thing that makes any sense to do. We must go on to Cambermere and seek out the local chapter of the Hawksfire. If I can consult with my siblings in the Order, we between us might be able to determine a rational course of action. And if nothing else, I must warn them of the danger in case they don't know of it, since it seems that mages of various ilk are being targeted. Forwarned is forearmed, or so the wisdom of our ancestors tells us. I think it the most prudent course of action."

"And if we need a place to lie low for a while and avoid whomever was after Nym, then the Hawksfire chapter hall or one of their other holdings might be the safest place for us to be. I agree that does make sense,"

Faraine said. "I don't like being cooped up in a city, but I can see the necessity. So yes, I agree with you, Aeson."

"Nym?"

She blinked, startled. "Yes? Oh, I see. You want to know what I think. Well, I can't think of any better plan at the moment, and I do need to be in a city for at least a few days. I need to perform where I can and make what coin I can, and I need to find a luthier and get my lute repaired, so...yes. I agree."

"Good, I'm glad we took a vote on it," Aeson said dryly. "Not that voting makes the plan any more logical than it already was. So, it's settled. We make straight for Cambermere and my Order, and then we see what my mage sibs know of this and what they can advise. And if it comes to it, if we do need to use Nym as bait, as she so bluntly put it, we'll have a lot more backup to help ensure our safety than we would if we tried to flush out our hunters-turned-quarry with just the three of us alone."

"Backup sounds good. I like backup," Nym mumbled, but the two were already beginning to discuss logistics and next steps, and she let them have at it, her thoughts drifting toward the oncoming dark moon night and what she'd have to say to her fae partner-of-schemes when she had the chance to speak to him again.

DREAMS AND CONFIDENCES

After leaving Tilsk, the trio made their way down the road at a faster pace than what they'd set previously. Nym thought it was probably to try to make up for the time they'd spent in the village, but no one seemed to be following regardless. If only that sort of luck would hold until they reached the city where Aeson's mage order kept a base, then maybe things would be all right. She could hope.

Over the course of the late afternoon, the terrain gradually became more rocky with the occasional low hill or sparse stand of trees. Nym noticed a few areas where stones had obviously been quarried out of hillsides, and here and there wagon tracks led off the main road. It seemed a lonely sort of area—one with few settlers willing to eke a living out of the stony ground unless they were actively engaged in the stonemason's trade. If there were farms, they must be closer to Cambermere where, presumably, the land was a bit more hospitable.

About an hour before nightfall, Aeson led them away

from the road toward the edge of a small wood, where they set up a rudimentary camp. Aeson seemed familiar with the area, which Nym found comforting. She'd never known how much she would miss the merchant caravan until she found herself magically removed from it, and she hadn't known the members of it for all that long nor traveled far with them before she met a fae bard who turned her world upside down.

Surreptitiously watching Faraine and Aeson as they sorted through the saddlebags for the makings of dinner, Nym wondered how long she'd be with these two. After tomorrow night, would she still be in their company, or would another three weeks have passed while everyone thought her missing?

A terrible thought occurred to her as she pondered Erevan and her supposed disappearance from the merchant train, then subsequent return so much later. Was it possible that her new fae mentor was responsible for the other missing people? Had he lured others out and then taken them outside of time, as he'd done to her?

But no. Even as she thought it, it didn't quite make sense. Erevan had said he was looking for stories and tales from the mortal lands, and to her knowledge, she was the only person on Faraine's and Aeson's list who was a bard or storyteller of any ilk. And Erevan *had* returned her to the world—albeit a bit later than she'd expected, and given all she'd read about the time-bending nature of the fae realms, that might not have been his fault.

Also, by the terms of their contract, he had no call to send someone to abduct her and bring her to him. He'd said he could always find her, just as he'd done that first night, and he'd already told her they'd be speaking on each new moon, so it didn't make sense that he'd send someone to retrieve her earlier than that. Sending a creature like the tarinx to kill her was very much counter to her being able to fulfill her end of the bargain they'd struck. He clearly didn't want her dead. If he had, he'd have killed her immediately and not made a deal with her that could put him in nearly as much jeopardy as it put her in.

Nym found herself strangely relieved that logically, Erevan could not be the person who'd tried to have her kidnapped. But that still begged the question of who else it *could* be. The goblin and the man who'd smiled at her so strangely at the inn had referred to their employer as "Himself." Nym was positive that she did not want to meet Himself, whomever that might be.

Aeson made a small fire before dark, to cook a meal and heat water for the tea they had, indeed, bought at the market in Tilsk. It helped to chase the chill from Nym's bones, and by the time she prepared to sleep near the doused fire, rolled up in the new cloak with her clothing bundle under her head as a pillow, she felt almost warm. They hadn't really spoken much that evening, the others seemingly lost in thought much of the time. But for once, Nym didn't really mind the lack of fireside tales and music. She was a bit lost in thought herself.

They set watches during the night so that while one stayed on guard, the others could sleep. But all that night and following day of travel passed uneventfully— so much so that Nym was beginning to wonder whether all their caution and haste was truly warranted. She had yet to meet with Erevan, though, so she remained wary. It wouldn't do to let her guard down just when she might most need to be alert and ready for anything.

The second evening as they made ready to camp, Nym battled nerves and worry, trying to chase thoughts of Erevan and his expectations out of her head. It proved impossible, no matter her efforts. Aeson had taken them into a small ruin that had been nearly swallowed by a grouping of trees trying to become a forest. Most of the stones were scattered and broken, vines growing everywhere and trees thriving right in the middle of what had probably once been the main hall of a small noble holdfast. But some parts of the walls still stood, tumbledown though they were, and they provided some shelter from the wind that had begun to blow in the late afternoon. The person on watch would be exposed part of the time, but that could not be helped.

Nym was doubly grateful for the presence of the walls because she still had no idea how Erevan would contact her. If he woke her with a musical summons in the middle of the night like he had before, then the walls could help provide a sight barrier to her sneaking off to meet with him. She had no wish to deceive her companions, but that, too, could not be helped. Her agreement with Erevan preceded her agreement with Aeson and Faraine, and it was by far the more perilous of the two.

"I'll take the third watch," she called to Aeson, who grunted in agreement. No watch at all might have been better, but she'd no doubt Ereven would figure out some way to hold her to their promised meeting.

The absence of any moonlight made the night seem more threatening somehow. She'd never been one to be afraid of the dark before. But now that she knew there were things such as tarinx in the world, the darkness that had once seemed safe and comfortable now seemed to harbor all manner of potential dangers, even for one with elven eyesight and long experience in making her way in the dark.

As soon as the others had doused the fire and she and Aeson had climbed into their bedrolls while Faraine stood guard, Nym fell into a fitful sleep.

She'd been sure she wouldn't sleep, but she did. She soon fell into a lucid dream that led her through a dark forest surrounded by a ring of violet light. Everywhere the light touched, whatever lay in wait beyond it seemed to hang back and avoid contact. Something about it reassured her, and in any case, she felt safer within its glow than she would have outside where the nameless things waited.

The light guided her relentlessly to a small hut that stood in the middle of a clearing. Nym hesitated, all the tales of witches' huts hidden deep in the woods coming to mind and clamoring for attention, but if she refused to enter, would the light that seemed to be her only protection leave her surrounded by other things she already felt clearly were a threat?

But then, all of this was only a dream anyway, wasn't it? Maybe nothing she did here really mattered.

Briefly, she realized that she could have chosen to wake up. She couldn't have said *how* she knew that, but she felt the knowledge deep within herself, much as she'd known she could have resisted Erevan's summons that night with the caravan. Well, if she could wake herself from this lucid dream whenever she pleased, there was no clear reason to avoid confirming its probable purpose. She approached the door to the hut and pushed it open.

Erevan was sitting on a chair beside a blazing fire, a kettle of something that smelled of cider and spices set to heat in the coals. He looked up as Nym entered. The door swung gently shut behind her, but she managed not to jump when it did.

Erevan looked like no witch Nymariel had ever heard of. And in his elegant clothes that were obviously fit for some fae noble's hall, he should have looked out of place in this hovel, with herbs hanging from exposed beams in the ceiling and a tiny round table taking up part of the space, laden with an array of simple food that would probably never grace that same noble's table. But he looked entirely at ease here, a study in contradictions. Nym came to the conclusion that she had a lot to learn about his world and how it worked—or at the least, a lot to learn about *him*.

"Mulled cider?" Erevan asked. "Or would you prefer tea?"

"Neither, though it was considerate of you to offer," Nym said, glancing around the space and finally settling on a simple chair at the other side of the fireplace.

"It won't harm you, you know," he said casually.

Nym blinked. "What won't harm me?"

"The cider. The tea. Or the food on that table. I assure you, none of this is a means for me to trap you here in the Otherworld and prevent you from leaving, physically or otherwise. I *need* you to leave again. I need you to come, and go, and repeat that process over and over, to bring us both what we want from this bargain we've made."

Nym nodded finally, and accepted the cup of cider he poured and held out to her. Thinking back over what she'd just been through, it was entirely possible that even if she *were* trapped here, she'd be safer with Erevan just now than she was back in the mortal world. At least, that was true at the moment. After he tired of her and their arrangement? That might be another story. But in this moment, some deep instinct told her she was safe with him, and she had to trust her own instincts, or she might just as well give up now and let the unknown enemies take her.

"Something troubles you," he said, and she felt his intent gaze pierce her as surely as if he'd fired a dart made of pure thought into her forehead. It didn't feel like an intrusion so much as a *connection*, and not necessarily an intentional one. It felt more as though this sort of mind-to-mind communication were as natural to him as breathing. He probably didn't even see it as invasive.

"A lot has happened since last we spoke, even though it has only been about a week in the mortal world since I...re-emerged."

"Ah; about that," Erevan said. "I summoned you into the dreamspace tonight so that no more time would pass in your world than absolutely necessary while we are speaking. After this night, you will not hear from me again until the next new moon in your world, as per our agreement. And we will likely communicate in dreams in future, when such is necessary. I am sorry that our last meeting took you physically out of your world for such a long passage of time, but trust me on this; it could have been worse. We will do all we can to avoid it in the future. There are precautions we might take, ways we might play with time so that such a thing does not happen again. I am not, contrary to common belief, given to spiriting mortals away from their own surroundings just to serve my whim. But the need is great, and so therefore we find ourselves here."

"Fair enough." Nym took a cautious sip of the cider. It tasted like no mulled cider she'd ever had before; tangy and sweet at the same time, with so many different spices that she had trouble sorting them all out on her palate.

"What else troubles you? For I know there is more behind your eyes."

"Something is hunting me. Or maybe some*one*. I don't know why. I thought I was careful to use the *wyld* in only small amounts, but maybe I did it wrong." Nym knew her voice held all the bewilderment she still felt over her most recent performance.

"Explain."

Nym met Erevan's gaze, and the kindness and obvious concern she saw there took her aback. Before she could decide what to say, the whole story came tumbling out, from her emergence back into the deserted caravan campsite to her time at the Ring and Dagger, her narrow escape from the kidnappers and the tarinx, and how she came to be traveling with Aeson and Faraine.

Through it all, he listened quietly, only interrupting to ask her to clarify details when necessary. When she'd finished, he studied her for a moment before sighing and reaching for a bottle of wine that suddenly appeared near to hand. He popped the cork and took a long swig from the bottle, then put it away and leaned forward, still studying her closely.

"I must have made a lot of mistakes if I'm already driving you to drink," she pointed out, earning a rueful chuckle from him.

"No, no, it is not you. There is clearly more afoot here than either of us are able to see right now. I will see what I can discover before our next meeting. For your part, you must be very careful. Trust no one fully. Even those who seem trustworthy may have a hidden agenda or be themselves deceived. I do not believe that you erred particularly in your use of the *wyld*, though we can certainly work on your fine control of how much you use in your music. I think whomever targeted you was likely after the magic itself, not reacting to the fact that its source was fae."

"Aeson and Faraine think that someone is going after magic-users too," Nym said. "As far as we can tell, all of the missing people they are trying to locate were able to use magic to at least some degree. Aeson is also worried because he is a mage, and he is concerned for others in his order."

"As well he should be, by the sounds of this," said Erevan, frowning.

"But, *I'm* not a mage. Not really. I'm just..." she trailed off.

"What are you?" Erevan challenged.

"I'm a bard. A bard who uses magic you gave me."

Erevan laughed. "You think I *gave* you that magic, or the ability to wield it? I didn't give that to you, my dear bard. The *wyld* was always a part of you. Perhaps you are more mage than you think."

"I...well, but I..." Nym frowned. "I'm sorry, Erevan, but that's not actually reassuring right now."

He laughed again. "No, I should not think it would be, under the circumstances. But you will have to hone and train it nonetheless, and the sooner the better."

"That was another thing I wanted to ask you," Nym said, more eagerly than she intended. "Can you teach me to use the *wyld* to help protect myself?"

Erevan studied her for a moment longer, a half-smile playing about his lips. "I suppose that my teaching you this would come under the aegis of safeguarding your life, and thus protecting your ability to carry out the bargain we've already made. I see no need for us to make an additional bargain to cover this request."

Nym felt her eyes go wide at the realization of what might have just happened, and then Erevan broke into peals of laughter that had Nym wanting to join in, though none of this was truly funny.

"The look on your face just now was more than payment enough, if any such payment was ever needed. Yes, dear bard, I will teach you some small magics that will help you in your own defense, should such be needed. But again, I caution you against using it too lavishly and too overtly. Use it for small wards and small protections instead—things which will give you advantage in the defense of your own life or that of your companions. For were you to use greater magics, I fear that you would call down upon yourself notice such as we would both deeply regret. Secrecy is your friend and constant guardian just now. Heed me on this."

"I will do my best," Nym said, relief making her feel weak. He was going to help her. That was good; it was what she'd hoped for. Perhaps more than what she'd hoped for, if she were to be honest with herself.

She paid close attention as he began to teach her what she needed to know. He didn't even ask her to repeat any stories or songs for him, though she supposed that was due more to the fact that she'd barely had any time out in the mortal world between this visit and the last, and less because of tonight's lessons themselves or the time they took. To her surprise, they got along well, as though they were old friends and not two people bound by a magical agreement. At least, she didn't *think* the easy comeraderie was her imagination, though she knew better than to rule it out entirely. Some small part of her was shocked to realize that she didn't want the session to end.

When she popped abruptly out of the dream and back into her body, she was still lying wrapped in her cloak in the ruin, and Aeson was shaking her shoulder to wake her to stand her turn at watch.

TEN

HAWKSFIRE

The city of Cambermere was the most welcome sight Aeson had seen in many, many days of traveling. Larger than Kalas, its tall spires and towers, wide main streets and spacious market squares boasted more loudly than a drunkard of the region's wealth and prosperity. Guards dressed in the livery of the noble house of Redmane patrolled the outer walls that ringed the city, and several gates with heavy iron portcullises positioned at regular intervals protected the access points from any would-be invaders.

Aeson guided his two companions unerringly across the city to the sector that housed the massive stone chapter house of the Order of Hawksfire. He'd spent many a day in his youth here on its campus, training in the arts of swordsmanship and arcane magic. Both required a control and discipline that he valued highly.

He hoped he'd managed to disguise the palpable sense of relief he felt at coming back here, to perhaps the one place he might actually think of as "home." Here, he'd find answers, counsel. He wouldn't have to worry quite so much with so many of his brethren here, even with the elven bard beneath their roof and unknown pursuers possibly still on her trail. Any would-be kidnappers would find themselves greatly outmatched here, and maybe with other minds set to the problem of who the mysterious kidnapper was, and *why* magic users were being abducted, they'd finally make some progress in finding a solution.

At his direction, his companions dismounted and shouldered their belongings. He turned Seralo and Caeros over to the initiate who came to take them to the stables, then began to climb the steps to the main entrance.

Aeson nodded to the guard at the door, and led the two women inside to the capacious hall. He noticed that Faraine looked visibly uncomfortable with all the walls around her, which seemed a bit ridiculous at first, until he realized that perhaps this was the largest and most impregnable building she'd ever seen. It could be intimidating, he supposed, to one who'd grown up in a small woodland hamlet whose largest building was probably the village inn.

From what she'd said, Nymariel was also from a small village, though with her elven background and her chosen profession, she was showing no signs of feeling intimidated by the grandeur of Hawksfire Hall. Her talent as a bard and performer was apparent, and she held herself with all the grace and dignity of a noble, though he knew her beginnings were as humble as any. In many ways, she was still an enigma, and Aeson found himself more than a little relieved that both she and Faraine had agreed to come here with him. Here, he'd be able to share the burden of keeping everyone safe with his siblings in the Order.

In the meantime, until he could speak with some of his superiors, he and the women could finally relax a little. They could eat an excellent meal. Have a bath. See to the repair and maintenance of their weapons. Nym would, of course, want to have her lute repaired, if it was possible to do so. She'd have to go out into the city for that, but even there, she could be accompanied by several of his Order sibs, and she'd be as safe as he could make her.

Right up until they needed to use her as bait. She hadn't been wrong about that, though the necessity still bothered him.

As they passed a group of Order initiates and their mentors, someone called out a greeting to Aeson. He nodded and waved, not calling to mind the fellow's name, but responding to the greeting with pleasure nonetheless. It was so very good to be home, among friends and allies.

Aeson frowned again as his thoughts went back to Nym and the question of her role in all of this. It might be better if one of his brothers were set up as bait for whomever kept stealing magic users away. But that might not work. Every mage-knight in the Order and no few of the initiates were usually clearly recognizable as skilled fighters, which tended to make people think twice about antagonizing them. Perhaps that was why he'd heard no reports of any member of the Order going missing as yet. It was a small blessing, perhaps, but it also meant that one of them could probably not take Nym's place when the time came to lure out the kidnappers.

But all of that could wait for the moment. Aeson and his guests were nearing the kitchens, and the scent of hearty stew and baking bread wafted out, making his mouth water. Trail food was good enough, and he was used to it, but the notion of a generous meal prepared by the Hall's fine kitchen staff was appealing enough to cause him to turn aside from his original direction—the barracks—and bring his companions into the warm, bright kitchen instead.

"Aeson! It's so very good to see you!" Melly, the head cook and chatelaine, hurried up to him and threw her arms around his neck in a hug, smearing flour on his tunic—not that he minded. Her hair was greyer than he remembered and she had a lot more wrinkles, but her figure was just as stout and her smile just as kind. That obvious kindness combined with her businesslike manner tugged at his heart, causing a flood of nostalgia. She was, after all, the closest thing to a mother he'd had since he left home all those many years ago. He suspected many in the order felt the same.

"Melly, you are a welcome sight, flour and all!" he said, laughing, spinning her around off her feet as though she were a young girl and not the formidable woman who'd smacked him with a rolling pin on more than one occasion when he was a boy caught misbehaving in her kitchen.

"Flatterer. Now get you to the table in the Hall, and I'll send out a server with some food for you. Best stop and wash first, though; I can tell you're just off the road."

Aeson hesitated. "Ah, Melly…would it be possible for

us to eat in here tonight? Or maybe in the staff dining room, instead of the Hall? My companions aren't used to...all of this." He indicated the building with a grand sweep of his arm.

Melly's sharp gaze took in the two women, both of whom looked exhausted and more than a little bedraggled. Her expression softened. "Of course, Aeson, of course. You poor dears. You must be—"

She broke off, staring at Faraine as if she'd seen a ghost.

"What is it, Melly?" Aeson asked, worried.

Melly studied Faraine for another long moment before answering, while Faraine fidgeted and looked terrified.

"Oh, I'm sorry, dear. Please don't mind an old woman's foolishness. You just remind me of someone I once knew, is all. The resemblance is so uncanny, it startled me. But then, it's likely to be no more than my poor memory just embellishing things, so don't give it a second thought." Melly laughed and shook her head, as if appalled at her own fancies. Faraine gave her a nervous smile, but Aeson could tell she was unsettled.

Briskly, Melly beckoned to a young woman wearing a chambermaid's dress. "Leanne, come here, please. I need you to take these two to the servants' wing and find rooms for them, preferably close to one another. No need to set them up in the Order barracks when they'd be more comfortable here with us. See to it that they have hot water to wash with, and bring them back here when they're ready. I'll arrange the dinner."

Aeson caught a sharp, questioning look from Faraine and nodded, knowing that she'd interpret it correctly; it was safe for them to go with Leanne. They were among people he trusted. Nym's expression betrayed nothing beyond curiosity and a kind of speculation, as though she were sizing up the staff as a potential audience later. He'd no doubt the kitchen staff would enjoy a good tale or two, and he couldn't see the harm in it, as long as she didn't expect them to pay her. But first things first. Rooms, washing up, food, and then perhaps tomorrow, after he'd had time to speak to the Chapter heads, they could determine the next best course of action.

Aeson watched as Leanne headed out of the kitchen and down the hall leading to the servant's quarters, his two companions following her. Even though she had to be sore from riding pillion without a saddle for the better part of three days, Nym's walk was as jaunty as though she were enjoying a stroll in the palace gardens. She seemed to have struck up a conversation with the chambermaid already, while Faraine stalked along behind in silence, head turning from side to side and often looking back over her shoulder as if she were trying to watch all possible attack points at once.

Aeson shook his head in bemusement. They both seemed to have a kind of bravado that they wore like a costume over whatever they were really thinking or feeling, but each wore it differently. It was amazing that they already seemed to have the beginnings of a friendship developing. He'd not have laid odds on that; they seemed so dissimilar in temperament. Had he not been observing them for the past several days, the growing bond wouldn't have been apparent even to him. Not that friendship was his strong suit.

Oh, he was close to a few of his brothers in the Order, but it was a different sort of friendship, if it could be called such. He knew he could count on any member of the Hawksfire to watch his back and support him in a fight, and several were good for an evening of cards or drinking, but to take them into his confidence in a more personal sense? Aeson sighed, low and under his breath so no one would hear and ask him his thoughts. He'd left behind all of his past when he'd joined the Order. As far as any of his Hawksfire brothers and sisters were concerned, he didn't really *have* a past. And that was as it should be. Every child adopted into the ranks of the Hawksfire left behind whomever and whatever had come before. It ensured that everyone in the order was fully committed and free of regrets.

Or at least, it was supposed to. Aeson had never submitted to the blocking of his memories the way the others had. On the day when the instructors were to put the memory block spells in place for his class of initiates, he'd feigned illness. He didn't deserve to forget that day in his youth when he'd learned how costly magic could be, and how great the responsibility was for those who could wield it. That knowledge was what had driven him to the Order, and he didn't deserve to be relieved of it.

Melly returned and interrupted his musings as she thrust a mug of hot tea into his hand, pushing him toward a chair by the fire. "Aeson, you look nearly done in. Sit and warm yourself for a spell, while I send someone to get your old room ready for you. You've been on the road so long this last time, it's probably covered with dust. But we'll set that to rights in no time."

"Thank you, Melly. You're too good to me, as ever."

Melly brushed off his thanks. "Oh, it's nothing I wouldn't do for any of my younglings. Though there are few enough of *those* about in these halls this past decade and more. Well, maybe children just aren't as willing these days to let go of whatever things they've done in the past. Takes a lot of commitment to be a knight of the Order of Hawksfire."

She bustled off, muttering about the falling numbers of initiates and how demanding the adult members had become of late. Bemusedly, he watched her go for a moment, then turned his attention to the mug of tea she'd handed him. Children unwilling to let go of whatever they'd done that had brought them to the Order's door? It hit home, but what Melly didn't know about him could never hurt her. And his commitment wasn't in question—never had been.

Aeson remembered all too well what he'd done in his past. Even now, decades later, it was as clear as if it were yesterday. He never spoke of his childhood to anyone, not even by indirect reference. He could never reveal that he was aware of his past prior to entering the Order, or there would be too many uncomfortable questions about why he'd never had the memories blocked. They kept him honest, and they kept him penitent. It would have been all too tempting to allow the memories to be blocked so that his earliest awareness was of his induction into the Hawksfire, but he always needed to remember why he'd chosen to come here in the first place. It was important.

The Grand Master had always taught that the pre-Order memories from childhood were removed as a way to give an initiate a fresh start, and to ensure their loyalty. It didn't matter what their lives had been like prior to entering the Hawksfire; all of that was forgiven, forgotten, and gone. The only thing that mattered was what they did with their lives going forward.

But Aeson's memories, however painful, were a part of what made him who he was, and sealing them away seemed like cheating, somehow. A free pass that he didn't deserve. With intense focus, he soaked up the warmth and good scents from the brick oven as Melly's bread baked. Thus comforted, he let the forbidden memories wash over him, as he had so often since he'd first come here as a scared and grieving boy.

It had been about this same time of year, when it happened. He'd been no more than eleven. His friend, Padraig, had been with him as he ran though the field behind his father's farmhouse. They'd cut across the field and slipped into the woods, exhilarated at the crisp air and falling leaves. Everything seemed possible; everything was an adventure.

They played about with sticks that they used as swords, then took to running and tumbling in great piles of leaves. Then Padraig had boasted that he could lift and throw a larger stone than Aeson could. Aeson took him up on the challenge; he'd been practicing, lifting heavier and heavier loads on the farm, and his muscles were starting to show something for his effort. Padraig was always something of a boaster, and it was time he had to eat his words, for once.

The idea was to stand at forty paces from one another and heave a stone toward the other's general direction. Of course, the one in the path of the stone was supposed to dodge, but the heavier the stone, the more difficult it was to heave one far enough to go past those forty paces anyway. The heaviest stone Padraig could lift only went part of that distance when he heaved it, but it was a good enough throw; he'd been practicing for the stone toss that was held on the village green every fall.

Aeson tried to lift Padraig's stone and only just managed it, staggering under its weight. It was hard to carry, much less toss any distance. Padraig had jeered at him, questioning Aeson's strength, his balance, and even his competence. Then he questioned Aeson's parentage, implying that his mother had slept with a wimpy scholar to get him, saying that was why Aeson was so weak.

That had been the last straw. Something inside Aeson snapped. All the insults, the insinuations, the teasing that for years had assaulted him on all sides from the other boys in the village—it all was just too much. They thought he was something to be ridiculed. They thought he was somehow inferior, weaker, less worthy, just because he was the smallest boy in the village. Well, he'd show them. He'd show them all.

Strength flooded him, and he heaved the rock, feeling the air currents take it as a tingling sense of power and well-being coursed through him. His aim was impeccable, that day. The rock, seeming far lighter than it should, flew with uncanny accuracy, straight toward Padraig. It hit the other boy right between the eyes, and he dropped to the forest floor, limp.

Aeson had run up to Padraig where he lay, wide-open eyes staring at nothing. Screams, loud and ringing and terrifying, left Aeson's throat, and by the time his father and some of the other village men came running up, his throat was raw with the screaming.

He'd owned up to everything that had happened—all of it. And not a sevenday afterward, he found himself on a cart bound for the city, exiled from his village for killing his friend. Yes, it had been an accident; even the most hidebound elders of his village saw the scene for what it was. But he was exiled nonetheless, and he found that he was glad to go. He had to get away from those people with their staring eyes and accusations, away from the hurt gazes of his parents and older brother, Jaimie.

They didn't want a mage in the family; they didn't know what to do with one. And, to be honest, he didn't really know what to do with himself. He'd admitted the truth of what had happened, and been punished for it. It felt as though it wasn't just his magic they were rejecting, but his very being—all that made him who he was. And there was just no coming back from that, no matter how much hurt and pain he'd seen in his family's eyes. One would think *he'd* betrayed *them*, somehow.

Once the caravan boss had delivered him to the gates of the Order and left, Aeson had squared his shoulders, climbed the steps to the door, and knocked three times as he'd been directed. The door had opened, and his new life began. He could say he'd never looked back, but that would be a lie.

Even after all this time, he'd never regretted keeping

his memories. The Order's teachings were right; magic could be both gift and curse, but whatever else it was, it was a responsibility and a sacred charge for those who could wield it. Too much power was even more likely to be misused, and so Aeson had always been grateful for the leash on his power that the Order provided.

This was the right way; it was the only way that made sense to him.

Faraine had no great desire to be alone in this unfamiliar place, but she dutifully followed Leanne down the long hallway of the service wing. The servants' quarters were all adjacent to the kitchens for ease of access, and while Aeson and Melly had been greeting one another, Faraine had also noticed another couple of doors leading off the kitchen, presumably for access to the wine cellar and who knew where else. Perhaps the stables? If that were the case, she could check on her horse later. No matter whose home one was in, it was always prudent to familiarize oneself with all possible exits, just in case trouble came knocking.

Melly's obvious startlement at her appearance bothered Faraine. Had the woman somehow glimpsed certain secrets that she would rather keep hidden? Or did she truly remind Melly that strongly of someone she'd known before?

It begged a whole raft of questions.

Leanne stopped beside one of the doors that opened off the long hallway. A quick glance through the door showed Faraine a very simple room with a comfortable-looking cot, a washstand, and a small wardrobe.

"You can use this room while you're here, and your friend will have the one just to the left," Leanne said with a shy smile. "Please let me or Mistress Melly know if there is anything else you need. Any guest of Brother Aeson's is a friend of ours. He's always been kind to all of us on the serving staff, and he dotes on Mistress Melly. And she's always been like a mother to him and all the children here."

"Thank you," Faraine managed, which seemed to be enough. The chambermaid was already showing Nymariel to her room, which looked identical to this one except for the color scheme of the patchwork quilt on the bed, the pastoral scene depicted on the small painting on the wall, and the matching towels that hung from the bar on the front of the washstand.

From where she stood just inside her room, Faraine could hear Nym and the chambermaid chatting. Despite herself, she envied the bard her natural ability to make small talk and win people over, even when she was not using whatever magic charm she'd used on the audience back at the Ring and Dagger in Kalas. Some things just came more naturally to some people than to others.

At least, Faraine assumed that Nym wouldn't need to use magic just to talk to people. She seemed to have a natural affinity for what people wanted to hear, or for what they needed. That in itself wasn't too uncommon; plenty of people seemed to have that ability. The unscrupulous ones used it to their advantage at the expense of others, almost as a rule.

Nym, however, seemed to be truly at ease with people, and seemed to genuinely care what they thought. For all her willingness to magically bilk people out of some coin during a performance, Nym also seemed determined to give her audience their money's worth. Faraine wasn't sure whether that was admirable or ridiculous. How many cons actually had a conscience? It made Faraine's mind want to tangle itself in knots, just thinking about it. Nym was a living paradox. A likable one, but a paradox nonetheless.

Faraine had just pulled her thoughts back from her woolgathering and stowed her few belongings under the bed and in the wardrobe when the paradox walked into her room and sat down on the bed, looking up at Faraine expectantly.

"Can I help you?" Faraine asked automatically, a little startled.

Nym smiled and brushed a hand through the air as though brushing aside the question. "I just came in here to ask *you* that. You seem a little on edge since we got here, and I was wondering whether you were okay after the way Melly seemed to recognize you. It seemed to startle her as much as it did you, and I wondered if you knew what was going on."

"Straight to the point, eh?" The quick reply was out of Faraine's mouth before she could stop it. She immediately felt guilty. An overture of friendship didn't deserve a snarky brush-off. "I'm sorry. You're right; I'm a little out of sorts. I was already feeling out of place and uncomfortable, and then Melly's reaction to me just...I don't know...scared me, I guess. I don't know why."

Nym was watching her closely. "No, it's more than

that. When you saw Melly's reaction, you got the strangest look on your face. Like you were half afraid she'd root out a deep, dark secret, and half hopeful that she really did recognize you for some reason."

"No, I...wait. You know, I think you're right! I hadn't figured out my *own* reaction to that encounter until you said that just now. Hopeful. Yes. For a moment I *was* hopeful, because for about a split second I thought that maybe Melly had seen my brother before. But that's crazy, right?" Faraine sat down on the bed, shaking her head at her own foolish notion.

Nym shook her head, too, but with emphasis. "No. *Not* crazy. Do you and your brother look much alike?"

Faraine nodded, that strange feeling of hope building in her heart again at Nym's unexpected support. "We do. We have the same father, the same nose and forehead, same skin color. We had different mothers, but we both take after our father. My mother died when I was five. When I was seven, my father remarried and then my brother was born. Both my brother and I seem to take after our mothers in terms of talents or abilities. But we take after our father in looks. No one could ever tell we were half-siblings, the family resemblance was so strong. So I'll admit that when Melly reacted as though she'd seen a ghost, it gave me hope that maybe, just maybe, she'd seen my brother pass through at some point."

"And that could give you a clue toward finding him, but it's also a worry, because...oh, I see," Nym said, eyes widening. She got up, looked up and down the hall, then closed the door before returning to sit on the bed beside Faraine.

"Because if Melly *has* seen my brother, then it's possible that he actually ended up passing though the Order and becoming a member, rather than being kidnapped by whomever is targeting magic-users. And since all of the members of the Order have their memories of their time prior to induction blocked away..." Faraine's voice was little more than a whisper, and at the end, she trailed off altogether. It was all just too much to consider. And yet, she had to.

"Then in that case, he wouldn't remember you, and you showing up here could present a complication," Nym finished.

"Yes," Faraine said, relief that Nym understood and didn't think the notion foolish making her nearly giddy. "So, you see my dilemma."

"Perhaps you should tell Aeson," Nym said after a moment.

"I will. But maybe not just yet. Melly may have been correct and just mistook me for someone else. She may not even remember who."

But Nym was shaking her head. "No, Faraine. Melly doesn't seem like a woman who forgets her kids, and all of the children who pass through this chapter of the Order are her kids, in her mind. She wouldn't forget a young man who passed through no more than a year ago. That's about when you said he had disappeared, right?"

"Correct," Faraine said, mind reeling. "Well, let us just keep this between ourselves for the moment. I'll see what I can find out by having a look around when I can sneak away, in the quiet moments when no one is watching. And if you want to help me, you can try to suss out whatever you can about the most recent boys who've passed through here when you're playing bard for the servants. Servants know a lot more than most people give them credit for. They're one of the best sources of information in the entire kingdom, or so my uncle used to say when he visited. He served as chamberlain to a local lord, back near where my family lived."

"Sure, I'll help all I can. And what do you mean, *playing* at being a bard? I am a bard. There's no playing, save what I do on the lute. Or...what I *did* on the lute, before I wrecked it by falling on it."

"Poor Nym! We'll make sure to try to do something about that tomorrow," Faraine said, smiling despite her worry. She surprised herself by reaching out to pat Nym on the shoulder. "And you're right; I apologize. I didn't mean any disrespect, madame bard."

Nym gave her a good-natured mock scowl from under raised eyebrows, and before she knew it, a giggle slipped out of Faraine's mouth. A *giggle*! This bard was a bad influence on her. She'd have to be careful not to let her guard down; caution was still vastly important. But friendship was important too, and she had the feeling that both she and Nym had had far too little of that in their lives.

Friendship was a tempting thought, but it was early days yet. She'd give it time and see what happened, no hurry. And in the meantime, she could certainly use Nym's natural charisma to her own advantage, just as she'd been using Aeson's sword arm. One could never have too many allies, whether or not they became actual friends.

ELEVEN

THE MUSIC OF LOSS

Nym eyed her audience, letting them squirm for several moments of suspense before she picked up the thread of her tale. Tonight's was a tough crowd, comprised of mostly kitchen staff, a good handful of young initiates, and a much smaller number of children whose parents were kitchen or stable workers. Her tale drew them all in, though, as surely as a fish on a line, reeling them in little by little until she reached the penultimate scene that had them hanging on every word. The tale wound to an end with every set of eyes fixed on Nym, grins spreading from ear to ear, their delight evidence that she'd done her job well.

And she'd done it all without using the *wyld*, tempting though it had been to weave some into her voice for added nuance and flavor. The sections of the tale where she sang a little, acapella, would have been the perfect place to try it. But this was right in the middle of the repressive Order of Hawksfire, and she didn't dare yield to the impulse. It wasn't as though she were doing it for coin anyway; surely none of these people could afford it.

No, she was doing it for the sheer joy of it, and in gratitude for the wonderful meal and hot bath she'd been able to enjoy earlier in the evening. Now, in the last hour before the children's curfew bell rang, she'd yielded to the kitchen staff's requests for a private performance—albeit gratis—and they certainly all deserved it.

Besides, it gave her a chance to hone some of her other skills, with no lute to disguise any thin spots in her performance.

The lute. She'd have to try to get out into the city tomorrow, to see if she could find this luthier that the carpenter in Tilsk had told her about. She might be able to perform without a lute, but she missed it as much as if it were an old friend. Which, in a lot of ways, it was.

"Excuse me, mem?" A small hand plucked at her sleeve. Nym looked around at the child who stood at her elbow, and smiled.

"You may call me Nym," she said. "Did you need something?"

The boy scuffed the toe of his shoe against the floor, looking down at his feet. "I know you're finished with the story and all, but I was wondering something." He flushed, still scowling at his feet.

"That's all right. What do you want? If it's not a story that takes too long, I could tell maybe just one more, if you've a favorite."

"It...it isn't really a story, mem. Not really. It's just...I was just..." He swallowed, then looked up at her face. His eyes were wide, vivid blue, and so earnest that it made Nym's heart ache. "I was wondering whether you might sing a song my mother sang to me. Tomorrow they are going to remove my memories, and I just...I just wanted to hear that song one more time, before...."

Nym blinked back sudden tears. "Of course! I'll do my best. What is the song? Can you sing a little for me, so I can see if I know it?"

The boy nodded and complied, his voice still high and clear as he sang the first verse of a lullaby Nym didn't recognize.

"I'm sorry, but I don't know that one. Maybe you can teach me, and then we'll sing it together? And would you tell me your name? Bards like to know where they get their songs from."

He nodded eagerly. "Dannel. My name is Dannel."

"All right, Dannel. I don't have an instrument at the moment, so I'll need you to tap the beat out for us, like this." Nym lightly tapped her hand on one leg.

Dannel followed suit, changing tempo slightly, and beginning the verse again. Nym repeated it with him, then waited for him to go on to the next part of the song. The child patiently obliged, and together they sang and repeated all of the verses of the song until she had it memorized.

"Will you sing it for me yourself, now?" he asked finally when she'd learned the last verse.

Nym nodded, and began the song again, this time letting her voice rise a bit more loudly so that it carried to the other children who remained in the room. Looking at Dannel bravely trying to hold back tears, Nym instinctively reached for...*something*. Something to comfort, to heal, to make this last night of his childhood just a little less dark. He might not even remember this tomorrow, but for tonight, she wanted him to have what peace and comfort he could.

A little of the *wyld* crept into the music, making it haunting and sweet, carried on Nym's voice alone, and she found herself having to hold back some of the magic when it flowed too strongly. It was as though the absence of any instrument made the magic stronger somehow, and it was all Nym could do to keep it to the smallest trickle. She hadn't meant to use it at all, but it had happened anyway, as though Dannel's sadness somehow demanded it.

When Nym fell silent again at the end of the song, she glanced around at the rest of the children. Some were openly weeping, even a few of the older ones who had no doubt already lost their own early memories. And Melly was surreptitiously wiping tears from her eyes with the corner of her apron.

A smattering of applause began, which was cut off when Melly hastily began to gather the children up and shoo them off toward the initiates' dormitories.

"Not a peep, now, lambs. Off to bed straight away, and not a word from any of you about this last bit of singing. I've let you stay up past your bedtime, and we wouldn't want to get Mistress Nym in trouble for that, now would we? No, of course we wouldn't. Off you go, quickly now."

The children filed out of the kitchen, obviously taking great care to walk quietly and not to speak above a whisper. *Apparently, it isn't just the bard who might be in trouble if they were caught*, Nym realized.

Dannel was the last to go, and he looked back at Nym with such gratitude and sadness on his face that she thought her heart might burst.

Alone in her room that night, despite the comfort of a mattress underneath her and four walls around her, it was some while before Nym could coax her mind off the children and their situation here. Sleep was slow in coming.

When she woke the next morning, it was to the sound of a bell, ostensibly calling the residents of the Hall to breakfast. Melly sent a chambermaid to collect Nym and Faraine and bring them to the kitchen, where they ate with the serving staff. Aeson was nowhere to be seen, but Melly assured them that he was eating with his Order brethren in the main hall, and would see them later, after he'd had a meeting with the Grand Master in residence to tell him whatever news he wished to impart.

That meant that for the time being, Nym and Faraine were on their own. Faraine volunteered to go with Nym into the city to find the luthier that Tilsk's carpenter had recommended. Upon hearing their plan, Melly insisted on making up a lunch packet for them to take along, and requested that they also stop at a seamstress' shop in the same area as the luthier, to pick up a packet of thread and cloth that Melly had on order.

It wasn't until they were well on their way across the city that Nym remembered that Aeson had intended to send them with an escort. But the city was large enough and the streets busy enough that she doubted anyone searching for them would readily find them in the teeming crowds. Just to be safe, they pulled the hoods of their cloaks up to obscure any clear view of their faces;

the brisk autumn wind was just chill enough today to justify it in the eyes of anyone who happened to glance their way.

They made it to the luthiers without incident and without having to solicit anyone's attention for directions, in part thanks to Melly's clear and concise description of the market district.

A tiny bell hanging over the door chimed as they walked in. Everywhere Nym looked, harps with beautifully carved pillars stood either on the floor or on tables, and lutes, lyres and gitterns hung from racks on the walls. Wind instruments ornamented with silver chasing lay in gleaming cases, and cannily crafted tin whistles stuck up out of the top of a large pottery vase. It was a bard's dream of a shop, and Nym could only stare for a moment in wonder. No dragon's hoard full of gold could possibly rival this, as far as she was concerned.

A tall, slender man with long brown hair came out from the back room, his eyes taking in the two women and the lute bag Nym carried. Pulling the instrument out, she offered it to him without comment. He took it, inspecting it with a practiced eye, long fingers feeling the damaged soundboard and running over the rounded bowl of the back, checking to see whether any of the laminated sections had separated.

"Are you Davic Mercery?" Nym asked, though it was already clear they'd found the luthier.

"That's me, yes," he said, still studying the ruined instrument, holding it up to sight down the neck, turning it about to examine it from all angles.

"You were recommended. I'm hoping you can repair this for me. Performing without it makes me feel as though I have one hand tied behind my back," Nym said.

Davic sighed. "Well, it is true that I can repair it, but that is not the limiting factor. The real issue is that the repair is going to be expensive. Almost as expensive as simply buying a new lute. This one's good days were long in the past even before this damage happened. How much were you hoping to pay?"

"How much would the repair cost me, at the minimum?" Nym didn't want to suggest a price and then find the luthier quoting her own price back to her if the amount she stated turned out to be higher than what he actually required for the repair.

Davic handed the lute back to her and looked at her levelly. "Twenty gold. Would have been less, but the damage to the soundboard is affecting the neck too. The whole thing is about to cave in."

"Twenty! Oh...I'd hoped it would be less," Nym burst out, thoroughly dismayed. Twenty gold pieces. She didn't have even half of that, and she'd had no opportunity to take any paying gigs since leaving Kalas. "I don't have that much now. I might be able to get it, though. It will just take me some time."

Davic nodded. "Well, then, bring this poor thing back when you have the gold. Meantime, I have a flute I can sell you to tide you over as an instrument. I'll even give you a deal on it. It's been on a back shelf for a long time, and I need to clear a few things out to make room for new merchandise. What do you say?"

Nym considered. The expense of a flute would delay the lute's repair even longer, and she had no skill with a flute. But on the other hand, having a second instrument could come in handy, and she was fairly sure that Erevan would know how to play. He could teach her, if he also considered her having a playable instrument as part of safeguarding her ability to hold up her end of their bargain. And if not, she'd find a way—teach herself to play if she had to. There was no way she would get herself into any additional deals with Erevan, no matter how much she might need his help. She'd been lucky so far. Luck wouldn't hold out forever.

"I'd like to see it, if it isn't too pricey," she told Davic.

He nodded and went into the back room while Nym and Faraine waited. It seemed to take him quite some time to locate the flute in question and return to them, but as soon as he pulled it from the long wooden box where it resided, Nym knew she wanted it, whatever its price. She'd just have to convince Aeson that she needed a few evenings of performance time in whatever taverns and inns in the city he felt were obscure enough that she wouldn't draw notice of the wrong sort. Though she might have to start by telling stories in the market square for tips, and that might prove more problematic.

She'd figure it out, somehow.

The flute was made from wood so dark it was naturally black, and polished so smooth as to feel like glass. When Nym blew into it, it produced a sweet, high but mellow tone that resonated in the small instrument shop, faintly vibrating the strings of the harps and lutes on display.

Davic was watching Nym with an odd, almost regretful look. "I'll sell that to you for thirty silver. That's the best I can do. It's still a bit dear, but not so much as a lute."

"Eighteen," Nym countered.

"Twenty-five."

"Twenty. I'm buying it off a back shelf where it's been forever, remember? It's on sale, or so you implied."

A faint smile played about Davic's mouth. "All right; sold at twenty. Here, take it. I'll even throw in a travel case for it, just to remind you to bring that lute back when you can afford the repair, or even just to come back for a new lute, which is what I'd actually recommend."

"Pleasure doing business with you, though I'm sorry the lute repair wasn't in the cards just now." Nym counted out the twenty silver and took the flute and its case from Davic, then shouldered her broken lute in its soft case and left the store, Faraine hovering nearby with a guarded look on her face.

"Well, that did not go the way I hoped, but at least I got something for my trouble," Nym said as they headed down the street toward the seamstress shop.

"There was something off about that man," Faraine grumbled. "I didn't like the way he was looking at us. And why did it take him so long to find that flute? He had time to eat a sandwich back there while we waited."

"I don't know."

They found the seamstress shop easily enough and gave the proprietor Melly's name. A few short minutes later, they were on their way back toward Hawksfire Hall with package in hand. However, Faraine insisted on pulling them down several random streets on the way, so that they ended up arriving back at the Hall in the late afternoon after having taken a rather circuitous route. She wouldn't even stop on the way to eat any of the lunch that Melly had packed, insisting that they could eat it as soon as they were back safely at the Hall.

"You're either paranoid, or you saw something that's got you spooked," Nym said when they were finally inside the walls of the Hall once more and ensconced in Faraine's room with the door shut, after having dropped off Melly's package with one of the chambermaids.

Faraine took a big bite of her sandwich, chewed, swallowed, then waited a few more seconds before she spoke.

"Nym, I know that you're not naïve. You're smart, you have good survival instincts, and you notice a lot of details that most people don't. But I think you may have a blind spot where other musicians are concerned. I was listening very closely while Master Davic was in the back room. He didn't rummage through anything, so if he was searching for the flute, he was searching with his eyes only. And I also heard him speaking to someone back there. It sounded like he was talking about us, though I couldn't tell for sure, and I thought I heard them reference Tilsk and the carpenter you spoke to. You told Davic someone had recommended him to you, but you never said who that was. So, paranoid I may be, but I don't trust the man, and I'm not sure we did so well by being there today. In fact, I have a bad feeling about it."

Cold fear settled like a ball of ice in Nym's stomach. "If it's as you fear, then Master Mercery was likely in it for the money, which seems to fit with his inflated price for a lute repair. He sells me an old flute that he wanted to get rid of anyway, and then he reports on my whereabouts to someone else who will probably pay him for that information. In essence, he gets paid twice. Just wonderful. We'd better find Aeson and let him know."

"He ought to be finished with his conference with his Grand Master by now. I'll find Leanne and ask her if she can locate him and send him to us. That way, we keep this as quiet as possible, and we don't draw attention to ourselves."

Nym nodded grimly. She looked down at the sandwich in her hand, Melly's delicious bread suddenly tasting like wood ash in her mouth. All she'd wanted to do was get her lute repaired, for pity's sake! Faraine was right; she needed to be even more on her guard. Whomever was after her seemed to have ears in the most unlikely of places, and they seemed to know too much about her, if even shopkeepers and musicians were reporting her whereabouts.

She and her companions needed to find out who was behind these abductions quickly, before anyone else went missing. Least of all herself.

TWELVE

DISILLUSIONED

Aeson paced back and forth in front of the Grand Master's door. After breakfast this morning, he'd come here to secure a conference and been told to wait—that Grand Master Zebermar would see him before lunchtime. Lunchtime came and went and no one came to summon him. And still he waited. Now it was late afternoon, and still no summons.

Aeson sighed. You'd think they would want to hear his report. That was what they sent him out into the world for in the first place, wasn't it? They sent him out so that he could bring back vital information of concern to the Order. Yet this Grand Master saw fit to keep him waiting all day, and he'd skipped lunch because he'd been following instructions to wait.

The Order of Hawksfire assigned a senior member to each chapter hall, to make sure things ran smoothly and the more inexperienced members of the Order had a seasoned veteran to turn to if they found themselves in need of guidance. A few years prior, Aeson himself had been asked to head up one of the Chapters, but had refused. He had no head for bureaucracy, however necessary it might be. His preference was to be out there trying to deal with the evils in the world, protect people, right wrongs...it all sounded so idealistic when he thought of it like this. But it was true.

However, no matter how idealistic he might be, no amount of patience could account for the fact that Grand Master Zebermar, who traveled frequently between Chapter halls, had seen fit to ignore Aeson's impending report in favor of something else that apparently seemed more important, though there had been no other traveling Order sib reporting in to the Cambermere chapter in over a month.

It had been his good fortune that Grand Master Zebermar was in residence here at the moment, or so Aeson had been told by the Hall steward. Good fortune. Perhaps. But how much good fortune could it be if the Grand Master continued to ignore him? How many more lives were put in danger with every hour he had to wait to warn the heads of the Order?

There were four Grand Masters in the Order of Hawksfire, and the heraldic arms of each represented one of the four elements of earth, air, fire, and water, though that didn't necessarily represent each Master's actual magical aptitude. The arms were mainly for show; the four elements looked well-balanced and impressive in a parade, which the Order put on only if the general populace seemed to need the reassurance. The four Grand Masters shared the responsibility of guiding the members of the Order, also serving as check and balance for each other. Whatever he told Grand Master Zebermar today must be conveyed to the others before they could form a response to the threat, and time was of the essence, in Aeson's opinion.

He'd never met any of the other Grand Masters, though he'd seen them from a distance on a number of formal occasions. They were all said to be formidable with their abilities. One of them, Master of Earth Alsa Chendoni, was newer to her post than the others, though she'd been there since before Aeson joined the Order. She'd replaced the original Master of Earth, an enigmatic person named...what was it? Jarrah. That was it. Just Jarrah; they had no known surname that Aeson had ever heard. Now that he thought about it, he remembered Melly speaking of Jarrah on occasion; apparently they'd been friends once. Jarrah had left the Order over some disagreement with the other Grand Masters. Aeson didn't know much more than that, but he'd often wondered what the disagreement had been about.

Another half hour of alternately pacing and leaning against the wall, and Aeson had come to the conclusion that Zebermar would not see him today. He growled under his breath in frustration. More people could be going missing while he wasted his time pacing a hallway! And even his Order siblings might be in danger at some point! How long until whomever was abducting magic-users decided that taking a member of the Hawksfire was worth the risk?

Aeson's stomach rumbled loudly, reminding him of how long it had been since he'd eaten. Perhaps nipping down to the kitchen to grab a bite to eat while he waited would not take too long. The dinner hour was fast approaching, and he had no desire to skip *two* meals today.

He had just taken a step in the general direction of the kitchens when the door to the Grand Master's study opened, and when Aeson turned at the sound, Zebermar himself stood in the opening, his sharp gaze making Aeson freeze in mid-motion.

"Brother Aeson! It is so good to see you back again after so long away! I am sorry you have been waiting for so long, but other matters have arisen which demanded my attention. Please, come and tell me all your news! With any luck at all, we can go through all you need to impart before the ringing of the dinner bell."

Finally. Aeson gave the Grand Master a nod and followed him into the well-appointed study. The walls were lined with reference books and scrolls of all sorts, even though the Hall boasted a very well-stocked library. The ones in this room had all been curated by the various Grand Masters personally over the years, according to the tastes and interests of each, and now it was all overflowing, some tomes even stacked upon the floor here and there.

At one side of the room nearest a tall arched window, a large oaken desk was situated to best catch any incoming light, and a comfortable dark-blue-cushioned chair stood behind it. It was to this chair that Grand Master Zebermar went to sit, gesturing Aeson to take a smaller but similarly cushioned chair on the opposite side of the desk.

Gingerly, Aeson sat. Both chairs and the desk were carved all over in elaborate geometric designs vaguely reminiscent of arcane sigils, to the unpracticed eye at least. It was visually busy, but not restful. All harsh planes and angles—though perhaps it represented the Order and its tenets very well indeed, for all that.

"Thank you for seeing me, Grand Master," Aeson said, trying to keep any hint of annoyance out of his voice.

Grand Master Zebermar regarded Aeson from under a pair of bushy grey brows. He meticulously straightened the books and papers on his desk, then folded his hands and waited.

Aeson began with the first of the investigations from several months prior, and the ones that followed. Following some impulse that he could not put a name to, he left out his meeting with Faraine and the fact that Faraine was looking for her brother. Instead, he explained that he'd run into the two women on his travels and had agreed to provide them safe escort to Cambermere, establishing himself in the role of protector. Let Grand Master Zebermar make what he would of that.

Mages in the Order weren't prohibited from taking lovers—not that either Faraine or Nym would stand for that kind of nonsense from him. But some deep instinct warned him that allowing such an implied fiction might prove to be prudent, and he'd never found his instincts to be untrustworthy. In fact, often as not, if he ignored his gut, he usually came to regret it.

Grand Master Zebermar had listened quietly all through Aeson's recounting of his investigation, and now he was nodding, seemingly almost to himself.

"You say you brought these two young women here under your protection. Where are they now?"

"Safely under this roof, Grand Master," Aeson replied. "I thought it best, until they had a chance to determine what they wished to do next. There is every chance they will want to secure quarters in the city. Cambermere's walls and security are second to none, after all."

"Very wise, Brother Aeson, very wise. However, a matter has been brought to my attention that you may not be aware of. It presents a dilemma, and it involves one of your...guests."

"One of my guests? How so, Grand Master?"

Zebermar leveled a steely gaze at Aeson, the bushy brows only serving to make him look sterner. That gaze had made many an initiate quake, Aeson included.

"The red-haired elven girl—the bard. I'm told she was entertaining the children with stories last night. A frivolous indulgence, and one I will have to speak to Melly about later. But in essence, not so great a problem in and of itself. What I wish to know is whether she did ought else last night, with regard to the children."

"I don't believe so, Grand Master." Aeson frowned. Why this line of questioning? What had Nym done now?

"Did she perform any magic tricks for them, perchance? Any sleight of hand, any rhymes or verses, or the like?"

"Not to my knowledge, Grand Master. Why do you ask?" Aeson knew his frown had only deepened, but he was truly perplexed.

Why should it matter whether a bard told stories? He knew her lute was broken, so it was unlikely that she'd have performed music—not that he was going to mention music to Zebermar now that he'd shown such an odd interest in Nym's affairs.

Having gotten to know Nym a little on the road, Aeson was loath to share her secrets and inadvertently convince the Grand Master that she was something that needed to be dealt with. Even if Zebermar had somehow inexplicably found out that Nym used music to coerce audiences into giving up a bit of extra coin, that was hardly a threat or an outright danger to others, least of all children who had no money to begin with and didn't tend to frequent inns and taverns.

Aeson's face must have shown his confusion, for the Grand Master sighed and settled back in his chair, gazing at him over steepled hands. "The outlandish gibberish that reached my ears concerning the bard must be false, then. It seems she did nothing that might cause an entire group of initiates to be suddenly resistant to the memory-binding spell." His tone suggested his words were completely opposite to his thoughts.

"Resistant to...what?" Aeson was completely bewildered now. What the Grand Master was saying sounded ludicrous at best. Nym, somehow causing the children to rebel against the memory-binding? Just by telling them a story about a farmer and a magical peach, as one of the small boys had been enthusiastically talking about at breakfast this morning?

"I do not mean resistant as in *refusal*, Brother Aeson. None of our initiates would *refuse* the memory-binding. I mean resistant as in being somehow immune to the spell. Every single child who was due to receive a binding this afternoon had some sort of—I don't know —arcane film clinging to them like a second skin, almost like a ward. One which prevented our master of initiates from effectively binding their memories, at least until they realized what was happening and performed a ritual cleansing first. It was strange, to say the least. Nothing like this has ever happened before."

"That is odd, Grand Master. I don't believe that the bard has that sort of ability, so this is certainly the work of some other as yet unknown agent. We will have to investigate, of course."

"Of course," Zebermar said smoothly. "We cannot have our tenets and protective practices being disrupted. Very well, then, if you have finished your report, you may go."

Aeson rose, but hesitated. "But, Grand Master, does not the notion of mages targeted by an unknown kidnapper concern you? What if our own Order members were to become targets as well? It might be prudent to assign us travel duty in pairs in future, to ensure our safety."

Grand Master Zebermar leveled a glare at Aeson, and he knew instantly that he'd overstepped. Something about the Grand Master's energy seemed to pulse and flare. For a moment, Aeson had the sense of barely leashed power—more power than any member of the Order should wield. But it was gone just as quickly, and all Aeson could sense was the usual, familiar levels of magical energy. He had to be imagining things, which was probably no wonder, given all the uncertainty of recent days. He clearly needed a good dinner and a few nights' sleep in a real bed.

Zebermar was still frowning at him. "I will remind you, Brother Aeson, that it is at my discretion and that of the Council of Four that any of the Hawksfire policies are changed. I do not think any of our members as yet would be at any risk from this, save perhaps the youngsters, and they are more than adequately protected in the Chapter Halls. I will share your concerns with the other three Grand Masters, of course, but until then, policy will continue as normal. Take your own precautions to keep yourself safe in your travels, if you are worried. But do not presume to dictate our decision for us."

"I am sorry, Grand Master; I did not mean to imply any negligence on your part. I merely wished to convey my concern for the members of Hawksfire in general, and make certain that you knew all that I had discovered, that the threat these kidnappers pose seems to be growing. And..." he trailed off.

"And? There is more?" Grand Master Zebermar looked slightly mollified at Aeson's apology, but still annoyed.

"Aside from the missing persons, I have heard a great many rumors among the populace. All across Valterra there have been reports of strange shadows and fell creatures stalking people in the dark places, from the forest depths to the alleys of cities. Fear among the people is growing; they feel a rising threat that they cannot put a name to."

Now Grand Master Zebermar smiled, giving a hearty chuckle that set Aeson's teeth on edge. "Rumor of...shadows? Monsters in alleyways? What sort of foolishness is this? Tales fit for a campfire on the Night of Soulhallow when autumn gives way to winter! Children and fools invent such stories to scare themselves and explain why nighttime is dark. I would have thought one such as you would put no credence in such tales."

"I did not at first. Not until a night recently in one such city, where I encountered one of the creatures in those tales and struck it down, albeit with some difficulty. Then, I believed."

As succinctly as possible, Aeson described the tarinx and how he'd lopped off its head, leaving out the presence of Nym and Faraine in the stableyard. Adding that information would only make Nym's position all the more suspect. When he'd finished, Grand Master Zebermar stood, regarding him levelly.

"You have made your observations and your opinions clear, Brother Aeson, and your encounter with this creature is indeed concerning. You have given me much to think on. You should go now, and I will make arrangements to consult with my fellow Grand Masters and determine how best to proceed. Your diligence has been noted. Oh, and Aeson? We will have a feast to celebrate your return; I look forward to your attendance in the Hall this evening. That is all."

Thus dismissed, Aeson bowed and left the office, but he could feel Grand Master Zebermar's gaze on his back all the way across the room and out the door. Mouth tightening into a thin line, he turned in the direction of the kitchen. Feast, was it? Whatever pompous foolishness Zebermar had planned, Aeson wanted none of it. Whatever else he did, he had to warn Nym about the Grand Master's suspicions.

Perhaps the time has come for us to leave, he reflected tiredly. He certainly wasn't getting the reception he'd expected here, apart from Melly's motherly welcome. Home seemed to have become just another morass of politics and bureaucracy, not to mention power plays by those who were supposed to hold their positions with honor. How disappointing.Aeson hadn't taken more than three steps down the hall when he heard the sound of heavy boots approaching behind him.

Faraine looked up from grooming Caeros, blinking at the late afternoon sun slanting into the stall through the small window. It was perhaps an hour or two before the dinner hour, by her estimation. After the errand and subsequent talk with Nym, she'd come to the stable to think and reassure herself that the horses were well taken care of. But thinking hadn't gotten her very far. All it had done was bring up more questions.

Sighing, she put down the brush and made to leave the stall when a small noise caught her attention. She peered over the stall door to see a not-quite-adolescent boy—one of the stable staff's children, most likely—loitering nearby, apparently waiting for her.

"Hello," she ventured, moving out of the stall and latching the door behind her. "Were you looking for me?"

"Not you exactly, but...I was hoping you knew where the bard lady was," he said, looking nervous.

"Nym? She was out in the garden with Mistress

Melly just a bit ago, so she's likely to be in the kitchen now. Why? Did you need something from her?" Maybe he wanted a song, too. Like the boy from the night before. Faraine had been in the corner, listening, and she'd seen how Nym interacted with the children. People really seemed to love her. At least, they loved her when they weren't trying to abduct her, or when they weren't reacting badly to whatever magic she used to inspire them to give up extra coin.

"I don't want anything from her, mem. She's a real nice lady, though, and she really helped Dannel. That's why I wanted to tell her something. I think it's important."

"Tell her what?" Faraine felt her brow furrow. Children weren't terribly comprehensible to her, but this boy seemed to be rather anxious.

"I heard something today, mem. When I was in the Hall running some errands for Mistress Melly. I stopped to check on Dannel just a little while ago. I wanted to see how he was after they took his memories. He's been my best friend here, but I wasn't sure if we'd still be friends, and I wanted to see if he remembered me. But as I was heading toward his room, I heard some of the Brothers talking. They didn't notice me. They were talking about Dannel and the other initiates—said the memory spell wasn't working right on them, and that they think the bard is to blame for it. I don't want her to get into trouble, mem! I like her, and Dannel liked her, and—well, I thought I ought to warn her that some of the brothers are planning to come and get her after curfew tonight."

"Come and get her? Why? And why after curfew?"

The boy's nervousness increased. "I...I think they said they didn't want to alarm anyone or get anyone riled up, so they were going to wait until after the initiates had gone to bed to take her to the Grand Master's office to question her. But it didn't sound like that was all they were going to do, and...it made me afraid for her."

"Thank you for telling me. I'll do my best to make sure that Nym doesn't get into any trouble." Faraine paused, thinking quickly. "Where do you and the other stablehands take your meals?"

"Sometimes in the kitchen, sometimes in the tack room. Depends on what we're doing and how busy we are. Mistress Melly usually keeps a kettle on for us if we're working late, or sends food out if we ask."

"All right. Then I have a special request for you, but I need you not to tell anyone, if you want to help Nym. Can you promise not to say anything, or to let anyone know that you helped me?"

"Sure, mem, I can do that."

"I need you to say you want to eat in the tack room, and take your food there early. Then get this horse and the big dun in the next stall, saddle them, and take them off the Order grounds. Out the back, though, not the front where the guards are posted. Is there somewhere either close to the city walls or outside where you can put them safely? Somewhere they won't stand out and no one would think to look for them? I don't want to leave them here right now. And do you have a friend who would help you with this, to account for the extra saddle?"

The boy was nodding eagerly. "I can get another boy

to help me, and I don't need to tell him why. We have a place outside the walls. We take horses there to exercise all the time, or to put some out in pasture and bring others back. There's even a little shed there, where we keep extra tack in case it's needed for us to exercise the horses in pasture. If I take yours there and bring two others back that look not too different, no one who sees me will even realize yours are gone. I can put the other two in the stalls where yours are. I don't think any of the Order knights know what your horses look like, anyway. They just keep track of how many stalls are filled. A horse is just a horse to them, nothing special, and not even a friend." He gave a little snort as if to illustrate what he thought about that sort of mindset.

"That's exactly what we need. Thank you for your quick thinking," Faraine said. "Now, tell me where this pasture is and how to get there. I'll also need to know what parts of the city lie closest to it."

She listened closely while he gave her a description of the layout, keeping a sharp eye out for any potential intruders. It wouldn't do to be seen talking to the boy, and she didn't have much time to warn Nym and Aeson and get them all away. And there was still the problem of how the three of them were to get outside the city walls if the Order inquisitors were to alert the gate guards, but at least the horses would be clear if and when their riders managed to make their own escape. Still....

"How do you and the others get out of the city when you don't want to be seen?"

The boy grinned. "Well, I wouldn't give up that

secret, but if you need it to save the bard lady I guess I can let you in on it. Though you won't like it much."

"Try me."

"There's an old entrance to the sewers down closer to the market square, with just some loose boards covering it, and then a grate. It locks, but the lock was broken a long time ago and nobody's noticed. If you take two left turns down the tunnel, then a right, another left, then two more rights, you come out downhill from the North gate, close to the river. The pasture is across the river and just a little east from there. It's shallow under the main bridge, though; that's where we cross when we're not on official business. Taking the horses is official business. Going for a swim or scrumping apples in the orchards isn't."

"All right. Well, you have our thanks, and I'll be sure to tell Nym how you helped her. Best get going; it won't be a terribly long time before supper, and the light fades more quickly this time of year."

"Right." The boy darted off, presumably to recruit help for the horse transfer.

Faraine thought it was a pity that she hadn't been able to offer him even a few coppers for his help, but she would leave nothing behind that might be magically traceable, if she could help it. Resolutely, she turned back toward the kitchens.

Nym was there as she'd predicted, speaking quietly to Melly while they both peeled potatoes. Melly was looking upset, but also was putting a great deal of effort into her dinner preparations.

Faraine drew Nym aside at the first opportunity, as Nym was emptying a bowl of potato peelings into a pan on the stove, where they could be boiled for the starchy water and then put into the compost.

Swiftly and in a low tone that wouldn't carry, she told Nym what she'd learned from the stableboy. Nym's eyes widened in alarm, but then her body stilled. In a voice of utter calm, she asked, "Have you told Aeson?"

"No, but I was about to. You should go and pack up your things quickly. Then we need a way to get out of the Hall during the dinner hour without anyone noticing."

"I can help," Melly announced quietly, appearing suddenly at Faraine's elbow. Faraine jumped, but Nym didn't seem overly surprised. What had she and Melly been whispering about while they were peeling potatoes?

"I can get you out by way of the wine cellar. And Faraine is right; you should go as quickly as you can," Melly continued, to which Nym merely nodded as though they were discussing the dessert course. Faraine envied her composure.

"Praise your resourcefulness, Melly. I'll get my things."

"And I'll get Aeson. He can't be far, if he's been waiting to speak to the Grand Master all day." Faraine made to leave the kitchen, but just then, the door opened and in strode a tall, gaunt man with pale skin, bushy grey eyebrows, a long, hooked nose, and a dark goatee with red in the center like a stripe down the chin. His garments were understated, but he exuded an air of authority that made Faraine's stomach clench with sudden apprehension. This could be none other than Zebermar, however much she wished it wasn't.

"Ah, just the people I wanted to see," he said in a cheery tone as his gaze fell on Nym and Faraine, easily picking them out from among the crowd of busy kitchen staff. "Aeson has been telling me about his travels with the two of you, and I would like very much to get to know you better. I expect you to dine with us tonight in the main hall. Mistress Melly, please see to it that our guests are appropriately attired. Brother Aeson is already making ready and will join them in the dining hall."

"Yes, Grand Master."

On the heels of his pronouncement, Zebermar swept from the room, as haughtily as if he were a king —one who accepted no counsel and would not take no for an answer.

As soon as the door closed behind him, Faraine looked helplessly from Nym to Melly. "What do we do now? I can still try to find Aeson and let him know what's going on. Maybe we can still make a run for it."

But Melly was shaking her head, looking distressed. "I've seen this sort of trap before, loves. It seems clear to me that the Grand Master already suspects Aeson is hiding something from him, and he's going to want to know what. That means he already considers Aeson a potential rogue. The punishment for anyone who goes rogue in the Order is severe, right up to the point of having their magic fully drained, not just leashed. I will not stand by and watch that happen to the boy I raised —not if I can help his friends rescue him. Zebermar knows that you won't want to leave without Aeson, and so he's got him sequestered somewhere until the dinner bell rings. He'll be guarded right up until then, so you won't be able to get within a cloth-yard of him. We'll have to find another way."

"But how, Melly?" Faraine felt her grasp on calm slipping away.

Melly sighed. "Go to the dinner. Dress in the best you have with you, and try to look as though you both dote on Aeson—like he's the sun that rises in your morning sky. Act as though you're both awed to be in the Hall and to be with a knight of such strength and prowess as Aeson."

"You think the Grand Master will try to poison us?" Nym asked, mouth tight with tension though she stood calmly, as though she were discussing a feast day performance she wasn't particularly looking forward to.

"Poison, no. Drug, yes. They'll want you to be biddable and answer any question they ask you. And there isn't anything I can do to warn Aeson. But it's not him they want—not really—other than as a wayward son who needs discipline. We'll deal with this as we may. I'll give you an antidote for the drug I think he'll use; you can sprinkle some in your food or drink; just don't be seen doing it. Remember, I've been here at the Hall a very long time. I know their ways." Melly's mouth pursed as though the very words she spoke tasted sour.

"But, if we could just get word to Aeson somehow..." Faraine began, almost pleadingly. She'd never been good at performances. Keeping secrets was one thing; openly lying and doing so convincingly was another.

"We won't be able to warn Aeson of any possible plot, but we can hope he'll catch on somehow," Melly continued. "If we can come up with a distraction of some sort—one that requires the Grand Master's attention and will get him out of the room—you may be able to make your exit then, before the guards come for you. He never allows them into the dining room; he's too fond of making a dramatic statement when he has someone arrested. But we'll get you all through this, somehow. No one hurts my children without me trying to do something about it. Now you girls go and get ready for this dinner. Think of it like a performance in a play." She patted Nym on the shoulder.

"Or we could run for it now, and Aeson can follow when he's able," Faraine muttered, then immediately felt ashamed of her momentary weakness. Of course she wasn't leaving Aeson behind—not when he might have his magic stripped for trying to help them.

Melly regarded her calmly. "You could indeed leave Aeson to his fate and just go without him. You *could* choose to do that. It depends on how much loyalty you feel to a man you barely know."

"I'm sorry. I'm just not used to depending on other people. Until I met Aeson, I was always alone, ever since my brother..." she broke off, tears gathering in her eyes. "But no, I won't leave Aeson. He's the first person to be kind to me, to even offer to help me."

"Your brother." Melly was staring at her, brows furrowed. "Your brother. Did he look much like you? Same nose, same eyes? Slender, just a little taller than you? And was his name Jerric?"

"Yes! That's his name! Have you seen him?" Faraine burst out, causing a couple of the other kitchen staff to look their way. Hastily, she lowered her voice. "If you know where he is or what happened to him, could you tell me? I mean—just in case we actually make it out of here? I've been looking for him for a year now."

Melly's eyes filled with tears. "Oh, child. I thought I recognized you, but I hoped I was wrong. A young man passed through here more than ten months ago. He was about your age, maybe a little younger. His name was Jerric, as I said, and he mentioned he had a sister. Yes, I think I've seen him. I'm so sorry."

"Sorry! Why? Did he become an initiate in the Order, and won't remember me now?" Faraine knew they needed to dress for dinner as the Grand Master had ordered, but she was so close to finally finding out what had happened to Jerric.

"No, dear. He wasn't an initiate. He was a prisoner. They were sending him off to be processed. Said he'd done something that justified having his magic drained, and they were moving him from the holding cells here to a more secure location. At least, that's what the lads told me. I took him food once; that's how I met him. After, they forbade me from taking food to the prisoners again. Now they always send it with an Order sib; it's been that way for the past six months. I get the feeling they don't want the staff to know too much about the criminals that pass through."

Faraine felt herself bristle. "My brother isn't a criminal. He was abducted from our village! And now I think I know by whom."

Nym put a hand on her shoulder. "Faraine, he's already gone from here; without a clear idea of where they might have sent him, we can't do anything to help him right now. But we *can* do something to help Aeson."

"What if Aeson is in on this scheme?" Faraine

demanded hotly. "What if he's known about it all this time and lured us here just so we would also be captured? All that talk about finding the kidnappers, and how no one should be too powerful, and magic should be used responsibly!" She stopped, out of breath and on the verge of tears.

"No, Faraine, think! Haven't you paid attention to Aeson since you've known him? I've only known him for a few days, and I know that he's a man of principles. He's a true knight, mage or no. He'd never stoop to being part of a scheme that aims to abduct people and drain away their magic—to whatever purpose." Nym's voice was low, but firm, and Faraine found herself listening in spite of herself.

She wiped the treacherous tears away with her fingers. "You're right. I know you're right. I just never expected to find Jerric's kidnappers here, of all places."

"I don't think Aeson expected that, either," Nym said. "Now, let's go get ready to play at being Aeson's little lightskirts. Bet you two silver that he blushes the first time you simper over him."

"You're on," Faraine growled. But she followed Nym back to the servants' hall and their rooms, where they dressed in their nicer clothing and bundled all the rest of their belongings up, leaving all of them under her bed. There wasn't time to hide them any better.

Then, head held high and hips swaying like her life depended on it, she followed the serving girl into the great dining hall, where a great many men and a scattered few women and middle-gendered folk had gathered at the long table, laden with what looked like a full harvest feast. For such an austere hall with such rigid rules and tenets, this was surely an atypical evening meal, and it looked as though all the Hawksfire mages in residence other then the very youngest children had gathered to attend.

Let the farce begin, she thought, fighting off a nervous shudder. *Strike the pose and perform like an actor, and maybe we'll get through this.*

THIRTEEN

DINNER AND A SHOW

Nymariel sauntered into the Hall, looking around as though awestruck—which wasn't entirely an act. The high vaulted ceiling with carefully positioned round windows reminded her of the depiction of an elven High Hall that she'd once seen in one of the innkeeper's books back home. None of the Hawksfire mages she saw appeared to be elven, however.

In the middle of the Hall, a long table with a series of high-backed chairs on each side stood laden with platters of food and sweating pitchers of chilled wine. Roasts, ham, fish, a bounty of different fruits and vegetables—it was more food than Nym had seen in one place in a very long time. Only a couple of the harvesttime feasts back home had come close, but this one seemed extreme by comparison. Humans knew the concept of excess better than any other group Nym had met. It seemed far too lavish a spread to be a welcome feast just for Aeson, even if that were a fiction to disguise what the Grand Master thought was an elaborate trap.

As she sashayed toward a seat near Aeson, she fingered the folded cloth in her pocket, in which Melly had wrapped her share of the antidote to the truth drug they were about to ingest. She'd get some into her very first bite, if at all possible. She had no intention of giving the Grand Master any more information than she possibly had to. But just in case, she had taken a small extra precaution before even entering the room.

Humming under her breath as she dressed for dinner in the second-best clothing she had with her—the plain but clean tunic-dress and light breeches—she had tried infusing just a trickle of the *wyld* into a very small charm that Erevan had taught her. If someone threw a lot of magic against it, it would break, but if she'd done it right, it should help her resist any subtle magical tampering the Grand Master might be planning. Whether that would also help with the drug, she wasn't sure, but it never hurt to be as prepared as possible.

Pity she hadn't been able to do the same for Faraine, but if the other woman had sensed her doing it, there would have been questions Nym wasn't prepared to answer. Using a touch of the *wyld* in her music to entice a crowd but not on any one specific person was one thing, but using it directly on a specific person without their consent might be asking for even more trouble that any she'd yet experienced. In any case, she was still learning these *small magics*, as Erevan had called them. There was undoubtedly a subtlety to it that she hadn't yet mastered.

When she saw the gathering and all the crisply

ironed tunics and resplendent gold and silver chains around mages' necks, a small part of her regretted not wearing the wonderful bard's shirt and coat that Chalia had made over for her. But that was just vanity. She didn't want this Grand Master to see her in it and possibly mark it in his memory; it was meant to stand out in a crowd, and she didn't want him to associate it with her in particular if he ever heard it described in the future.

She'd nearly reached Aeson's chair when one of the Grand Master's attendants took her by her arm and led her to a different chair, not close enough to Aeson for her to so much as whisper to him during dinner. Faraine had been shown to a more distant chair as well. Nym noted that her own chair was the closest to the Grand Master's of the three, but not quite close enough that she might be able to physically reach him. He wanted to keep an eye on her, and he intended to do it while also maintaining his own safety.

Coward. He can't just say what he's after or make a direct accusation; he has to drug it out of us and make us as uncomfortable as possible in the process.

When everyone attending the dinner had entered and was seated, the Grand Master signaled the staff to begin serving. Nym tried to watch him without being obvious about it, surreptitiously while appearing to be interested in her plate. Under the table, she was able to reach into her pocket and pinch a bit of the antidote powder between her thumb and forefinger, and when the Grand Master turned to a server to complain about the wine, she quickly spilled it onto some roast potatoes, not caring how evenly she distributed it.

When the Grand Master looked back down the table, Nym had speared the piece of potato with her fork. She put it in her mouth and chewed, trying not to seem as though she noticed his look of approval upon seeing her eating.

When next she caught Zebermar's eyes upon her, she made sure to turn an adoring look upon Aeson, which made him blink in bewilderment. Nym was gratified to see that despite her insistence that she was terrible at acting, Faraine was also doing a creditable job of craning her neck down the table to look at Aeson every so often. If her posture and facial expression seemed a little strained, she nonetheless gave the impression they required. Though, now that Nym watched it happening, she'd have been hard put to say that the looks of anguished yearning Faraine was giving Aeson were all feigned. That, or she was a better actress than she purported to be.

Intriguing as that might be at any other time, Nym forced her attention back to the task at hand. During one of those moments when the Grand Master's attention was again focused briefly on a server, she managed to make eye contact with Faraine, who gave her the tiniest of nods to let her know that her own use of the antidote had been successful.

Aeson, however, was completely without any such aid, and after a while, he began to lean a little in his chair as though he were drunk. But Nym knew it was not the wine that was making him slur his words and display less tact than he normally would have done. As large a man as he was and as much as she'd seen him drink back at the inn in Kalas with no noticeable effects, he hadn't had nearly enough wine to be as impaired as he was from the alcohol alone.

Melly's antidote had better be strong, Nym thought grimly, forcing herself to eat enough of the dinner on her plate to convince Grand Master Zebermar that she was affected too. She began to beam at Aeson whenever possible—wide, beatific smiles, accompanied by a bit of clumsiness with fork and spoon to make it look as though she were affected similarly to Aeson. Faraine seemed to be making an attempt to do the same, laughing a little too loudly at some joke one of the other mage-knights told and sloshing some of her wine onto his shirt in the process.

The Grand Master told a joke then, directing most of his attention to Nym, and she made a pretense of laughter as well, letting her gaze become unfocused to add to the impression of being affected by the drug. She had to take her cue from Aeson; his demeanor and actions would have to guide her performance, since he was the only person at the table who was actually under the drug's influence.

Abruptly she realized that the Grand Master had spoken to her directly. She forced her gaze back to his, blinking as if she were having trouble focusing.

"Whazzat? Sir?"

"I was commenting that you look lovely tonight, and I wondered how you and Brother Aeson met."

Dangerous territory, that. It all depended on what Aeson had already told Zebermar, and they'd had no chance to ask him about the interview beforehand.

"I saw him from a distance first, but as soon as I saw him I just knew he'd be...be someb'dy worth my time," she slurred. Then she giggled. "He was so...*so* pretty! Isn't he pretty, Gran' Master?"

"I cannot say, young woman. My tastes do not run to men such as Aeson. But I can see that you must be very enamored of him indeed." Grand Master Zebermar's tone was dry, but it was also plain that he now considered Nym too impaired to be expected to make sense. He looked just a little dismayed, as though he thought perhaps the drug had worked a little too well. But Nym suspected that with any truth drug, there would also be a time when a subject would be at precisely the right level of impairment that they would then willingly divulge any information he asked from them.

She was trying to figure out how they might make their exit before the end of the dinner when Zebermar looked at Aeson and suddenly asked, "My dear Brother Aeson, tell me, if you can; how came your lady friend to allow something to damage a lute in her possession? I'm told that she visited a luthier here in the city, and that she also sought a repair in one of the villages before you arrived here. Most musicians of any skill never let their instruments out of their sight, much less allow them to be damaged. That suggests an interesting story, and I would hear it, from your perspective."

Aeson frowned in confusion and looked as though he were about to answer, clearly having trouble focusing on the Grand Master. He took another drink, then stared at the cup in his hand as though he didn't recognize it. Nym thought frantically. How could she stop him from giving away her secrets? Anything he said was likely to land them in far worse trouble than they were already in. Then suddenly an idea occurred to her. It was crazy, but it might just work.

"Gran' Master, sir!" she called loudly over the din of conversation.

When he looked at her, expression mildly annoyed, she turned a bright, happy smile on him. "Yes, young woman?" he said, one bushy eyebrow raised nearly to his hairline, a look so comical that it made Nym nearly want to burst out into genuine laughter, had they not been in such a dangerous predicament.

"Did Aeson tell you—I am not just a musician. I'm a *bard!* An' I can *prove* it! Here, give some room, an' I'll...I'll...*sing* for you!" She jumped up, knocking her chair over, swaying on her feet. She had no instrument, but she grabbed a spoon from the table and began to tap it against a mug half full with ale, making a clattering rhythm of sorts.

If anything, the Grand Master now looked more alarmed than annoyed. "Hold there, young woman, I don't think that is necessary just now. Why don't you sit down again, and we'll—"

Nym began to sing, as off-key and raucously as she could, at the top of her lungs. The choice of song didn't matter, really, so she settled on an old sea shanty she'd heard once. Still singing off key, she began to climb onto the table, brushing aside plates and cutlery with her foot while looking as clumsy as possible. Once up, she staggered around, stomped her feet and sang with all her might, trying hard not to wince at her own deliberately jarring and off-key notes. It was a travesty of a bard's routine, and it was perfect.

Faraine jumped to her feet and began to clap in time with Nym's spoon rhythm, letting out a whoop of joy now and then as the tune became a raucous song of debauchery and exploits fit to make a sailor blush. All the mage-knights certainly did. Some of them guffawed openly, whooping and clapping between peals of laughter, while others shifted nervously in their seats, eyes downcast. One left rather abruptly, a hastily-snatched round loaf of bread clutched in his hand, held in front of his crotch like a shield.

The dinner party disintegrated into an uproar, some of the guests looking as though this were the most fun they'd had in many a long day, and others looking as though they wished desperately to be anywhere but here.

Angry now, the Grand Master signaled to his attendant, who ducked out the door and returned with two of the guards. They grabbed Nym and hauled her off the table, still singing at the top of her voice until she fell to giggling and sagged in their arms.

"They're all useless like this! Take them. Take all three of them to...to sleep it off for an hour or two," Grand Master Zebermar roared, clearly out of patience with her and the goings-on. Just as she'd hoped he'd be.

But something was off about his energy, Nym realized suddenly. Through the *wyld*, she could sense a barely repressed fury, and a tingle of magic that battered at her senses, hit her wards and recoiled, then hit again, harder, before pulling away, as though he'd leashed himself at the last moment. Even as the guards escorted her away, she could feel Zebermar's burning gaze on her back.

The guards half-dragged, half-carried her out of the dining hall, followed by more guards escorting a loudly protesting Faraine and a clearly bewildered Aeson, who looked none too steady on his feet.

Nym's moment of triumph was short-lived, however. The guards hauled them to a stone staircase leading downward from the hall adjacent to the dining room, clearly willing to drag anyone who could not keep their feet on the stairs. At the bottom they turned down another hallway, this one lit by torches at intervals, and finally stopped at a small archway that led into a row of cells comprised of iron bars.

They opened the one at the far end with an empty cell opposite and shoved the three into it. With expressions of disgust, they shut and locked the door, then set off down the hall again. Nym could hear their footsteps echo until they passed through the archway into the hall beyond the prison. She hadn't been in the cell for more than a few moments when she felt her carefully placed personal wards crumble. Apparently, she hadn't made them correctly, or had forgotten something she needed to do to maintain them. If that was the case, she supposed she ought to consider herself lucky that they'd lasted through dinner.

Dimly, her mind racing and the beginnings of a headache coming on, Nym glanced around the cell. One rickety cot stood against the far wall, scattered musty straw covered the floor, and a bucket stood in the far corner. The bucket was empty, but the smell emanating from it betrayed what it was meant to contain.

Nym began checking the bars that formed the cell to determine whether any were weak or loose, but they were all too solid, and her hands began to cramp, so she gave up. Discouraged and slightly dizzy, she went to the cot and sat down. Aeson just stood where he was, still looking completely disoriented, but Faraine came over to the cot and sat down beside Nym.

"Don't blame yourself for how that went. *I* thought your distraction might work too, you know. In a way, it worked perfectly, other than us winding up down here. And I don't know what else you could have done to keep Aeson from telling them everything they wanted to know."

"I don't know if I made things better back there, or worse," Nym said, wiping her forehead with her sleeve. She was sweating a little, even though the cell block was chilly. "I don't know what to do now."

Faraine looked determined. "We're getting out of here. That's what we're doing."

"What? How? I don't see how we could possibly get out of here, unless you know how to pick locks. I don't, but I'll try, in a little while. I just need to...sit here awhile first." A short rest would help. They still had a little time to find a solution, and if she just rested for a few minutes to clear her mind, maybe something would come to her. If only she could concentrate! The headache was getting worse, and that didn't help. Maybe she really had had too much wine, after all.

"You won't need to pick any locks," Faraine said firmly. "There is one thing I can try. You did your part in getting our inquisition delayed by a couple of hours. Quick thinking there, by the way. Now it's my turn to do the next step." She didn't seem to be suffering any discomfort, and all of her feigned drunkenness was gone.

Then Nym remembered what else she'd ingested besides the wine. Apparently, Melly's antidote worked better on humans then it did on elves, and with fewer side effects. Nym hadn't asked Melly what the ingredients in the antidote were, but it seemed she must be allergic to one of them. Her skin had begun to itch a little, and she had an unpleasant metallic taste in her mouth. Surely Melly hadn't poisoned her, though! Not after all her help and kindness, and her obvious motherly affection for Aeson. And it didn't *feel* as though she'd been poisoned. Not exactly. But something wasn't right, regardless.

Faraine gave her and Aeson a level look. "There is something I need to tell—well, show—the two of you that I hadn't intended to reveal just yet. But given the mess we're in, I think if there was ever an appropriate time to trust and be trusted, that time is now."

"Wha' you mean, Fara? Raine. Fara Raine." Aeson was still slurring his words. He blinked at Faraine, then suddenly smiled. "You're so beaut'ful, you know? You're so—"

"Stop that! You don't know what you're saying right now," Faraine snapped. At Aeson's hurt look, she relented. "Sorry. I appreciate the compliment. All right now, folks, here goes. We're about to get to know one another just a little better. Don't try to kill me, please. I'm not an enemy." She nodded once as if to reassure herself, then fell silent.

The air suddenly shimmered where she had been

standing, and all at once, a black cat stood in her place. It yowled and turned around, ducking out of the cell and through the bars, then trotted off down the corridor, leaving Nym to wonder if she were hallucinating on top of the headache, dizziness and itching skin. *Gods, Melly, what was in that antidote?*

Nym was still puzzling over it when the cat returned, carrying a ring of keys in her mouth. She dropped the keys on the floor, rose onto her hind legs and became Faraine again, clothes and all.

Grinning, Faraine looked from Nym to Aeson and back to Nym again, then shrugged and reached for the cell door, inserting key after key in the lock and turning them until she found the one that clicked.

"Where..? How..?" Nym gave up and shook her head, rising determinedly to her feet. Aeson, for a wonder, was still standing, though he didn't look particularly alert.

"I'm a cat shifter. That part is obvious now, right?" Faraine was looking up and down the row of cells.

A few of the other occupants noticed and some began to plead with her. Nym noticed that most of them had the same look on their faces that Dannel had had the previous night.

"Cat shifter. A werecat?"

"No, not a were. Just a shifter. And it's all cats. Anything feline. Not just housecats."

Nym shook her head in wonder. "All right; we'll continue this discussion later. Right now, we need a new escape plan, and quick."

Faraine frowned. "I hadn't thought beyond getting

us out of the cell. But Melly had a way to get us out of the Hall via the wine cellars. That plan would still work if we only had a way of getting back into the kitchen without being noticed."

Nym glanced at the other prisoners again. "Say, Faraine, I think some of these folks were probably locked up here for all the wrong reasons, given our own experience. What do you say we right a few wrongs, since you have the keys already?"

Faraine glanced over at Nym, startled, then laughed. "A distraction worthy of your performance earlier tonight. Won't the Order have fun sorting all of *this* mess out?"

She began unlocking cell doors all down the row, and the corridor was suddenly crowded with a mass of prisoners.

"The guards are down that hall, fellow miscreants," Nym sang out, wincing when it made her head pound harder. "They surely can't stop all of us together!"

The other prisoners looked at one another, then at Nym; then with a collective yell, they surged down the hall en mass, crowding through the arch at the end of the prison corridor and onward out into the hall and the stairwell. As they did, Nym grabbed Aeson by the arm and towed him along in a half-crouch, letting the press of fleeing bodies and the din they made cover her and her friends' exit. As she'd hoped, the startled guards were too busy shouting and grabbing at whichever prisoner came nearest to pay heed to any three individuals in particular.

The mob of prisoners surged up the stairwell and out into the main floor hallway, but as they continued left, Nym dragged Aeson right, into an alcove. Faraine followed, flattening herself against the wall next to Nym and Aeson, putting a hand firmly over Aeson's mouth to forestall any stray exclamations he might make.

As soon as they were fairly sure the guards had passed and were occupied with rounding up the escaped prisoners fleeing madly in all directions, Nym and her friends made for the service corridor that led off the main hall to the kitchens. Just at the entrance to the kitchen, they spied Melly, looking this way and that as though she were waiting for something, or someone.

"Melly," Faraine hissed from her hiding place, and the old cook gave a start, then looked visibly relieved when she spied Faraine.

Nym still wasn't sure whether Melly was entirely trustworthy, but since Faraine seemed to have taken no harm from the antidote, she had to assume that her own discomfort was just an unfortunate reaction to an unknown allergen in the mix.

"Oh, miss Faraine, you gave me quite a fright!" Melly said, wiping her hands on the front of her apron. "I was about to come down and get you out myself, rules or no rules, but I see you've been every bit as resourceful as I'd expect a friend of Aeson's to be. Now follow me, quickly."

The three followed Melly through a door into the wine cellar, which apparently had two levels, an upper and a lower, the lower of which was reached by means of a trapdoor. Once they'd all descended, Aeson mostly sliding down the ladder rather than climbing down it, Melly led them to a small rack of wine kegs. The rack appeared to be on small rollers to make it easier to move, and behind it there was a small bolted door. Melly threw the bolt and opened it, and the three fugitives stood blinking at the dim, dank-smelling passage revealed behind it.

"The stablehands don't know about this entrance, so they can't reveal it if questioned. Torches are in a barrel to the right of the door, and your saddlebags and other things are already here; I brought them as soon as you went in to dinner. No telling what mischief the Grand Master might get up to, rifling through all your things. I've also left a parcel of bread and cheese and a few other things you might find useful."

Nym swallowed her guilt at her earlier suspicions. "Melly, we owe you a debt of kindness we may not be able to repay for some time. Just please be careful yourself, so they won't suspect you helped us."

Melly waved away the sentiments. "I told you there isn't anything I would not do for one of my children. And the high-and-mighty, self-righteous Grand Master is *not* one of my children. Now, get you gone, quickly. Keep Aeson walking and the drugs should wear off by morning. Just go, so this night's work won't be for nothing. And I do hope you find your brother, Faraine, dear," she said over her shoulder as she turned to go. "Go straight on down this tunnel to the first crossing, which is just under the marketplace entrance. Then follow the same turning instructions the boy already gave you, and you should be out well before dawn. I expect your little prison break distraction will keep them busy here for a good while, yet." She sounded satisfied, as though justice had been done.

Nym hoped it had. She hoped they hadn't set a band of true criminals loose on Cambermere. But she had no doubt that the Order would waste no time in getting the escapees rounded up again. And she also had no doubt that it wouldn't take the Grand Master long to discover which three prisoners were now missing. She could only hope that Melly's part in the escape wouldn't be found out. She felt a little guilty for the position they'd put the cook in, but going back would not help Melly, or any of them, and getting caught again would make a mockery of her efforts on their behalf.

The small door shut behind them, and a moment later the sound of a bolt sliding home sent Nym and Faraine hurrying to shoulder their perishable belongings and as many of Aeson's as they could carry. The rest—all the things that were relatively sturdy and hard to damage, they loaded on Aeson as though he were a pack animal. He stumbled along, still unsteady on his feet, mumbling a little between snatches of the song Nym had sung at dinner, delivered very off-key, and deadpan. All of it would have been hilarious if they weren't trying to escape through a sewer in the dead of night and remain undetected.

Nym lit a torch, grimacing at the way it rubbed against the newly-tender skin on her palms, then began to lead the way down the tunnel, keeping to the narrow walkway along the side. While she was grateful that they wouldn't have to wade in sewage, she found herself holding her breath every few minutes—as much to listen for sounds of pursuit as to have a periodic break from the stench of the sewers themselves.

FOURTEEN

SONG TAKE FLIGHT

They followed the main tunnel until they came to an intersection with a grate that served as a bridge between the two sides of the sewage channel. Nym followed Faraine over it as they took the first left-leading tunnel available, Faraine muttering "Left, left, right, left, right, right," in a low tone as though she were afraid that she might forget the sequence.

Nym was alternately sweating and chilled as she trudged along behind Faraine, who had traded duties with her so that she now held the torch while Nym towed Aeson along. Part of her was amazed that he wasn't protesting their guidance. But then again, he was still alternately singing and muttering, and while he seemed able to carry the few saddlebags they'd hung on his shoulders, his steps were none too steady.

Somewhere between the third and fourth turns in Faraine's sequence, he abruptly dropped the saddlebags and staggered toward the sewage channel, where he vomited into the filthy water, narrowly missing Nym's boots. She staggered back with a muttered curse, and Faraine, several steps ahead of them, halted and turned around.

"We need to keep going," she hissed urgently. "They could easily be following us by now!"

"Tell that to Aeson," Nym said, gesturing to where he stood, leaning precariously out over the water, anchored only by Nym's hand gripping his sword belt at the back.

Faraine sighed. "Halfway there, friends. We're halfway there. Aeson, if you can pull yourself together and keep moving, we'll be out where the air is fresh and the water is clean—or at least, cleaner."

"Pull m'self 'gether?" he asked, frowning at her as though he might be seeing two of her. "I'll try, 'Raine. You know I'll try. Have to keep you...safe."

"We'll all be safer when we get out of these tunnels," Faraine insisted, but her voice was gentler. "Are you able to move on now?"

"Load me up," he said, obviously making an attempt to seem steady.

"The saddlebags didn't fall in the sewage. That's a blessing," Nym muttered, but if she were being honest with herself, she felt none too steady on her own feet. They were making relatively good progress, but it was slower than she'd have liked, and she understood Faraine's nervousness. There was no guarantee that Melly's scheme to get them out of the Hall hadn't been discovered, and anyone pursuing them was likely to be in much better shape than she and Aeson were in at the moment.

"I've loved you for a long time, F'raine," Aeson was muttering now, staring at Faraine's back. "I couldn' tell you 'cause I was s'posed to protect you. But then you had to end up pro...prec...p'tecting *me!* Zebermar's a snake, an' the Order's a lie, and it was all lies, the whole time, and I b'lieved them! Ten times a fool, and ten times a—"

He broke off in an unintelligible mumble before falling into a morose silence. But the purging seemed to have helped clear some of the drug from his body; his steps were steadier and he no longer seemed to need anyone to guide him along the walkways.

Faraine made no comment, but Nym noticed that her back was ramrod straight and she walked along without a backward glance until they finally came to the last turn in her litany. Whatever she thought of Aeson's drugged confessions, she kept it to herself.

Probably wants to give him an out when he fully sobers up and realizes what he's been saying, Nym thought, concerned and amused both together, despite her itching skin and pounding headache. Vaguely, she wondered whether she had a fever, but as they walked, the shivering and sweating gradually lessened and then stopped. The antidote was probably clearing her system by now, thank the gods. Both she and Aeson needed to be as functional as possible when they reached the mouth of this last tunnel.

And gods send there won't be any guards or Hawksfire stooges waiting by the river! We still only have two horses, and that's going to make for slow going unless I want to take the chance of stealing one of the Order mounts. At this point, it mightn't be much of a choice.

Ahead of her, Faraine stopped, peering cautiously

out of the sewer opening. Ahead lay the river; Nym could hear it burbling along even above the noise of the spillway, downhill from the four filter tanks that had been built into the hillside leading down from the city walls. She couldn't remember what she'd read about Cambermere and its builders; many of the human cities, if not most, had no such system for treatment of their sewage.

It wasn't elaborate, but it did tend to keep the solid waste contained and composted for the most part, and the way the last two tanks had been designed caused the water that remained to pass through a series of fine meshes enhanced with magic before it joined a shallow finishing pool and eventually, the river. It all served to render the water—if not pure—considerably less offensive in content than it might have been otherwise.

The fresh air that hit Nym's face as soon as she reached the mouth of the tunnel was a welcome relief. Her headache eased marginally almost as soon as she'd left the sewer—or perhaps that was her imagination. Either way, she breathed in her first deep breath of air since they'd entered the tunnels.

The others seemed similarly revitalized. Faraine put out the torch she'd been carrying, but she didn't leave it behind, instead stuffing it into the tangle of saddlebags and other gear hanging off Aeson's back. Cautiously, alert to the slightest sound or movement, the three crept from the tunnel and down the slope, careful to walk down the series of stairs and landings that had been built for the purpose of maintaining the drainage tanks rather than leave footprints in the bare earth of the slope. Furtively, they made their way slightly upriver from the tunnels toward the bridge. That took them much closer to one of the gates than Nym would have liked, but if they wanted to retrieve Caeros and Seralo, they'd have to cross where the stableboy had indicated, directly below the span of the bridge.

It made little sense to Nym to have a bridge tall enough to walk beneath in a spot where the water came no higher than her knees, but she supposed that the level must have been much higher at one time to justify the height of the span. That, or the springtime would bring in a lot more water flow with the snowmelt from the hills farther east. The road ran parallel to those hills on the south side of the river, but Nym had spotted them in the distance as she and her companions had traveled to Cambermere from Kalas.

When they drew near the bridge, they spent several moments studying it to make sure no one seemed to be about, but they couldn't see any guards anywhere close to it. The only people Nym could spy were the guards stationed just outside the city gates, and they were far enough away that unless someone tripped, fell into the water and screamed about it, they wouldn't be noticed. As quietly as possible, the three slipped down the bank into the water, crouching low just in case they'd somehow missed a sentry.

Cold water got in over the tops of her new boots, but Nym ignored it and slogged after the others. She was shivering again, but due to the cold water this time and not fever. Aeson seemed to be mostly recovered from the drugs now, but he was uncommonly silent, not speaking at all except for necessary whispered communications, and those were sparse. He moved stealthily across the river, his steps making scarcely a ripple. Faraine moved on across like a silent shadow, face intent in the darkness lit only by the rising crescent moon.

On the other side, the three kept low, creeping as quietly as they could out from the relative cover of the bridge arch into a stand of trees and bushes that lined their side of the river. It was sparse, but any cover at all might be useful if anyone happened along. Nym held her breath as they made their way upriver from the bridge, where the trees began to increase in size and thickness. Maple, willow, and even birch made up a copse that led uphill from the river in the direction that Faraine led them, presumably toward the pasture the stableboy had told her about.

Nym spotted the cleared area through a gap in the trees before they reached it, and through the shadows she could easily make out the shapes of horses. Some dozed with their heads hanging low, others cropped the late fall pasture grass, and a few stood with heads up, watching the treeline. Did horses set watch at night for predators, like sentries?

Brushing aside the random thought, Nym crept to the edge of the trees where a wooden fence separated the pasture from the copse. She ducked through the opening in the fence, looking around for the promised shed.

Then she spotted it; a squat rectangle just off to the right at the far side of the pasture, its roof covered in sod that had probably been removed from the fence line when the poles had been set.

"Over there," she whispered to Aeson, pointing. Faraine had already spotted the shed and was making her way along the fence line to get to it.

Every few feet they all halted, waiting, listening for any hint that they weren't alone with the horses, but they heard no noises save for the hooting of an owl in one of the taller trees, and the crickets chirping in the brush among the trees ringing the pasture.

The pasture only had one tree; the rest was open. But the clearing seemed natural rather than cleared by human hands, and the grass was certainly plentiful, especially for this time of year, still green in spots when most of the summer's growth had faded and turned brown.

Faraine gave a low warbling call like a night bird, and moments later, Caeros came strolling up from among a group of other horses, Seralo following.

The shed had a lock, but it had been removed and was lying on the ground near the door. Silently blessing the stableboy who'd helped them, Nym wasted no time in grabbing a bridle from where the spares hung on pegs. There was an extra saddle as well, but if she was truly going to be so bold as to steal a horse and tack, she wanted to be sure she could convince one to trust her first.

On impulse, she replaced the first bridle she'd taken with another, a hackamore style, which had no bit but guided a horse with pressure alone. Bits had always seemed rather barbaric to her anyway, though Faraine's and Aeson's horses seemed not to mind them. Their saddles had been brought and put in the tack room as promised, so Nym left them to their preparations and went back out into the pasture, quickly scanning the horses there to see if one appeared sufficiently docile.

The first horse she approached laid its ears back and sidled away from her, and while she was able to get close to a few others, most just walked off when she tried to slip the hackamore over their heads. She didn't want to alarm them, so chasing one down or trying to force the issue was not an option. She knew how to ride horses from her days with the caravan, but she'd never really known one well, aside from Aeson's and Faraine's mounts. Now she had to make a strange horse trust her and allow her to ride away on it?

She had almost given up on the notion of stealing a horse when she noticed a white mare standing near the lone tree, watching her quietly. The mare was solid white except for her ears, which were some darker color that even with elven eyesight, Nym couldn't quite make out in the dim moonlight. The idle notion that the ears would be red in sunlight crossed her mind, though she couldn't have said where the thought came from. The mare reached out to nuzzle her, lipping her hand lightly as though searching for a treat.

Nym hesitated. This horse didn't seem at all alarmed by her presence, and she seemed friendly enough, but the white would be noticeable in the darkness. Still, none of the other horses seemed approachable, and she couldn't take all night deciding.

Faraine came up, carrying the spare saddle and Nym's saddlebags, Caeros following behind her. "We've got to move, Nym," she hissed. There's no time! I spotted something moving down by the river, and

Aeson thinks he saw a torch down toward the bridge. I think we might be in trouble. Get that horse saddled and let's get out of here while we still have half a chance."

"I'm going to call you Wyldsong—Song for short—at least until we get to know one another better, unless you happen to like the name. Okay, girl? I hope you don't mind," Nym murmured to the mare, ignoring Faraine's incredulous look. "What? I don't know her actual name, but I can't just call her Horse."

Nym slipped the hackamore over the white mare's head and fastened it while Faraine put on the stolen saddle and fastened Nym's saddlebags onto it, her fingers moving quickly and deftly even in the dark. She shoved Nym's lute bag and crossbow at her and mounted her own horse, turning him back toward the direction of the shed.

All hesitation gone, Nym grasped the reins and hastily scrambled into the saddle. She hoped the mare was good with a hackamore and that she wouldn't be stubborn about leaving the herd. But the white horse turned immediately as soon as her rider was settled, following Caeros toward the spot where Aeson stood waiting, the top two boards of the fence lowered to allow the horses through. Seralo was on the other side already, and Caeros was quick to follow. They'd just cleared the gap and Nym was about to do the same when they heard a shout from the far end of the pasture.

"Hurry!" Aeson growled, keeping his voice low.

Song crowded forward through the gap until she was close to Caeros' flank. Aeson hesitated just long enough to replace the two fence boards to make it harder for anyone to get past, then vaulted into his saddle and urged Seralo into the trees.

The shouts were closer now as people hurried toward the tack shed. Torchlight cast moving shadows over the pasture, where the other horses were now milling about, some whinnying in alarm at the sudden chaos. When Aeson booted Seralo into a gallop, Caeros followed, and Song sped after the others with no urging. In the dimness under the trees, the two lead horses blended into the night significantly better than the stolen mare, whose white hide must surely stand out in the darkness.

From behind, Nym could hear the sounds of mounted pursuit. Of *course* the Order would pursue. They had a pasture full of mounts to use, after all. With any luck, there would only be a few on horseback at first, though, since the entire herd had been surprised and alarmed by the sudden intrusion of shouting humans. Maybe the confusion would work to their advantage somehow.

The trees were still sparse enough that the horses running at full speed through it had no trouble with their footing, but Nym knew that if they kept on like this as the woods got thicker, they'd have to slow or risk one of the mounts stumbling or breaking a leg. The only good thing about moving into denser undergrowth would be that their pursuers would have to slow as well. But the thicker woods were some distance off yet, and now the enemy knew which way they were headed. There was little choice otherwise, though. Any change of direction just now would take them out of the scant cover the trees provided.

Song vaulted over a deadfall, throwing Nym forward in the saddle, then back. She gripped the horse's sides hard with her legs and managed to stay mounted, but the damaged lute that she'd hastily slung over her shoulder slipped down her right arm.

A few lengths further into the copse, she heard the *thwap* of a bowstring, and an arrow struck a tree just to their right. Song gave a shrill whinny and dodged to the left, and Nym's lute went flying off her arm to land somewhere in a stand of gorse. There was no time to try to go back for it. The shouting had intensified, and she thought she heard the sound of dogs, though they were still some distance behind. Then something else whizzed past her ear, and Nym's eyes went wide as a bolt of crackling green lightning shot past in her field of vision to strike another tree. The mare jerked, but didn't startle; she just kept running in the general direction the others were taking, though they were barely-seen dark shapes dashing between the trees just ahead. Nym held on with all her might, heart pounding in her ears like counterpoint to the sound of the mare's hooves.

The mage-knights were out in force, and she and her companions were the foxes to the Order's hounds. Melly's face popped into Nym's mind, and she hoped the woman was all right, that her part in the escape hadn't been discovered. But with this sort of response and rapid pursuit, it was probably a vain hope, and their own safety was far from assured.

Moments later a pulse of energy that she recognized burned into Nym's senses. And with her personal wards down, it stung and battered at her mind, making her wince at the pain. So she hadn't been wrong about what she'd sensed from Grand Master Zebermar in the feast hall. He was back there somewhere with the rest of the pursuit, and he was trying to wear away any shields or personal defenses they had.

She had the sudden horrible feeling that he knew something about the magic she wielded, though she didn't see how he could possibly know. But that was a concern for later, after they managed to get away from here.

"We need to hide, girl," she murmured, hunched down low over Song's white neck. "They can see your white coat too well in the dark, and I think they sense our magic. They won't stop unless we can lose them somehow."

The mare snorted, and a tingle ran through Nym. The energy of *wyld* surged through her in a torrent, chaotic and untamed and yet somehow familiar. It chased away the last of the headache, but the real wonder took form right before Nym's eyes. The mare's white coat rippled suddenly, and the white was flooded with the color of mist and shadow. Even those had-to-be-red ears changed, and suddenly Nym was riding a dark dapple grey, the mare's new coat blending seamlessly with the mist that sprang up around them. Realization hit her with a jolt.

Oh, gods! I stole a faery horse, faery horse, faehorsefaehorsefaehorsefaehorse...! Too late, Nym remembered the legends—what that white hide and red ears signified. The horse she'd stolen wasn't even a mortal horse! She was a creature of wind and *wyld*, and now she flowed through the forest as though she were the wind itself, easily passing Caeros and Seralo and gathering them up in her wake. As the baying of the hounds increased in intensity, the fae mare ran straight into a wall of mist that loomed in front of them. Nym felt a surge of pure energy though her very being, and then all sound of pursuit stopped as though the entire world had been muffled in soundproof white nothingness.

FIFTEEN

INTO THE WYLD

Time seemed to slow, and then Song burst through the white mist, slowing to a canter and then a walk as she carried Nym out into a deep forest glade. The other two horses burst through only moments later, but there was no sign of the pursuers who had been close on their heels. Nym breathed a sigh of relief as Song came to a stop at last, but her relief was short-lived.

The forest had changed. Somewhere during that mad scramble through the mist, they'd come into a dense wood of tall, old trees that reached high into the sky, which sparkled with stars—unfamiliar stars. Nym peered up at them, hoping she'd just temporarily lost her bearings, but there was no denying it. These *were* different stars, not the ones Nym had been familiar with since childhood. Realization stole over her, and she laughed, softly. Of course. She should have known.

"Well, Wyldsong, I did say we needed to hide," she said aloud, albeit ruefully. "You've hidden us; that's for sure. I guess I need to be careful what I say around you from now on—if you still want to travel with me, that is. I'm just glad you brought our friends through as well."

"What is going on, Nymariel?" Faraine asked, sounding shaken.

Nym shrugged. "It's nothing I did. Song brought us here. I guess when I told her we needed to hide, she took me seriously. If it's any consolation, the Order probably won't be able to pursue us here."

"Just where is *here*, Nym?" Aeson was patting his mount's neck absently, though it seemed the action was more to comfort himself than the horse.

Nym sighed. There was no help for it. Dodging the question would not help them—not when they needed to be able to trust one another more than ever.

"We appear to be in the Otherworld, also known as the fae realm, Wyldenmore, or—as we elves call it— Lyre."

"The fae realm? But how...why did...Nym, *what did you do?*" Faraine was as close to losing her composure as Nym had ever seen her. Even Aeson was looking at her askance.

"I didn't do this," Nym repeated calmly. "It was Song. She brought us here, through a barrier only she could sense, and it let us in because it let *her* in."

"The horse? But that's crazy, Nym! Even for a person who makes up stories, I'd have thought you'd come up with a better explanation than to blame this on a *horse!*" Faraine's voice had risen in volume, and without seeming to realize it, Aeson moved Seralo closer to Caeros and put a hand out to touch her shoulder. She jerked away, but not as though she didn't want him to touch her—more as though she were embarrassed at her outburst.

Aeson was frowning, but he seemed calm. "All right, wherever we are and however we came to be here, we need to find a place to go to ground for a short while. We need to get our bearings if possible, rest the horses, and eat some food that isn't drugged. Nym, since apparently your horse knows more about this place than we do, which direction do you suggest we take?"

Nym was about to protest that she knew next to nothing about Lyre and had nothing to triangulate with, but Song began to walk, moving forward confidently through the darkness among the massive trees. Nym noticed with a shock that her coat had gone from dapple grey back to white. Or maybe she had been hallucinating the dapple grey during their escape from the Order? That was possible. Certainly, neither Faraine nor Aeson had made any mention of a change in appearance in the mare, which they most certainly would have done, had they noticed such a thing.

The other horses fell in behind Song placidly, as if they'd already decided that she was the leader of the small herd of three. Nym could feel her two companions' eyes on her back as they moved through the forest, winding deeper and deeper through the darkness until Song came to a downward-leading slope. The mare took some track that even Nym's eyes had trouble making out in the darkness, but after a gradual descent, the way led into a clearing of sorts where a rocky outcropping to the right promised some degree of shelter from wind or rain, and where a fire might be made without being seen for any great distance. There was even a large tree near the outcropping that, when Nym peered at it more closely, appeared to be dead and hollowed out, the shell of it forming a round room of sorts. Unless her perception was off, at least one person could fit inside it—maybe two.

Dare we light a fire here? Nym wondered as she dismounted. Song gave a soft whicker and nudged her in the back.

With no more to go on than that, Nym decided to take the whicker for assent. She unloaded the saddlebags and her other belongings from Song, then removed the saddle and the hackamore. Song nuzzled her again and of her own accord went to join the other horses, who'd been similarly relieved of their trappings except for the fact that they wore halters. They'd also been hobbled to keep them from wandering far.

Aeson greeted Song's lack of restraints with a raised eyebrow, but the mare showed no sign of wishing to wander off—at least for the time being.

"I couldn't stop her if she really wanted to go," Nym explained. "She belongs to this world. She is home, and we are guests in her home. For me to assume that I own her in any way would be a very big mistake."

"I...see," Aeson said, his voice suggesting that he did not see, but that he was trying very hard to give Nym the benefit of the doubt. "Just so you know that if she does decide to wander off, then we're down a horse again, and in extremely unfamiliar and potentially hostile territory."

"Oh, I am aware," Nym said softly, watching Song.

"But it changes nothing. Song makes her own choices." *I stole a fairy horse. Or maybe I was stolen by one. I'm not sure which.*

They made camp against the outcropping, under a slight overhang. Aeson dug a small pit for the fire so that it would not be as easily seen from a distance and could be covered over when it was no longer needed. In addition to a bedroll for Nym, Melly had given them an extra set of saddlebags full of provisions. There was bread and cheese, but the bread was a dense sort of trail bread that kept far better than typical bread, and the cheese was tightly wrapped in waxed cloth. There was also a packet of loose tea, a small amount of dried meat, and bags of dried apple slices and mushrooms, oats, and rice.

"Bless you, Melly," Aeson murmured, then fell silent as he laid a fire with broken branches and deadfall that Faraine had gathered from nearby while he tended to the horses. When it was ready, he struck flint and steel to kindle a small but cheerful blaze. All the while, he maintained a contemplative silence, methodically sorting through Melly's carefully wrapped supplies to find a small pot in which to cook a soup of rice, dried meat and mushrooms.

Nym recognized what he must be feeling. She felt it too, though she'd only known Melly for a very short time. If the Order had harmed her.... No. It didn't bear thinking about. There was no way to know whether they'd suspected Melly or any of the children.

"I re-locked the shed when we came out," Faraine said, as though she'd caught the drift of Nym's thoughts. "I didn't want them to suspect the stablehands had anything to do with our departure."

"Good thinking." Aeson sighed and stared into the soup he was making, but Nym wasn't sure he really saw it; his expression seemed far away. After a few moments, he shook his head as though to chase away morose thoughts. "We'll need to refill the waterskins when possible. I suppose your new friend there knows the way to a water source." It wasn't quite a question.

"I don't know. Shall I ask her?" Nym couldn't quite keep the sarcasm out of her tone. If neither Aeson nor Faraine wanted to believe that Song really was a fae horse, then what did it matter whether Song knew where water might be or not?

Aeson shrugged and went back to his task. Faraine merely looked uncomfortable, and busied herself with taking an inventory of all of their supplies. Grumbling under her breath, Nym stalked over to Song and began to stroke her soft nose. Song nudged her gently, and her eyes seemed to stare straight into Nym, as though she were seeing beneath the surface. Nym snorted to herself at the notion, but Song's blue eyes gazing into hers nonetheless made her wonder.

"They want me to find water that's safe for us to drink, girl," she said softly, so none but the horse could hear. "Or to be more precise, they want *you* to find it. Maybe if you do, they'll believe that you really are what I told them you are. I'm not so sure they even believe we're in the Otherworld yet. But if they don't start believing soon, we could all be in even more danger than we were out there with the Order of Hawksfire chasing us. And also, I need a guide to get us out again —unless you can conjure up another of those handy mist barriers to take us back to the mortal realm?"

Song snorted as if the idea were ludicrous. Nym smiled ruefully, scratching behind the horse's ears. "I thought not. But I also thought it couldn't hurt to ask."

Song nudged Nym's hand, lipping it gently without biting. She acted just like any other horse Nym had ever known, and for a moment, the notion that she was fae seemed a little far-fetched, even to Nym. But then Nym noticed the mare's eyes, glowing faintly blue even in the darkness.

"I believe in you," she whispered. "Even if they don't believe me, I believe in you, and I believe you came to me for a reason. I will trust you if you trust me, and you helped me, so I'll return the favor if I can. But we still need a path back out into the mortal lands sooner rather than later, and we need to know what we're really dealing with out there. Otherwise, I have the feeling we're all in some kind of danger that we don't fully understand."

The mare tossed her head, looking for all the world as though she were nodding. Nym remained with her until Faraine came to let her know the meal was ready, but she had the feeling that some sort of unspoken agreement had passed between her and Song, whatever she was, and whether or not anyone else chose to believe it.

As she approached the fire, Aeson handed her a bowl of the rice concoction he'd made, and the three ate in a strained silence for several moments before anyone spoke. Finally, Aeson cleared his throat as if steeling himself for an unpleasant conversation.

"I owe both of you an explanation and an apology,"

he said, surprising Nym. "Firstly, I am sorry for what happened back there. I trusted the Hawksfire as if they were my own kin. I had no reason not to, until today. But now I find myself deeply ashamed and appalled that I wasn't able to see the corruption there before now. I could make the argument that I've been away for several months and have not kept up to speed on what has been happening internally to the Order. But that would be an excuse, and a pale one at that. You both questioned me when you met me, asking why I'd give up part of my power. I truly did so for the reasons I told you. But I never explained what happens to the power that is siphoned off from the members of the Order."

Nym stayed silent, eyes wide. She'd been expecting recriminations about her belief that Song was a fae horse, and she'd been expecting to be blamed for their unexpected realm-hopping, but she had not been expecting a confession from Aeson.

Aeson continued. "The power they bleed from us to keep us all at the same capacity goes into the Arboricanum, a special receptacle for magical energy, where it is stored in case it is ever needed. Think of it as a vast pool or reservoir that the Order could tap collectively if and when we ever needed to defend the world against a threat so powerful that our combined strength without it would not be enough. But once we give up some of our power to the Arboricanum, we are blocked from being able to recall it at will, just as we are blocked from accessing our memories. It would take another spellcaster, and a powerful one at that, to break those bindings and allow any of us access to either, once the bindings are set.

"And there is one more thing. When I was of an age to have my memories bound, I decided that I didn't want to lose mine, so I feigned illness on the day of the binding ceremony by imbibing some herbs that made me sick. By the time I *recovered*, the ceremony was long over and no one remembered that I had not been there. In all honesty, I don't know why it was missed, though at the time I thought it was because I'd been clever. But however it was overlooked, I still have all of my childhood memories—the good, and the bad. I have always deemed them necessary, because they remind me of why I came to join the Order in the first place. I have never thought myself to be worthy of being allowed to forget my mistakes."

He went on to explain what had happened in his past, when he'd used his powers for the first time and another boy had died. Nym listened to it all in thoughtful silence, though Faraine stopped him at certain points to ask for clarifications.

When he finally fell silent again, the three all sat staring at one another for a long moment. Then Nym roused herself, looking from him to Faraine and back. "Your memories of that accident when you were a boy are part of what made you the honorable man you are today," she said. "I don't think you would be the same if you'd had them removed."

"I don't either," he said, relief clear in his tone. "Losing the memory of pain, loss, or wrongdoing may give one a fresh start, but it also removes the perspective and wisdom that can come as a result of those experiences. It may make the Order more homogenous as a whole, but it also prevents much in the way of innovation or perspective, or...questions. Questions that perhaps people like Grand Master Zebermar would not want people to ask. But I was able to question, and when I did, it brought all of this down on our heads. For that, I am sorry. Had I thought to examine my own beliefs sooner, perhaps the two of you need not have become enmeshed in whatever is going on within the leadership of the Hawksfire."

"I was already enmeshed," Faraine said finally, causing Aeson to jerk his head around to look at her. She crumbled a bit of bread into her bowl, then set down the bowl on a flat rock near the fire. "While we were there, Aeson, I learned that the reason Melly thought she recognized me was that my brother had been there too—he was a prisoner of the Order some months ago. Melly didn't know where he'd been taken. But I think they may have taken him in the first place because he refused to join the Order, and then they trumped up something to charge him with and probably drained him of his power like Melly said they do to convicted prisoners. By now he's probably in a work camp somewhere, powerless, and forgotten. Except by me, and apparently by Melly, who felt sorry for him."

Aeson made a soft sound of distress, but Faraine wasn't finished. "I have a confession, too, though you already know what it is—unless it somehow escaped your notice, Aeson, when you were drugged. I'm a cat shapeshifter. I can take the form of any feline, large or small, if I've ever seen even a picture of one. I can't cast spells as such, but if you need a good cat, I'm your woman."

She blushed as she said it, as though she'd suddenly realized how that last part had sounded. Nym grinned but kept her comments to herself.

Faraine continued. "My brother had magic, and I have the shapeshifting. Our abilities are different because we had different mothers. My mother was the shifter, and she died giving birth to me. Then my father remarried, and my stepmother had my brother. She was the mage. Our father, well...he's a blacksmith. That's all. A very good blacksmith, but just a blacksmith. For a long time, he had trouble forgiving me for my mother's death, though it wasn't my fault. My stepmother was kind to me and tried to make up for my father's neglect, but she could only do so much. He finally came around and we repaired our relationship, but then my brother went missing and I...I had to try to find him. His absence broke our parents' hearts. I'm sorry I didn't tell you about my shifting sooner, but it's hard to know who I can trust with the secret. Most folks who find out think I'm some sort of were-creature, and they naturally want to put an end to me. But what I have isn't catching. It's just...a part of who I am. Of *what* I am."

When she stopped speaking, she picked up her bowl again and began shoveling food into her mouth as though it were her only profession.

Nym sighed. "Well, since we're all baring our souls, I have to tell you that I truly did not bring us here. It really was Song, and she really is a fae horse. I don't know how she did it or why, and I don't know why she was there in that pasture with the other horses, unless she just likes to visit with mortal horses now and then. I didn't mean to choose a fae horse; it just happened. But she let me ride her out of there, and she seems to have saved our hides at least temporarily, so...there it is.

"The rest of my background, you already know. I'm a bard, and I'm still learning my way. I have never met my father; never even seen his image. I seem to be able to use a little magic, as you've already guessed. But I don't know much about my abilities, and I couldn't say much about them even if I did. All I can do is ask you to trust me, and I can promise to do the same for you. I hope that's enough."

The others stared at her for several moments, long enough that Nym began to fidget uncomfortably. She was used to being weighed and measured by other people, but not by people whose opinions actually mattered, and whom she needed to be able to depend on to have her back in a crisis.

"It's enough, Nymariel," Faraine said. She nodded firmly. "I believe you about Song. I'm sorry that I doubted your word. I won't again."

"I believe you also, for what it's worth," Aeson said. "I'm certainly not one to judge you for your past, when it's not your past that got us into this mess."

Don't be too sure, Nym thought, but she didn't speak it aloud. Instead, she said, "Now that we're all officially on the same team and stuck in the same mess, we need to try to figure out what we've stumbled into. What's really going on with the Order, and how does Faraine's brother and, presumably, any other missing magic-user come into it? We don't know enough yet, and we can't just run blindly—even presuming we can get out of Lyre and back into the mortal realms relatively quickly. The one saving grace of being stuck even temporarily in the Otherworld is that the Order won't be able to track us here. At least, I assume that's why Song brought us here when I said we needed a place to hide."

"*Does* the Order have a way of tracking you, Aeson? Unless someone gave our plans away, they seemed awfully quick to find us at the pasture. Is there some sort of magical tracer in play so that you and your Order siblings can find one another from a distance?" Faraine was frowning. "I keep having the feeling that we're missing something."

Aeson went still, his eyes wide. He set down his tea mug carefully, as though it were fine porcelain. "Actually, there is. Another thing that I took for granted as harmless, but now might get us killed. Damn!"

He rolled up his sleeve to the elbow and turned his palm upright. There, at the wrist, was a compass-shaped tattoo with a stylized flame in the middle, the shape of a hawk silhouetted on top.

"I guess the Order thought of everything," Nym commented wryly. "They have you all leashed, in more ways than one."

"Well, a leash may be broken," Aeson growled. "And whatever breaks the leash may just return to bite the masters in the arse."

Nym laughed at that, and after a startled moment the others joined in—even Aeson, though he looked a little abashed.

"There is something that's been bothering me, Aeson," Nym said when the laughter died down. "When we wrecked the dinner and spoiled Grand Master

Zebermar's plans...I thought I sensed him using magic to scan my aura and energy, and then it felt like he was trying to batter down my personal shields. It was strong —much stronger than I expected, or I'd have prepared better. And then later, when they were chasing us in the woods, I felt it again. I don't know how to judge the amount of power you members of the Order can wield, but...he just seemed very strong. I wondered whether you had any insight on that."

"You sensed that, too?" Aeson sounded shocked. "I thought for a moment that I sensed something similar when I was speaking to him in his study, but it was such a brief flash, and I assumed I'd imagined it. He's not supposed to have any more power at his disposal than any of the rest of my Order siblings."

"So the Grand Master is bound like everyone else?" Nym asked, and Faraine nodded as though Nym had voiced her own question.

"I...we were always told it was so. But after his actions today, I am not so sure. I don't really know what to believe anymore," Aeson said quietly.

Nym frowned. "Could he be taking extra power for himself in some way? Might he have access to some of the power that the Order siphons off of all of the mage-knights?"

Aeson looked devastated. "I...suppose it's possible. If he's wielding more power than he should have at his disposal, than that would mean he's getting it from somewhere, and the only way I can think of for him to do that would be if he's tapped into the Arboricanum, which none of us are supposed to be able to do. It would be a betrayal of all of our laws and tenets."

"Well, I think the betrayal part has been obvious ever since he tried to drug us and then threw us into the dungeon, so it doesn't really surprise me if he's dipping his hand into the coffer, so to speak," Nym said. She felt bad when Aeson looked even more miserable.

"There are a lot of things that I now realize I've been blind to. I've...got a lot to process," he said finally. "But for now, I suggest we focus on where we are right now and what we need to do next. I promise we'll resume this conversation as soon as our situation is a bit more stable. I won't ignore any failings or betrayals from the Order. I may not like what I've learned tonight, but it was truth that I needed to hear, and I won't take it lightly."

"Fair enough," Nym said, and Faraine nodded bracingly, though she looked as though she would rather have gone to Aeson and given him a big hug instead.

The rest of the evening they spent planning as best they could. There had to be a way out of Lyre, and if all else failed, Nym knew, she only had to wait until the next new moon in the mortal realms and Erevan would find her. He could probably let them out, then.

And won't he be surprised to find me here, Nym thought grimly.

SIXTEEN

IMPROMPTU RESCUE

The moon that Nym could see in the Otherworld was in the same phase as the moon in the mortal realm. She and the others had laid their bedrolls on the ground inside the hollow tree, but only two of them were inside sleeping at any one time, the third on watch. Nym had taken the second watch, and there was still a little time before she would need to wake up Faraine for the third. They had let the fire die down but carefully banked the coals, not so much for warmth as to be able to start a blaze again right away as a potential deterrent for anything that might otherwise be tempted to creep into the camp in the night. Having a fire was as much risk as not having one, but Nym had to admit that she wanted a hot breakfast in the morning. Tea and toast, at least.

She scanned the forest, all her senses alert to the hidden life around them—the sounds of insects and night-flying birds, the sighing of wind through the trees higher up. Song dozed, as did the other horses, and Nym took her cue from their peacefulness that for the moment, at least, nothing was near that either wanted to eat them or capture them. That, or it was biding its time.

The waxing moon was a crescent in the night sky. It took Nym some time to figure out what it was about it that made it stand out to her. Then finally she realized. So many tales and legends said that the fae realm was a place of perpetual twilight. But many realms comprised the Otherworld, and Lyre, apparently, either had endless night or a normal progression of day and night. She hoped for the latter. An all-night realm would be difficult and dangerous to travel in, and even a weak autumn sun was better than no sun at all.

If only she could tell Faraine and Aeson about Erevan. She wondered whether they could sense that she was still holding something back. It was dangerous to keep the bargain and its terms from her companions, especially given the trouble they were already in from the Order. But it might be equally as dangerous to tell them, and she had made a promise.

She was pondering the problem when something made her freeze where she was, listening. There had been a sound like the creak of harness—yes! The creak of harness, and wheels rolling along the forest floor, snapping branches in the process. A quick glance toward the horses told Nym that they'd heard it too, and they stood with ears up, heads turning toward the sound. Song's eyes glowed in the darkness as she turned to look at Nym, but she made no sound, and neither did the other horses.

Quickly and as quietly as she could, Nym scooped

the dirt that they'd dug out for the firepit back over the coals, smothering them. In moments, she'd smoothed out the dirt and scattered pine needles and leaves over it the way Aeson did when he disguised a camp. Unless someone walked right over the erstwhile firepit and felt residual warmth beneath the ground, no one would be able to tell that there had been a fire in that spot.

Then Nym crept to the hollow tree and woke the others, telling them in a whisper what she'd heard. Instantly alert, Faraine got up and hastily began rerolling her bedroll, assembling her few belongings as quickly as she could. Nym did the same. Aeson followed more slowly, yawning but otherwise alert enough for a man who'd just had only about two hours of sleep after he'd stood the first watch.

Because they'd already rinsed and packed up the vessels used to prepare and eat dinner, there was little to assemble for departure, if such were necessary. The trio crept to the horses and quietly began saddling them, even Song, though she kept swiveling her ears back toward the source of the sounds that Nym had heard.

The creaking of wheels and harness was farther away, now, but still audible through the darkness. Nym shared a glance with Faraine, and Faraine nodded, though no words had been spoken.

"I'll go find out who that is and what they're doing. If I don't come back, just get going, as far away from here as you can. And if you hear a panther's cry, just grab my horse's reins and get away from here; I'll lead the pursuit in a different direction and catch up with you later—on four legs if I have to. I can track you by scent. Just don't shoot me by mistake if you happen to see a panther."

"But if we *do* see a panther, how will we know for sure—" Aeson began, but Faraine cut him off.

"Simple. If it's attacking you, it's not me," she said in a low growling whisper. The next moment, the air shimmered where she stood and a large black panther stood there, sleek and deadly, golden eyes shining in the night. Then she padded off through the underbrush on silent feet. Nym and Aeson waited with the horses. Fortunately, neither Caeros nor Seralo seemed particularly alarmed by Faraine's transformation, though Caeros stood intently watching the spot where his rider had disappeared into the underbrush.

Faraine returned a short while later, and as soon as she had regained her human form, she gestured the others to draw close.

"It's a party of goblins," she said in a whisper. "Or, what I think is Goblins. Some are larger, and wearing red caps, which seems to set them apart from the others. They appear to be transporting some prisoners —that's what the carts are for. I counted four prisoners between the two cages, and twice as many goblins. I don't know where they're bound, but if we were to head in the opposite direction, we could probably avoid their notice. However..." Here, Faraine hesitated. "The prisoners are mostly humans, though I think I saw one elf in the bunch. I didn't recognize any of them, but it seems interesting to me that a caravan of prisoners would be heading through the forest so close to where we came in. I know this is a whole other realm from ours, but...I think we should see whether we can find out more."

"I agree," Nym said at once. "I've just remembered a detail regarding the people who attempted to capture me in Kalas. One of them—the female—was a goblin."

"A goblin?" Aeson burst out in a startled whisper.

"Why didn't you tell us before?" Faraine asked, keeping her voice equally low.

"I didn't think it had any particular significance at the time, and I had only just met the two of you and didn't know if I could trust you. And by the time we reached Cambermere and got embroiled in the mess with Zebermar, it just...slipped my mind. I'm sorry," Nym said, exasperated with herself for forgetting that small detail.

"It's all right; we know now," Faraine said in a low voice, glancing back toward the direction the goblin prisoner train was taking. "But it means that we have all the more reason to try to rescue these folks and see what we can learn from them. It can't be coincidence that one of the people who tried to take you was a goblin, Nym. And if they're taking prisoners into the Otherworld, then that would explain all the disappearances, and why no one could trace them. No one from the mortal realm would automatically assume that their loved ones had been abducted by Goblins. I mean, there are all sorts of tales and the like, but no one in living memory has been reported taken by the fae— any type of fae. Not in over a hundred years, at least."

Nym stared at the ground. Taken by the fae. It seemed to her that there were all sorts of ways one could be "taken by the fae," and not all of them involved kidnapping.

"We seem to have two options at the moment," she said. "Follow them to wherever they're taking these prisoners and hope that we can rescue them upon arrival, or set up a distraction now and hope we can free them in the commotion."

"If we wait, we might find more prisoners than just those four," Faraine said hopefully, and Nym knew that she must be thinking of her brother.

"Yes, but what if the place where they're headed is far more secure? If they are bound for a fortress or similar—which seems likely—we may not be able to effect a rescue once they reach it. If we try now, we have a chance of succeeding, and at least four people are freed." Aeson ignored Faraine's scowl and appeared to be waiting for her reply.

After a moment, Faraine sighed. "All right! All right...we'll try now. Damn, but it's hard sometimes to do the right thing, even when you know it's right."

"We'll find your brother Faraine. Somehow, we'll find him, whether that's tonight or later," Aeson said quietly, but there was relief in his voice.

That only served to make Faraine scowl harder, but she squared her shoulders and tipped her chin up. "You'll need a distraction. I can arrange that. But it will be up to the two of you to get the prisoners out of the cages and hidden somewhere while the goblins are chasing the kitty."

Some deep instinct surged to the fore—the feeling that it should not be Faraine who took on this particular risk. A certainty, perhaps. A Knowing. And Nym could not have said how she knew; she just knew. Her heart sank, but she shook her head. "No, Faraine. You and Aeson will probably be better at dealing with the locks than I would, and if there's even a chance that your brother is in one of the cages, you need to be there."

The others gaped at her, but she held up a hand to forestall the argument they didn't have time for. No good had ever come from ignoring her deep intuition; she wasn't going to ignore it this time. "I'll be the distraction. I'll do my best not to get caught, but if I am, just get the others to safety, all right?"

"Nym, no! You can't—Faraine began, but Nym darted off in the middle of the protest, heading for the other side of the slowly-moving train of goblins and prisoners.

Swift, but quiet and as careful as possible. That was the way. Nym crept through the trees, always keeping the line of goblins and prisoners in sight. When she was roughly parallel to the middle of the column, she hid behind a pile of deadfall, making sure she could see around it. Then, singing quietly under her breath, she rewove the personal wards that had been shattered back at Hawksfire Hall, taking care to make them stronger this time. If she knew how to layer in a little illusion as well, that would probably help, but as it was, she had to work with what she knew.

Taking a deep breath, she began to sing softly, a haunting tune that sprang to her mind, meant to beckon, to entice. She couldn't remember where she'd heard it before, but it seemed appropriate now. Opening her senses to the *wyld* in the air all around her, she Sang, calling to the goblin captors to leave what they were doing and come to her. A small voice in the back of her mind questioned, doubted. Who was she to use the *wyld* this way, as though she were one of the fae Themselves? But need overpowered doubt, and she felt the moment the song reached the goblin's ears, the moment they stopped and began to confer with one another, and the moment they turned from the carts and started in her direction.

As soon as she heard the sounds of their approach, she darted off toward another hiding place, concealing herself behind a stand of gorse that stood in a different direction from where she'd been before. Then she Sang again, the *wyld* lending strength to her song. She'd had a hunch the music would work on goblins, but it had been just that—a hunch. Now they crashed toward her, calling out to one another in rough, gravelly voices.

Slowly but surely, she led them away from the carts, only pausing a few moments in one place, until the lights from the lanterns were distant. Only when she was fairly sure that she had led them far enough away that Faraine and Aeson must have been able to free the prisoners did she leave off the singing and try to double back. The goblins who had followed were stamping around, poking at bushes and underbrush, still a good distance from Nym, or so she estimated.

She'd started to move back toward where she thought she and the others had left the horses when a huge goblin stepped out from behind a tree, grinning at her. It wore a red cap that appeared to be soaked with blood, and it carried a wicked-looking pikestaff. From what lore she'd heard, Nym knew that redcaps were among the most dangerous of goblins. She reached for her crossbow, pulling it up and nocking a bolt in a smooth, practiced motion, but at that moment something hit her over the head from behind, and the already dark night went completely black.

Faraine nearly went after Nym when she dashed away, but reason stopped her. If Nym was set on being the distraction instead of her, then her best course of action just now was to concentrate on getting the prisoners free, trusting that Nym could handle herself. And Nym was right; there was a possibility that Jerric might be among those in the cages. If he was, he'd need to see a familiar face, and if he did, it might calm the others. Without the prisoners' cooperation, the entire enterprise was doomed from the start.

Faraine gestured to Aeson, and they slowly began making their way down the sloping ground ahead toward the wagons. As they drew closer, she could make out the harsh, guttural sounds of what was probably the Goblin language, interspersed with threatening comments in Trade Basic, a language common to most of the races that lived on this continent. Valterra, Myrecia, Arkesh, and the other human-held kingdoms and territories all spoke Trade Basic, albeit with regional variations. But she'd never had any opportunity to learn any of the elven or fae languages. Now she found herself regretting the lack. Not that she intended to strike up a conversation with any of these goblins, of course.

Gradually, she worked her way closer, and as she did, she began to notice a haunting sort of music drifting through the darkness, a song sung acapella, but somehow amplified so that it carried through the night. It was melancholy and beautiful, and it made all the hairs stand up on Faraine's arms and the back of her neck. It...beckoned. Cajoled. Asked for...something, and Faraine could not have said for what. Given that she recognized Nym's voice, she was certain the lure of the song was not meant for her, but it made her think of sirens calling sailors to their dooms in the sea. The resonance and power of it was fascinating and terrifying both at once.

Nym had never sung this song in her presence before; of that Faraine was certain. It was the kind of song that, once heard, could not ever be fully forgotten. And once heard, even if half-remembered and dimly recalled only years later, the song would still haunt its listener, driving them to try to find it again.

Faraine shivered. What was Nym up to, out there in the darkness? What kind of magic was she playing with? Whatever she'd done back in Kalas that had inspired someone to pursue and attempt to kidnap her, it was nothing to this. Even though Faraine had the sure sense of the song not being directed toward herself or Aeson, it took some effort of will not to allow her feet to turn in the singer's direction. One look at Aeson's face and posture told her that he was having a similar struggle.

It worked on the goblins all too well, though, which apparently was its intent. One by one their heads turned toward the sound, and one by one they left their posts around the carts and headed off into the trees on the other side of the trail.

By the time Faraine and Aeson arrived at the carts only three goblins were left, and they seemed torn between dashing off to join their fellows and standing guard as they'd apparently been ordered to do. Three well-placed arrows took care of that problem. Faraine didn't recognize what sort of shaggy four-legged beasts were harnessed to the carts, but they appeared disinclined to move any more than they had to, and stood with heads down, clearly taking whatever rest this unexpected stop afforded them. Even the commotion around them didn't seem to have alarmed them in the least. Faraine breathed a sigh of relief for that small mercy.

All of the captives were staring wide-eyed at one another, one or two shaking their heads, others scrubbing hands over their faces and ears as though to clear their minds or wake themselves from some dream, gripping the wooden bars of the cages in order to remain upright.

Faraine crept close to the first cage, one finger to her lips. Fortunately, no one cried out, but the captives stared at her with trepidation. That begged a question she didn't have time to ask, yet. Bending close to the lock on the first cage, she examined it. It appeared to be made of bronze. She'd hoped for a latch of some kind, but a lock would require either a key or some other way to spring it, unless she wanted to dull a blade trying to pry apart the metal.

"I'll be right back," she assured the nearest captive, then turned and darted toward the dead goblins. A hasty search of all three bodies didn't turn up any sort of key. Any key would probably have been with the larger goblins at the head of the group, and those were nowhere in sight now, having gone after Nym with the rest.

Muttering, Faraine left Aeson to stand watch, pulled out her narrowest knife, and began trying to pick the lock with it. Several exasperating moments later, she knew the effort was fruitless. Scowling, she beckoned to Aeson, and he came over from where he'd been patrolling the perimeter of the small prison train.

"I can't pick this," she murmured as soon as he drew near. "I'm not sure why, but it won't budge. Can you magic it open?"

"I can try," he said, equally low. "I'm not sure that using any magic in this place wouldn't give away our location, though, so as soon as I get both of these locks sprung, get the captives out of this cage and moving back the way we came. Keep an eye on them, though; we don't need them panicking or...making poor decisions. We'll have to hope that Nym is able to find us when she can."

Faraine nodded, though she couldn't help scowling a little at the idea of just running off and leaving Nym. But Aeson was right; these people needed their help, and Nym had seemed adamant about her role in the rescue. They had to trust that the bard knew what she was doing. She'd also caught the gist of Aeson's other concern—the one he hadn't voiced. They only had three horses. Even riding double, there wouldn't be enough transportation for everyone once Nym returned. The last thing they needed was for the now-freed captives to try to make off with the horses.

A quick glance toward the shaggy cart-beasts told

Faraine that they weren't an option. To begin with, she didn't know the first thing about them, and that unknown was far too great a risk if they wanted a clean escape. Then there was the possibility that they'd been magically harnessed and controlled, and setting them free of the cart traces might give rise to any number of problems. Best to just keep the focus and deal with one issue at a time.

While Aeson examined the first lock, Faraine peered into the two cages, searching each face, but none of them belonged to Jerric. Her heart sank, but she managed to push aside her disappointment. Jerric might not be among *these* captives, but that didn't mean he had not been taken by the same enemy. These people might know something that could help her. And even if they did not, they did not deserve to be hauled through the Otherworld in cages like beasts.

Aeson palmed the first lock, muttering under his breath while a faint blue glow appeared beneath his hands. Moments later, Faraine heard the sharp click of a catch releasing, and the lock sprang open. Immediately, Aeson let go of the lock and headed toward the second cage, presumably to repeat the process. Faraine quickly grabbed the now-opened first lock and removed it, stuffing it into a pocket. There was no sense in leaving it behind when it had just been touched by Aeson's magic. If there was even a chance that the magic he'd used might be traceable, they couldn't afford the risk. She threw open the cage door and helped the two occupants down. They still seemed a little disoriented, but it was hard to say what physical condition they were in otherwise.

"Are you able to run?" she asked them. They glanced at one another uncertainly, but both nodded. "All right; follow me if you want to get out of here."

She started off toward the trees where she'd left the horses, avoiding looking back until she heard the two men's stumbling footsteps behind her. Neither of them was Jerric, but they needed her regardless. Faraine grimaced. Until she met Aeson, she'd never felt responsible for another human being other than Jerric, and now there were multiple people depending on her, some of whom she hadn't even met properly yet. It was unsettling.

She reached the horses almost before she realized it. Caeros gave a low nicker and nosed her, hard. Grabbing all three horses' reins, Faraine mounted Caeros and sat waiting, peering through the trees to catch the first sight of Aeson.

The two men eyed Seralo and Song, and Faraine grasped the reins even more firmly. Fortunately, Aeson returned at that moment leading the other two freed prisoners, a human woman and an elven man. Aeson looked at the four unmounted people and frowned.

"We won't make much time with half of us walking, the rest riding double. But if Song will allow two of you to ride her long enough to get you a safer distance away, then she can probably double back for Nym...or one of us can. We'll just have to trust that Nym can stay out of harm's way for that long."

"We can't ride *that* horse," the woman was saying, pointing fearfully at Song. "That's a faery horse. We don't dare ride her. We'll just walk." Her brown eyes were wide in a slender face that would be pretty underneath all the dirt.

"Well, *someone* was riding her," the elven man said quietly, pointing to Song's saddle. "If we ask nicely, she may allow it. If not, then of course we'll walk. Gods' truth, I'll run if I have to. But I'm getting out of here one way or another. My family back in Cymbrona will be wondering where I am, and I am needed there." Slowly he walked toward Song, holding out both hands where she could see them. Then he bowed to her.

Song eyed him with curiosity, but she did not back away. After a moment, she took one step closer.

"Will you allow us to ride, my lady?" he asked as he straightened. "We promise to be respectful, and to disembark promptly when we are safely away from here. All honor to you and the steeds of the Folk."

Song dipped her head, then made a nodding motion. When the elven man reached for the reins and the cantle of the saddle, she turned slightly to allow him access. He mounted, then extended a hand toward the woman, who balked, backing away, shaking her head.

"No, I can't. I dare not. I don't want to be stolen away a second time."

Faraine blinked. Even though she'd said she believed Nym, she'd still had doubts. But apparently Song really *was* a faery horse. How had Nym known? Shaking her head, she extended a hand to the frightened woman. "Get up behind me instead, then, but let us get on with it or all our work will be for nothing."

Hastily, as though the offer might not be extended a second time, the woman caught hold of Faraine's hand and scrambled up behind her. Aeson motioned one of the remaining two men to mount behind him on Seralo, and the elven man helped the last man up on Song, who sidled a little and wrinkled her nose as if displeased by the smell, but otherwise behaved like any normal horse.

Leave it to Nym to make off with a faery horse when there were well over a dozen mortal ones in that pasture, Faraine thought with a mixture of concern and amusement. A part of her was tempted to dismount from Caeros and go after Nym right now, but Nym was a lot less helpless than most of these people seemed to be. All four of them looked half-starved, and Faraine was willing to bet that they were hiding injuries besides; their too-stiff motions favoring this limb or that gave it away.

She definitely couldn't leave Aeson to wrangle the group of strangers alone, less from the thought that they might band together, overpower him and take the two mortal horses as from the thought that if any of them fell from their saddles from pure weakness, Aeson would be hard put to deal with the problem alone. But the moment these people were relatively safe somewhere—anywhere—she was going back to track Nym and make sure she'd escaped the goblins as well, even if she had to go full panther-on-the-hunt to do it.

SEVENTEEN

CAPTIVE PERFORMANCE

When Nym came to, she was lying on a hard surface that jolted underneath her. Even without raising her head, she could make out the sound of wheels trundling across a forest floor and the footfalls of whatever sort of animal was pulling the cart. For she *was* in a cart; cracking her eyelids open just a tiny bit revealed that much. Grimly, she forced her eyes open all the way so that she could take stock of her surroundings. By the bars she could see in front of her face, she was clearly in a wooden cage—probably one of the cages that had been on the carts. That much made sense. But what of the others?

Body aching, she forced herself to sit upright. Her wrists were bound with coarse rope, but she was alone in the cage, and when she peered over the end of the cart, she could see that the cage in the cart following along behind her was empty. So Faraine and Aeson *had* gotten the other prisoners out, then. Good. But now she had to figure out how to get *herself* free. She hadn't meant to trade her own freedom for that of the other captives, but here it was.

The others will come for me, if they can, she thought. *But I almost hope they don't. There is no use in both of them getting captured trying to rescue just one person. One captured for four freed isn't the worst tradeoff, all things considered, though zero captured would have been better.*

She thought about trying to Sing again, but her mouth was so dry that when she tried to make a sound, all that came out was a squeak. One of the goblins came over to the side of the cage and poked her with a stick, grunting words at her in that harsh language they used.

She smiled sweetly at the goblin, which only served to make it jab harder with the stick, aiming for her ribs.

"All right, all right; stop that!" Nym backed away from the side of the cage. "There's no need to damage the merchandise. Whoever you're taking me to probably wouldn't like that, would they? Where are you taking me, anyway?" She used Tradespeech, hoping her captors would understand that much.

"You no need know where take!" The goblin scowled, but it finally tossed the stick aside.

"On the contrary, I *do* need to know. I won't be able to perform adequately if I don't know whom I'm performing for."

The goblin blinked at this pronouncement. "What per form? That not your only form?" He gestured toward Nym's body. For a moment, she was confused.

"My only form? Oh...you mean, am I a shapeshifter? No. I'm not a mage, either. So unless you intended to capture a bard to entertain your leader, I don't know why you decided to bother with me."

"You mage. You use *wyld*. We take all mages. Now stop talk. Talk again, jab with stick again. Then tie mouth shut. Yes?"

"You threw away your stick," Nym said sweetly, earning a scowl from the goblin. "Don't worry, I'll behave." *I'll behave exactly like any good captive should—with intent to thwart you at every turn.*

The goblin nodded at her with apparent satisfaction, which told her that she need not worry too much about whether goblins in general were capable of reading her thoughts.

The cart trundled along steadily through what remained of the night, finally emerging from the dense pine and fir into a rocky and more sparsely forested area as the light of approaching dawn began to grow in the sky.

Dawn and dusk. The between times. Wherever Faraine, Aeson and the former captives were, Nym hoped they'd be able to find a way back to mortal lands with the coming of the dawn. She, meanwhile, would watch and wait for her chance. If she bided her time, that chance would come. And in the meantime, she had the opportunity to learn more about the enemy— whoever they were.

The goblin had said she was a mage because she'd been using the *wyld*. Fine. Admittedly, she *could* use magic, which perhaps made her a mage in some people's eyes at least. Aeson and Faraine had said that the other people on their list of missing persons were also able to use magic in some way. So the most important factor in play was that this group of thugs and kidnappers was after magic users of any ilk for some as-yet-unknown reason.

Not only that, but goblins were working with humans on this undertaking, as she'd seen back in Kalas. And given her own party's detainment and subsequent pursuit in Cambermere, the Order of Hawksfire was looking more and more likely to be tangled up in the scheme somehow, passing non-order mages through their prisons, draining their magic. And then taking them...where? She needed to know more, preferably before someone tried to drain her of *her* magic. Except that she didn't *have* any innate magic; she just *used* magic—used the *wyld*—as she'd been taught. Right?

Nym pushed the uncomfortable thought aside. Later. She'd think on it later, when she didn't need to have all her wits about her to plan yet another escape from yet another precarious situation. It seemed as though almost all she'd done since she'd met Erevan and accepted his bargain was try to evade danger that wanted to pursue her at every turn. And yet, none of this was Erevan's fault. Was it? Certainly, he hadn't been involved when Aeson's Order decided to lock them up in Hawksfire Hall's dungeon. That had been the work of Grandmaster Zebermar. And for that matter, why would Erevan teach her any defensive magics at all and make a binding magical bargain if he only intended to have her captured and locked away?

None of this made sense. There had to be pieces of the puzzle yet missing, and she needed to know what they were. Grimly, she dragged her focus back to where she was at this moment and what was happening around her.

The cart had been trundling up a slight hill, and now it lurched up onto a flat space, then came to a stop in front of a wooden stockade with a heavy gate. She heard shouting from the goblins at the head of the train, and the gate creaked open ponderously, groaning on its hinges. It was so thick and heavy, Nym doubted she could move it on her own.

Most of the logs that formed the walls of the stockade had been sharpened into points, but every few logs, a bronze pike had been embedded instead. Upon these pikes severed heads of various creatures were impaled. Some had been there so long they were nothing but skulls, but some looked more recently added. Nym swallowed and looked away from the gory statement decor as she tried to locate any obvious openings or sally ports. She thought she spotted one toward the back of the stockade, but it was hard to be certain without seeing it more closely.

Tents that obviously served as barracks for the Goblins were scattered around the sides of the enclosure, and each group of tents had a campfire set up with spits and cooking implements, sacks, barrels and kegs that looked as though they'd been looted from the human realm.

One side of the stockade was clear of tents, however, and it boasted a stone structure that Nym first took for officers' quarters. Then she saw the bronze-barred windows, and the way the structure was half-buried in the ground so that only the windows showed above ground level. Nym had the feeling that it might actually have more extensive parts underground. The stockade had been built very close to a mountain slope on the north side, which could mean that there might be an entire complex underground, accessible through that one stone structure.

Her heart sank. How would she manage an escape if they stashed her underground? She couldn't turn into a cat like Faraine and make an escape through the bars on those windows, and any cells buried under the hillside wouldn't have even that much potential egress.

All of the goblins appeared more relaxed here, laughing and joking with one another and pausing to quaff mugs of whatever was in the kegs. Those who had been part of the prisoner train were the most sober of the lot, but they were quickly lost among the ranks of their kin. Nearly half of the number present in the stockade were redcaps, and those who weren't seemed to have the most menial duties—at least from what Nym could tell from the view she got as they opened the cage and yanked her out, then marched her across the open space to the low stone building.

One of the guards unlatched and threw open the stout wooden door, and the two others who had remained to guard Nym hustled her inside. As the door closed behind her, Nym had to fight off an instinctive sense of suffocation. The dungeon in Hawksfire Hall had been much wider and had higher ceilings. This space was cramped, rows of wooden cages lining both sides of the long, rectangular room. All were empty save one, but Nym couldn't see what might be beyond the ring of torchlight, at the end of the room that she'd guessed might lead into the hillside. Perhaps when morning came, there would be enough light through the barred windows for her to see whether that end of the room did indeed contain another door.

The guards opened a cage next to the occupied one and shoved her into it, locking it with a bronze padlock. Then they left, talking and laughing to one another, though one of them kept trying to hum the song she'd sung. Every time he tried, he earned a cuff on the ear from his fellow guard, but he persisted, though his attempted rendition of notes and tune were horribly off. Nym would have cringed at the sound, had some part of her not been amused by the guard's attempt and failure to reproduce her song. At the same time, another part of her was horrified that the song had apparently left such a lasting impression. That hadn't been her intention.

Or was it? Shuddering, Nym pushed aside the thought and tried to focus on her new surroundings. It was hard to decide whether to be terrified at being in this cramped space, or relieved that the goblins hadn't bothered to take her deeper beneath the hillside. Either way, her elven heart yearned to be back in the forest— any forest, even if it was a forest full of dangerous fae creatures.

The cell she was in contained a small pile of dirty straw and a bucket. Unlike the cell beneath Hawksfire Hall, there was no cot—nothing between Nym and the cold stone floor except the straw, and she had no intention of touching that.

Predawn light crept timidly in through the barred window. The goblins had taken the torch with them, but the light was still enough for Nym to make out a small figure in the cell next to her. Whoever it was sat with their back to the far corner, and they were huddled in on themselves, no doubt to ward off the chill. The

Otherworld at large might or might not have seasons, but this part of it seemed to mimic the seasons and days in the mortal realm, and the prison building was cold.

Nym used her foot to brush the filthy straw away into one side of the cell, leaving the other side only slightly less filthy. Still, it was an improvement. She considered wrapping up in her cloak and trying to plan...something. Anything. But a closer look at the other shivering prisoner changed her mind.

Even now that she had a proper cloak, she hadn't quite lost her former habit of dressing in multiple layers. Her wonderful bard's coat was still back in her saddlebags wherever Song was, but she had on the heavier breeches and tunic with a shirt underneath. She could endure a little time without the cloak, if it made her an ally.

"Here," she said, removing the cloak and beginning to pass it through the bars to the other prisoner. "You can borrow this for a while and get warmed up. I haven't been sitting here freezing all night, so I'll be okay. How long have you been here? I'm Nymariel, by the way. Nym for short."

The other prisoner stood slowly and crossed the cell to take the cloak from Nym's hands as she threaded it through the bars that separated them. Nym blinked in surprise. The person appeared at first to be a human female, but although the ears weren't pointed like an elf's, nonetheless Nym knew without a shadow of doubt that this was no human. There was something in the depths of that ice-blue gaze that reminded Nym of Erevan. Her breath caught in her throat. A wylden! What were these goblins doing with a captive wylden?

"I have lost track of the days, Nymariel," the wylden said. "Well met. You may call me Tiriana. I will not forget your kindness." She reached out a slender hand and took the cloak Nym offered, wrapping it around herself with a sigh of relief. "This is such comfort after so many cold days and nights. These borderlands are always so cold. I have never decided whether it is worth it to have them mirror the mortal lands just for a few warm days of sunlight, when the opposite of those days is such pervasive discomfort."

"You are not a winter-court fae, I take it?" Nym asked, carefully.

Tiriana looked at her, tilting her head quizzically. "Winter court? I suppose there may be some wylden who take on the aspects of the various seasons here and there, but I have never heard of such a thing as a winter court or the like. This must be a mortal world imagining. How little they truly know about us." She sighed. "But then, I suppose we have been withdrawn from mortal lands for a long time now, and humans live for so short a time that I am sure many have forgotten what little truth they knew. Elves live long enough, but their forgetfulness is deliberate."

"I cannot speak for other elves," Nym said quietly. "But for myself, I would rather remember. Unfortunately, I cannot remember what I never knew in the first place."

"Can you not?" It wasn't really a question. But then Tiriana smiled, and that smile was full of warmth, which surprised Nym. "I suppose the least I can do in return for your unselfishness is to help you remember what you say you never knew."

"I...uh...that isn't necessary. The loan of the cloak is something I would do for any fellow prisoner. I need no compensation."

Tiriana laughed, a musical sound that tried to evoke joy and hope in Nym's heart even as she tried to subtly reinforce her personal wards which were, miraculously, still in place. She must not have been subtle enough about it, because Tiriana's eyes went wide, and she stared at Nym openly, her face a mixture of amazement and delight.

"You can use the *wyld*," she breathed. "Then, we have a chance."

"What do you mean, we have a chance?" Nym asked, wary and confused.

But Tiriana seemed energized. "You still have your magic. They knew you had magic, but they have not drained you; they have left you intact. I cannot get us out of here without the use of my magic, but you—you still can."

"They drained your magic?" Nym asked, shivering now, and not due to the lack of her cloak. "How long did it take them to do it, after they took you? And is your magic the reason they brought you here?"

"Most prisoners are drained of their magic relatively quickly after they arrive," Tiriana said rapidly, the words tumbling out in her haste and excitement. "Some were drained before they were detained here. Most who come here have no access to their magic, and they are put to work in the mines, or sent on to other places farther inward...deeper into the heartlands of Lyre. Some are sent to toil in the Pelambrian Marshes, digging for peat or harvesting the foods that grow or swim there. Once they lose their magic they are fit for little else."

"Why are you still here, then, if you don't mind my asking, Tiriana? And why were you here in the first place? I didn't know there had been any wylden taken. I thought it had been only elves and humans. It may help us to figure out why they took your magic but then didn't send you out to their...work camps, I guess we'd call them."

"You may call me Tiri if you wish. I like this idea of a shorter name among friends. And to answer your question, I believe they did not send me out because they have some other purpose planned for me. I think they may be going to send me on to serve Himself. Though given how goblins think, that could easily be when they think my will is worn down and I am compliant from weakness. I would rather escape before that happens."

"I've heard that appellation for this unknown enemy before," Nym said slowly. "Just who is Himself? What does he want with mages?"

"No one seems to know his true name," Tiri said. "But as I understand it, he must be a mage of some renown or skill, to command so many. What he may wish to do with the magic drained is anyone's guess."

"There was a mage in the Order of Hawksfire, a Grand Master Zebermar, who sent men after me and friends I was traveling with. Could he be this...Himself?" Something about that notion didn't quite seem right to Nym.

But Tiriana was shaking her head. "No, I do not believe it is this Grand Master, though he could be involved somehow. Might Himself be one of your own people?"

"An elven mage?" Nym crossed her arms, considering. "He could be, I suppose. But if so, why bring magic users into the Otherworld, when we Elves live in the mortal lands? That makes no sense."

Tiri held up both hands in a placating gesture. "I am not seeking to drive a wedge between us by making such a suggestion. I only offered it as a possibility. In truth, no one seems to know just who Himself is, and no one seems to want to offer a name for him. He truly must be that formidable. It is a frightening thing. And all the more reason that you and I must find a way out of here. As soon as may be, for both our sakes."

"We agree on that, at least," Nym said. "Now, why did you think that because I haven't been drained of magic, I might be able to get us out of here? I've only ever used the *wyld* in my capacity as a bard, and this little bit of personal defense that you sensed. Aeson's the battle mage, not me."

"Aeson? Who is Aeson?" Tiri asked, then held up a hand. "Never mind right now; tell me later. For now, since you seem to use the *wyld* without fully understanding it, let us determine first how much you do know. Perhaps I can guide you in expanding that ability."

"No deals, no promises. Mutual escape purposes only," Nym said. "If you teach me what you think will help us both, I owe you nothing. Whether or not it actually works and gets us out of here, I owe you nothing."

Tiri blinked, but then she nodded. "No deals. No

promises. You owe me nothing. And I owe you nothing. I will still remember the kindness you first did me, however. It is the sort of thing that I do not forget nor make light of."

"Fair. Now, what do you think I need to know? How can I use the *wyld* to help us escape?"

EIGHTEEN

WELL MET BY MOONLIGHT

High in the hills of Lyre, it was not yet dawn, but the darkness lay quiet, anticipating. At a desk carved of ancient oak, within a tower of pale stone at the center of a hidden glade, a wylden bard sat writing. He had been there for much of the night, and only now that the liminal state of dawn drew a bit nearer did he take note of the passage of time—or at least the mimicry thereof that denoted the concept of *days* or *nights* in Lyre. Lyre mirrored the mortal lands, but was not mortal in itself. Time appeared to pass, but that was by design and in appearance only.

It had its uses, Erevan mused. Mirroring time the way this realm did made it possible for one to emerge into the same conditions in the mortal lands adjacent. Conditions such as certain weather, or phases of the moon—all could be accessed through Lyre. It was well known as a border realm. Once renowned as the realm where one could have the best delights of the mortal realm and few of its problems, a place of joy in creation itself, Lyre now lay in a watchful, uneasy silence. Where once green things flourished and traded pollen and traits with plants in the mortal realms, even that prodigious growth had slowed and begun to stagnate.

What few denizens of this kingdom chose to remember and most chose to forget was that Lyre, of all the fae realms, was supposed to be the guardian realm —the realm that stood in watchful defense of the most easily passible borders between the mortal realms and the realm of the ageless faery folk, the Otherworld. Where once trade and cultural exchange had flourished between Lyre and the powerful elven realm of Cymbrona, now the great forest trackways were quiet, the crossroads neglected. So many of Lyre's wylden had moved farther in, deeper, away from the borders. Only a few, like Erevan, remained this close to the mortal realms, and those who did were seen as eccentric.

Well, he could handle being thought eccentric, as long as he gained the respect and renown necessary to be admitted into the ranks of the court bards, where he might finally catch the royal ears and find a way to deliver the information that he now knew was so vital.

Ah, but first things first. Time might not be on his side no matter the realm he was in, but nonetheless without patience, he would gain nothing. Or, more likely, he'd gain the opposite of that which he sought. And to that end...he glanced once more at the stylus in his hand, blinking at it as if he'd never seen it before. His thoughts had wandered from his task, a thing that seemed to be happening more often of late. And the distractions just seemed to multiply at every opportunity.

It had become Erevan's habit to transcribe certain of

the new songs or tales he heard, though he easily committed them to memory the very first time he heard them. The transcriptions themselves—at least the ones he chose to commit to parchment—were intended as gifts for the King and Queen of Lyre, when next he happened to be in their presence.

In truth, the transcriptions were but a tease, a means by which to taunt the court bards. He knew full well that none of them would be able to match his tone and nuance in playing them; he had a deft and versatile style all his own, one honed by his tendency to practice the music he heard from the mortal world. The court bards had all the technical grace required to play the music, but they would be hard put to emulate the dense, earthy chaos present in so many of the human songs, or to evoke the sadness and grace mixed with delight that came through in elven works.

Playing this music right required attention to the emotion and intention behind the songs, and in this, most of the court bards were lacking, having spent no time at all with humans and forbidden to do so with elves. Erevan had the advantage, now that he had made a deal with a certain red-haired elven bard.

And you lead me a merry chase already, do you not, dear bard?

Erevan put down his stylus and tried to ignore the faint tickle at the edge of his consciousness. Because of the bargain he had made with Nymariel, he usually felt the ripples through the *wyld* whenever she was using it. It was easy to ignore. Or it had been, at first. But it seemed as though each time she used her abilities, they became stronger, and so did his sense of her.

The rate at which her power was growing might have seemed negligible at first, but he hadn't expected her to use it extensively. Certainly not half as much as she had apparently been doing. He had not anticipated that using it in any capacity at all would have gotten her into so much difficulty, so soon. Perhaps she had a talent for finding trouble. It was...perplexing. And highly, highly distracting. As was the lady herself—though that last thought was not one he could afford to consider too closely.

He still could not decide whether she was using the *wyld* so much because she was already addicted to the feel of the magic, or whether she really was in that much trouble from the other mortals and was just instinctively reaching for any sort of defense she could muster. He'd thought her to be of a singular, strong constitution—unusually strong for a mortal of any ilk. If she did prove to be so easily susceptible to the lure of fae magic, it would be disappointing, though not entirely unexpected. Many mortals had trouble in that regard, whether human, elven, or any other variety. But all his instincts had told him that Nym was different.

He'd already taught her far more than he'd intended to, and in such a short time! She had a way of wheedling the knowledge out of him, and he could not say whether it was due to her formidable aptitude for music, or a reason of another sort entirely. Insidious. Forbidden.

There were places even a wylden should fear to tread, especially when it concerned a mortal—any mortal, but especially an elf, given the centuries of enmity between their peoples. But something about her earnest emerald gaze, her humor, her warmth...it lulled him into giving her what she asked for, and keeping the price as low as possible. That, too, was perplexing.

Was it pure folly to admit that he rather liked the easy ebb and flow of their banter, and the way she kept subtly altering their bargain, just enough to gain his help without seeming to admit to needing it? He hadn't been this entertained in centuries. And for the first time in a very long while, he found himself wanting to know what was going to happen next, especially once they knew one another better.

She was not what he'd expected, this young elven bard. Far too beautiful by half, and too charismatic, for all her small-village past and general lack of courtly graces. A country bard, not a grand court maestro. But a bard for the people—maybe eventually *all* of the people. And as she learned, her ability would grow more than enough to see her welcomed into the halls of courtier and commoner alike, on either side of the veil. It was in essence the promise he'd made her, wasn't it? Even if she had no idea yet of just where that ambition of hers might lead.

But that was dangerous thinking. It was a dangerous path he'd set them both on. He'd known it to be so, but he'd set them on it anyway, because the price to be paid if he failed in his endeavor would be even greater than the price if she failed in hers. And if they ever decided to take their association a step further, to act on the connection already building between them....

No. Quash that thought, immediately. Focus on what needed to happen now, not what had happened before and what might happen later. Given his nature, it was tempting to let go of such concepts as *before* and *later* altogether and just stay always in the ever-present moment. The now. An endless space to be filled with whatever entertainment came readily to hand and a time in which troubles seemed far away in either the past or a future that need not be faced yet. But too many of his people had fallen into that trap for far too long, and apathy in this case could prove to be their downfall—not to mention the downfall of so much else.

The faint sense of Nym in the back of his mind suddenly became a torrent of awareness. It was more than merely distracting; it was insistent, demanding. She was pulling on the wyld as though she intended to wrestle it into submission. She was gearing up to do... something.

Erevan sighed. It seemed he couldn't simply ignore this problem and hope it went away, and ignoring it—pretending he hadn't sensed what he'd sensed—wasn't working. Responding to the flare of *wyld* he'd sensed from her only moments before would be a risk, but not responding might be even more so. He didn't want to tip his hand so early in the game. But she just kept... needing his help. And then, when he gave it, she put it to immediate and extremely creative use. No shrinking violet or delicate little flower, was Nym. If one handed her a sword, she was sure to use it, whether fully trained in its use or not.

Sighing, Erevan stowed away his writing implements and parchments and concealed them with wards he was certain no one would even sense, much less break. Then he went down the spiral stairs at a rapid pace, grabbed up his cloak from its peg by the ground-level door, and headed out into the darkness.

She was out there somewhere, his exasperating little bard. A not-so-subtle change in the flow of ambient *wyld* he sensed made him frown and hurry his step on the way to his horse, Zephyr. Then the full import of what he'd been sensing hit him all at once.

She'd used the *wyld* again, that was certain, but at a level of power he hadn't realized her capable of. It had been just a fraction off the level of a full Calling, and he had no idea where she'd even heard the song she used, much less how she'd summoned enough magic for it with no instrument other than her voice, which she shouldn't have been able to do. A shiver ran down his spine. However she'd done it, the song itself wasn't the worst problem he needed to address. The worst problem was that she'd done it inside the borders of the Otherworld, and he had no idea how she'd gotten there.

Nym's magic flared once more, then stopped altogether. In the space between one breath and the next, the *wyld* she'd summoned went quiescent, snuffed out like the flame of a candle. And what *that* might signify, Erevan didn't want to consider.

He saddled Zephyr with speed borne of desperation. If Nym were discovered, so would he be, and that would lead them both to ruin as surely as the sun would rise. He had to find her before that happened. Moments later, he was galloping Zephyr down one of the ley trackways toward the last place he'd felt the pulse of her magic.

Farther into the Otherworld, travel along the old straight tracks took very little perceived time; in fact, it was usually nearly instantaneous. In Lyre, because of the way the realm mirrored time in the mortal lands, it took a bit longer, though it was still much faster than threading one's way along the normal paths and trails, particularly in the forested areas. On a trackway—which mortals called a ley line—one could pass directly from one point to another, right through any tree or other naturally occurring object in between.

Normally it was the best and fastest mode of travel, and far surpassed the mortal idea of roads, which could meander around perceived obstructions, oft taking a traveler far out of their way. But none of these long-known and accepted details were helping Erevan now. It was as if the borderlands were mirroring the mortal world more closely of late, and even the trackways seemed to offer resistance, slowing his speed. In its way, it was as unsettling as all the rest of the growing strangeness.

When he drew relatively near the area where he'd sensed Nym's presence before she stopped Singing, Erevan slowed his speed to a cautious walk and guided Zephyr off the trackway. Carefully and with much delicate stepping on the part of his night-dark mount, he made his way toward the live presences he sensed ahead. This group seemingly had come from the direction he was headed for, though they were now a fair distance away and moving steadily in his direction. In a moment they'd be on him, but he didn't wish to make his presence known until he knew what he was walking into. To that end, he stopped, listening. Zephyr was listening too, ears up and swiveling.

He could hear the sounds of several people and at least three horses, though they were obviously trying to be quiet. Smart of them, not to gallop madly through the woods and draw attention that way, but nonetheless they were still readily apparent to his finely honed senses. Oddly, most of the energy he sensed from the group was human. First, he'd felt that Nym was in the Otherworld where he hadn't expected her to be, and now here was this group of humans and at least one other elf. There was a hint of fae in the mix, too, though he wasn't sure where that was coming from.

Given their proximity to where Nym had recently been, this could not be coincidence. But were these people friends or foe to her? If foes, he'd lead them a merry chase and make them regret that they'd ever crossed into the borderlands—assuming he didn't find it best to just eliminate them outright. If they were friends, though...well, he'd deal with that eventuality when he knew for sure.

Cautious, he summoned a Glamour through the *wyld*, taking on the appearance of a wizened and slightly disheveled older human man clad in a brown homespun robe and equipped for travel. Zephyr needed no instruction; his night-black hide rippled slightly and became dark brown and shaggy, like any such horse an itinerant hedge-wizard might own.

It was possible that these people had simply wandered through a thin spot in the barrier, and did not know where they were. He wasn't one to make sport of people who had done no wrong to himself or those he cared about, amusing though the notion might be on occasion. He'd make his presence known and speak with them, traveler to travelers, and then he'd decide what to do with them. Just what his decision would be would depend entirely on them.

Faraine glanced behind her for what must be the hundredth time, though it was much harder to keep a good eye on their backtrail while riding double. The group had made some progress at least. The path the goblins had taken was behind them and they were moving steadily away, though they'd refrained from galloping the horses—both to give Nym time to catch up and to reduce the chance that the train of Goblins would hear the drum of the horses' hooves on the ground. It was nerve-wracking, going at a fast walk, but if they were quiet enough, they could fade into the surrounding woods with relative silence, and any goblins that came back from Nym's clearly magical distraction would hopefully be confused and disoriented, unaware of which way their captives had gone.

That was putting a lot of faith in Nym's abilities, but Faraine was nearly certain that the faith was justified— if the eerie strength of that siren song had been anything to judge by.

Faraine caught the scent of the newcomer before she saw the shape emerge from out of the trees. Male, from what she could tell, and the scent read as human, although in the Otherworld, who could know for sure? But there was also the scent of horse, and the goblins hadn't been using horses. She relaxed fractionally, though her hands on Caeros' reins remained steady, prepared to urge the gelding into a gallop if she sensed a threat.

What now? she wondered, trying not to tense and send either her horse or her passenger into a panic.

The person who emerged from the trees to the left of their path was not at all what she'd expected. To the casual glance, he seemed quite ordinary. A grey-haired older man dressed in common brown homespun robes, he rode an equally nondescript brown horse laden for travel. The only thing that really set off Faraine's mental alarms was the fact of his very presence, here in the Otherworld. At least, she assumed they were still in the Otherworld. He had the look of a wizard, but to imagine that wizards just traipsed through the Otherworld at all hours of the night seemed a bit far-fetched to her. Nonetheless, his expression upon seeing their party seemed rather more alarmed than threatening.

Until or unless he did something to disabuse her of the notion that he was exactly what he seemed—a human traveler who might or might not be a wizard traveling through the Otherworld on some errand of his own—she would give him the benefit of the doubt to at least a small extent. A very small extent.

"Peace, fellow travelers," he said quietly, keeping his hands where they could see them. "Well met, I hope. It is unusual to see other travelers in the borderlands of Lyre. Where are you bound?"

"We are bound for the mortal lands," Aeson said, and Faraine could tell by his voice that he was as wary as she was. "You appear to have some knowledge of this area. Might you know of a crossing near here?"

"A crossing? That is complicated. It appears you have stumbled into this realm by accident, or so I assume. It would be quite a feat to stumble out again by accident. Fortunately, I traverse these borderlands sometimes to study the plants and other life I find here, and I know how to open the barriers to allow entry...or exit. Some among your party look as though they have need of such an exit." The man frowned, studying the extra passengers on the three horses.

"An exit would be welcome, provided there are no strings attached for such assistance," Faraine said hastily. She wasn't sure how much fae lore Aeson knew, but treating with anyone in these lands, no matter their appearance, could be fraught with risk, so she was taking no chances.

The man laughed, and it had a musical sound to it that set Faraine's mental alarms clamoring again. Wizard he might well be, but what more than that?

"You appear to have a steed of the Folk with you, and it appears that she carries passengers willingly. That seems a point in your favor. You also appear to have some knowledge of courtesy and caution. That is well, for there are folk here who would do you harm should you rouse their ire. But there are also those who pose no threat. The trick is in being able to tell which is which. Have you met with any who belong to the first category?"

"There are goblins back in the direction from which we came," Faraine said, thinking quickly. "I believe it truth to say that they were up to no good."

The stranger's mouth quirked up at the corners "Goblins are usually up to no good. Though from their perspective, they would doubtless view their mischief as very good indeed."

"This time their mischief included taking prisoners, torturing them, and transporting them to who-knows-where," the woman behind Faraine said, before Faraine could find a way to prevent her. Faraine reached down and pinched the woman's leg in warning. She gasped faintly, but made no other comment.

"Prisoners?" the stranger said, his frown deepening. "Well, if I were to happen to meet any of these goblins and their prisoners, what would be your advice to me on how to respond?" He was looking right at Faraine as he spoke.

A chill ran down Faraine's spine as she realized why he was asking. It was a chance. A slim chance, but a chance nonetheless, and all depended on how she responded.

"If I were a knowledgeable traveler such as yourself, I would help any such prisoners or other travelers in the area to make an exit into the mortal lands. Particularly if doing so would cause as much...mischief...for the goblins as they seem to be causing for others. And I would keep an eye out to potentially help any other prisoners they might collect in the future. I'd want to foil their plans as a means to keep the Otherworld free of such potential conflicts. But that is simply my own opinion, of course."

"And I did ask for your opinion, did I not?" the stranger asked, though it didn't really sound like a question. After a moment, he sighed. "Very well. Is this all there is of your party? Are there any others I might need to assist? Others such as these hypothetical future prisoners you say the goblins might collect?"

Faraine hesitated. There was really no help for it. If

this stranger was in fact what she now suspected him of being, he could easily overpower them with a flick of his wrist—even Aeson—unless she managed to fire a shot from her bow quickly enough. And she knew enough to know without doubt that she would never even manage to draw her bow. Fleeing was not an option now; their horses were encumbered, and one command from this stranger to Song might place Song's passengers in more jeopardy than they were already in. No, this stranger was asking for her honesty, and if she tried to deceive him, she had a feeling they would all pay for it.

She nodded, ignoring the urgent look Aeson was giving her. "We are missing one person. Our friend was lost back there, helping us evade the goblins. She's elven. Red hair, green eyes, slender. She's a bard by trade, and she was meant to catch up with us, but as she hasn't yet, I worry that she might have been taken."

The stranger sighed, shaking his head as he dismounted his horse. "You should have begun with that bit of information," he said. "Be that as it may, I will open the way for you to depart these lands. The white mare, however...she must be set loose as soon as you reach the other side. Do you carry your missing friend's belongings? If I seek her and find her for you, she may have need of them."

"They're...well...they're all on the white mare," Faraine said. There was no use prevaricating. She had a terrible feeling that she'd just offered Nym up on a platter, but given their current state of encumbrance, they had no chance to go track Nym down themselves, much less mount a rescue if one was needed.

"Of course, it would be *that* mare," the stranger said, almost to himself. Then he looked at Faraine and smiled. "I suggest you prepare yourselves. Unless you go straight in the direction I tell you, you may well find yourselves off track." He pointed eastward. "Head in that direction, where the sun rises in the mortal lands. Keep steadily on until dawn; do not stop. You will feel it when you cross the border. As soon as you sense the crossing is complete, turn the mare loose. Do not try to detain her, or it will go badly for you."

"But...what about our friend? I had intended to go back for her as soon as our passengers reached safety," Faraine said. No use hiding anything now. They were as exposed as they'd ever been, and there were too many lives at stake in this moment, not just Nym's.

"It appears you've mounted a daring rescue up to now, and you are to be commended on that," the stranger said. "But if you do not know these lands, you would likely not get far if she has indeed been taken by goblins. One of you alone, tracking your friend through the *wyld*...courageous, but not as likely of success as you may have hoped. Even if you were able to track her, say, on four legs rather than two, you still might not get far. And you would leave your other companions without capable defensive assistance."

Faraine opened her mouth, then closed it. Sweat broke out on her forehead, mocking the coolness of the air. She nodded, not trusting herself to say more. He was right. She hated him for saying it, but he was right. She'd have a devil of a time tracking Nym through a fae forest even in cat form, and leaving Aeson outnumbered among strangers was just as bad an option. Why had she agreed to let Nym be the distraction, even if it had worked all too well? And as to how the wizard had sensed her feline nature, she didn't even want to speculate. Aeson had traveled with her for nearly a year and still hadn't known until she told him.

The stranger smiled, not unkindly. "Your friend may yet have resources you are unaware of. That horse may be one of them. Heed my words, and do as I advise. When dawn comes, the way will open for you, and you must be well away from here by then. If I do meet your friend—Nym, was it? I will assist her however I may, and if fate decrees it so, I will send her back to you. Now, go. Do not look back. Away, steadily but swiftly, away."

Faraine nodded, gulped once, and guided Caeros in the direction indicated. Silently, she prayed the others were following and that none of them looked back, but for her part, she intended fully to do exactly as this *perfectly normal, friendly human wizard* had told her to do.

It was only after they were well on their way that Faraine remembered that while talking to the stranger, she had never told him the name of her friend.

NINETEEN

DAYBREAK

Nym listened carefully as Tiriana described the complexities of the song she was teaching her. They had to be very quiet; if they sang too loudly, it would doubtless bring the goblins into the prison bunker. It was difficult; more so than Nym had thought it would be, but under the circumstances, it was the only chance they had.

Nym sang softly, trying to match the lilt and flow of Tiri's voice. Tiri shook her head, repeated the phrase, then gestured for Nym to try again. In her way, Tiri was proving to be far more exacting a teacher than Erevan. But if this song could unlatch the door to their cages and then the door to the bunker itself, then they'd at least be outside.

Another song would create a fae glamour to make them invisible, and that one had to be sung in a whisper. Tiri had thought of everything, seemingly, though the process of first getting out of the bunker and then making it across the compound undetected was a bit more complicated than Nym would have liked.

They also had to time it exactly; the guards made routine patrols past the bunker; Nym could see their boots pass by on the muddy ground above, which was roughly at her eye level when she looked out of the barred window.

Their only saving grace seemed to be that the goblins had been tired after their journey and the chase after Nym through the woods, and had apparently been disinclined to do anything more than stuff her into the cell, much less take her to anyone who could drain her magic.

Though no doubt the Order of Hawksfire would have done that for them, had we not escaped them at the Hall, Nym thought sourly.

"Stop that," Tiri said in an exasperated voice. "Whatever you are thinking about, it has flattened your tone. You must keep your mind on the work. Think only of what you intend to accomplish. The Otherworld is a changeable place, Nym. It responds to your intention, and to your need. Even these borderlands will do that, though they are more stable in form than many of the inner realms. So you must take care how you frame your intent."

"Noted," Nym said, and went back to the musical phrase. She estimated they had only a few more minutes before the guard would make another round, and dawn was nearly upon them. She didn't know what would happen during the day, and escaping while the light was still dim sounded like a much better plan than doing so in broad daylight. But once day came, she might be out of time, for surely the goblins wouldn't just leave her sitting here all day before at least some of them thought to get her *processed*, as Tiri had called the permanent draining of magical energy.

Carefully, with as much focus as she could muster, Nym Sang softly again. A faint creak sounded from the direction of the bronze lock on their cage. It remained latched, but there had definitely been something going on.

"Good," Tiri said, nodding encouragingly. "Try again, but with just a little more power this time. You have to learn how to put the right amount of magic into your songs so that they only do exactly what you intend them to do. Audible volume does not dictate how much of the *wyld* you can thread into a Song. A whisper may carry more power than a shout; it is how you interact with the *wyld*—how you flow with it and allow it to flow through you—that determines the strength of a Song or any other working."

"Oh. I hadn't thought of it that way." Nym frowned, thinking. Perhaps this was why she'd been having trouble controlling the *wyld* when she performed. She tended to put her all into a performance, and with that amount of emotion and focus, she was probably calling too much of the magic into her music without intending to.

But what would happen if I did intend to? How much power could I summon if I really needed to? Erevan didn't want me to use a lot of it; he wanted me to keep it small and subtle, so I didn't draw attention to myself. But maybe there are times when subtle won't do. Maybe there are times when a quiet person needs to be loud, or a trickle needs to be a flood. Why didn't Erevan tell me this? And where is he now, anyway? He can sense me through the link he made. If I use the wyld, can I sense him, too?

The thoughts tumbled through her mind in a tumult of realization. She could sense him, dimly but unmistakeably. And there was a connection between them, she realized, beyond the mentor-student business arrangement and magical bargain—something she could feel now that she actively sought to connect.

It was only when Tiri gasped that Nym realized she'd been humming a tune that Erevan had taught her, one she'd never sung since the night they'd met. And her thoughts of him while humming that tune seemed to have had some effect. Tiri was staring at a visible concentration of light and energy that enveloped the bars between their cells, to the point that the bars were no longer visible. If Nym peered into that intervening space just right, she could almost see it coalescing into a smooth, rippling oval surface. There were trees within that oval of light. Forest. It was like looking into a painting, or a mirror to someplace else entirely, or....

"A portal," Tiri breathed. "Nym, that's a portal! Why didn't you tell me you could do that?"

"I didn't know," Nym said, though her voice came out nearly disembodied, thready. Glancing at her hand, she saw that she was nearly as transparent as the magic she'd raised. In fact, her whole body was growing so transparent that in a panicked moment, she thought she might be fading away.

"I'm going to jump through this space you're holding—this space you have *become*," Tiri said, her voice a mixture of fear and hope. "To translocate yourself, just keep your focus on wherever you were thinking of when you created that portal, and follow your thought through the energy to wherever or perhaps *whatever* that was."

Tiri suited action to words and darted through the shimmering oval. Peering through the energy, Nym saw her come out the other side. For that matter, she *felt* her come out the other side, and that was a decidedly odd sensation.

For a moment, Nym wavered, and her already transparent form wavered as well. It was terrifying; she felt herself beginning to drift, to come apart. What had she been thinking about when this had happened? Focus. She had to focus on....

Erevan. She'd been thinking of Erevan when this had happened. Thinking of how he was able to locate her, and that she should be able to locate him the same way. She focused on him more firmly; not on the admittedly attractive appearance he'd shown her, but on their interactions, on his patience, on the kindness he'd proven himself to possess. She focused on their agreement, on the bond he'd set between them, the things he'd taught her, the inexplicable feelings of familiarity and safety that she felt whenever they were together.

The first rays of dawn began to filter through the bars on the windows. Nym imagined herself hurtling through that portal, to wherever he was...and felt herself coalesce into solidity once more, her body suddenly heavy and more cumbersome than she'd ever felt it to be before.

She dropped to her knees from the sheer weight of her own body. It took several moments to remember how to breathe again. When she did, she looked up into Erevan's stunned face. His gaze traveled over her as if checking that she was in one piece, then past her, to settle on the only other person there with them in the forest glade into which they'd emerged.

"Tiriana?" he asked, and Nym was shocked by the emotion she heard in that one name, spoken aloud. Clearly, Erevan knew Tiri, and seemed to care deeply for her.

Tiri, for her part, looked as shocked as Erevan. For a moment, her mouth opened, then closed, no sound coming out. He seemed to be the last person she had expected to see.

"Where under the summer stars have you been?" he asked now, taking a step toward her, then stopping as if unsure what to do next. "Gods, Tiriana! I feared you were dead! I have searched for you for so many seasons in Lyre that I'd despaired of ever finding you again. And now you just drop through a portal, with my...with an elven woman?"

Tiri drew in breath and seemed to steady herself. "Erevan! I am not sure how this happened! I was waiting in that cage for so long without the use of my power that I had begun to despair, and then tonight the goblins brought in this elven woman. Her name is Nymariel, but I get the feeling somehow that you already know that. It was she who got us here. *Her* portal. I had thought to teach her how to open the locks on our prison, but instead she just...did this."

"I didn't mean to," Nym groaned, trying to stand on shaky legs. "At least, I don't think I did! I thought I was picking a lock. Creating a—ah—portal was not my intention."

"And yet, here you are. Here you *both* are. I can scarcely credit it, though you both stand before me. Well, one of you is standing." Erevan held out a hand to help Nym up, and she took the offered hand before she thought about it, shivering inwardly at the frission of sensation she felt when they touched.

The moment she was upright she noticed the clear resemblance between Erevan and Tiriana, right down to the lines of their noses and the slant of their eyebrows. Either they'd just happened to choose very similar appearances when deciding what form to take, or this was the way they typically looked when in a humanoid form at all. Either way, the resemblance made them appear to be....

"This is Erevan. He's my brother," Tiriana said, her sharp gaze darting between Nym's face and Erevan's. "I told you I would not forget your helping me. And not only have you provided me an escape from that awful place, but you have delivered me straight to my brother. That was above and beyond the call of compassion, whether or not you meant to be quite so thorough. This is...a rather unexpected development."

"Unexpected to say the least," Erevan said, as though he were still struggling with the concept of what Nym had done. But his gaze on Tiriana's face was that of someone who had seen a ghost somehow restored to the flesh.

"I've already said that I didn't mean to make a portal. I told you that I have trouble controlling the *wyld* sometimes. I didn't know I could do...this. And I'm not at all sure that I could do it again, even if I wanted to." Nym's voice came out quietly, suggesting a calm that she did not feel.

Erevan turned to look at Nym then, and she felt her entire body tremble under his gaze, though whether it was from her own reaction to what she'd just done or the emotion that now threatened to overwhelm her, she could not have said. Their eyes met, and she could not look away.

All else in the clearing, including Tiriana, seemed incredibly unimportant in that moment. Even with the unexpected reappearance of his apparently lost sister, Erevan seemed likewise affected. That only compounded the utter confusion that swept through Nym. What was happening? How had she been able to open a portal when all she'd been supposed to do was magically pick a lock? And more than that, why had her wild, instinctive portal brought them *here*? Why had her first impulse been to reach out to him, bargain or no bargain? Even as she framed the question, she knew she needn't look too far for the obvious answer.

Erevan was still looking at Nym, wonder in his gaze. "Perhaps it was the unintended result of need combined with untrained *wyld* that caused this. From your words, sister, it would appear you were teaching her to use the *wyld* to break down barriers, like the locks on the doors. It would seem that she broke down a different barrier entirely, but the need and the end result are inextricably related. She needed something desperately—or you both did, and the *wyld* responded to help make it happen. Or at least, that is my working theory in this moment. What do you think, Tiriana?"

Tiriana didn't respond.

"Sister?" Erevan turned, frowning.

But Tiri had disappeared. Nym, blinking in the light of the sun that had risen to dapple the leaves and branches of the forest with gold, couldn't see the fae woman anywhere. What she *could* see was her cloak lying in a heap on the ground and the utter shock, pain and bewilderment in Erevan's eyes when he realized that his sister was gone.

TWENTY

ATTITUDE AND APTITUDE

Aeson watched as Song, sans riders, headed back the way they'd come. The itinerant wizard who had assisted them in the Otherworld had been right. He couldn't speak for the others, but Aeson had known the moment they crossed the barrier between worlds, even though nothing in particular marked it except for a feeling of heaviness on this side and a sense of muffling, as though senses in the mortal world weren't quite as sharp. Images weren't as clear, scents not as distinct, colors less vibrant. In a way, it felt like a letdown, but then there was also that sense of the familiar, of being in a place where one truly belonged and which one understood.

They were home, in the sense of no longer being in a world not their own. But as to exactly where they were in the general category of *home*...that, Aeson had yet to determine. He just hoped it wasn't too close to any of the Order's holdings and the pursuit that they'd run into the Otherworld to avoid, especially with four unarmed people depending on them for protection—two of whom were now without a mount.

The man who rode behind the elf wanted them to keep the horse, and he'd grumbled a lot when the elf had made him climb down. But the elven man—Vesryn, he called himself—had given him a hard look that had put an end to the grumbling. It had been Vesryn who had spoken quietly to the mare, praising her for a smooth ride, for all the world as though he thought she could understand his words. Then he let her go, her reins tied together and draped loosely over the cantle of the saddle.

Mist gathered around the white mare as she walked. She stepped into that whiteness, through it. And vanished. The woman riding with Faraine breathed a sigh of relief, but Aeson frowned. Song had been their last tie to Nym, and he had a feeling that, troublesome as traveling with the bard had been thus far, they'd be better off *with* her than without her. Now that he found himself with very few allies, he wanted them all close to hand.

Vesryn squared his shoulders and resumed walking, and after a moment, the other man did, too. The group continued in the general direction they'd been traveling, but they made worse time now. Every hour or so during the morning, Aeson and Faraine stopped to switch passengers or to walk themselves.

All the switching around made things take longer too, but whenever their feet were on the ground, their horses' reins remained firmly in their hands, and both usually kept a hand on the bridle as well. Neither was willing to give over complete control of the horses to the strangers. Kindness and common decency were well enough, but they only extended just so far under circumstances like these. Aeson knew that both horses were far too well trained to respond to any attempted commands from whomever happened to be in the saddle as long as their owners held the reins.

He didn't think any of these four had been names on his list of missing mages. As far as he knew, none seemed to have the aptitude or fit the descriptions he'd been given, but then, if their talents had been small to begin with or their magic already drained, it was quite possible that he might not now be able to sense it. But he hadn't exactly put that to the test. He needed to know more.

"Vesryn, we understand that there have been a number of magic-users taken captive, likely under similar circumstances to all of yours. We've been trying to find and free those people at the behest of their families. Could you tell us how you came to be taken?"

Vesryn, who had just climbed up on Caeros behind Faraine, nodded. "I was no mage, if that is what you were asking. I had some small skill with the crafting of sigils and runes, but it was only useful for copying tomes and setting small charms to keep the pages well preserved. Minor magics at best, but useful for a scribe. I had locked up the scriptorium in my village one evening and was heading home when something hit me from behind. The next I knew, I was in one of the goblins' cages."

"And did they drain your magic?" Aeson asked.

"No. If that was their eventual purpose, they would have gotten very little for their effort." Vesryn's tone was wry.

"What about the rest of you?" Faraine asked. "Are any of you mages, or able to use magic in some way, like Vesryn?"

"The magic? *That's* what this was about? Oh, for the love of the gods! I wish I'd never even *heard* of magic," the woman burst out from where she sat behind Aeson. "Mages, magic...all of it is just so unnatural! I want no part of it. I wish they *had* taken mine away. I never asked for it, never wanted it. And now I'm in danger because of it? I...I don't know what to say!"

"I think you've said all that we needed to hear, mem," Aeson said, a bit gruffly. He wasn't about to mention that she was now riding behind a mage, with her arms about his waist to steady herself.

"Remma. My name is Remma. I'm from Breck, west of Cambermere."

"Well, Remma, I am sorry to hear that your talent is not to your liking. I assume that means you had not trained it at all?"

He could feel Remma's eyes boring into his back. "No! I would never! Filthy stuff, magic. It's dangerous. It—" she broke off. "Never mind. I think I've made my feelings clear."

"You have indeed." Aeson turned to look at the human man who hadn't wanted to let Song go. "What about you?"

The man scowled at the ground, and spat. "They took my magic. At least, they said they did. I didn't know I had any to begin with. If I'd known—if I'd been able to train it—no one would've ever been able to get the drop on me the way they did. Got me outside the tavern when I went out to take a piss. Clocked me on the back of the head, just like the elf, there. Only after they got me, they took me to some big building in a city— never told me which one. Said I was under arrest for being drunk and disorderly, and I had to go before a judge.

"Then they drugged me with something, locked me in some cells, and I must've passed out. The next morning, I was sick—never had such a bad hangover, ever. Passed out again. Next thing I knew, a bunch of creepy priests were all around me, I was tied to some sort of slab with crystals sunk into it, and they were chanting over me. I thought they were gonna sacrifice me to some old dead god or something. But then I felt this *whoosh*, and a pull, and then I was on fire. They pulled something out of me—I could feel it.

"I begged them to stop, but they ignored me. And then it was like I was a scarecrow with no stuffing, you understand? I haven't felt right since. I might not have known I had magic, but I didn't want to find out like this, just when someone stole it right out of me. Haven't been able to sleep since, for the nightmares of having my guts ripped out. I mean, I still have all my actual guts, but I feel like they're gone, just the same. *Something* is gone."

The man fell silent, and for several moments, no one spoke. Then "I'm sorry, Duncan," Remma said quietly, surprising Aeson. "I don't like magic. I don't. But I don't think I'd have wanted to go through what you did. I'm glad they hadn't gotten to me yet, if that's what they were going to do."

"We're trying to find the ones responsible for all of these abductions, Duncan. We'll drop the four of you off in the nearest village with what coin we can spare for you to find passage to your homes, and then we'll go back to our hunt. It would help if any of you could describe the people who took you, before the goblins. The priests you spoke of, Duncan. Did they have anything in common that you could identify them with?" Aeson caught Faraine's concerned gaze, but he thought he already knew what the answer would be. He braced himself for the blow he knew was coming.

"They were human. Uniforms on some of them, I think. Robes, like priests wear, you know? Or maybe...knights? But the ones I saw had these tattoos on them...here." He pointed to his arm. "Flame with a hawk over it. I dunno what it means, but maybe it will help you figure out where to look."

The third man was shaking his head. "I can't do much magic either. Just little stuff; nothing fancy. Parlor tricks, my friends call it. I've never trained it either. Didn't love it or hate it. Just knew it was there. And it's still there, but now I know it's made me a target, I'm not sure I want it either. I saw the people Duncan talked about. But they just grabbed me on the way past, like. They were riding through my orchard and one pointed at me; they grabbed me and stuffed me into the cart next to Duncan. He was in a bad way, and I was pretty sure he was what they were all so on about. Seemed like I was an afterthought. Like a mint after dinner, you know?"

Aeson shook his head. "So, out of the three of you, only Duncan's magic has already been drained, most probably because he had the most potential. Anyone who had smaller amounts of power was left with their magic. Interesting. What we don't know is whether they were saving the rest of you for later, or whether they just took you in the first place because they were trying to fill a quota."

"Fill a quota? Well, I find that exceedingly insulting," Remma said huffily.

Aeson bit back a snort. One moment, magic was dirty and she wanted no part of it, and now she was insulted because her talent hadn't been great enough to make them want to drain her dry immediately. He barely stopped himself from shaking his head in bemusement. He might never understand women.

The remainder of their journey was spent in relative silence, each seemingly lost in their own thoughts, but around midafternoon as they topped a low hill, Aeson spotted chimneys in the valley below, and soon enough a bustling small village came into view. Not a village with a chapter of the Hawksfire, he noted with relief.

The village was called Corram, and it sat several days' distance to the southeast of Cambermere, with a fair few other small villages and hamlets in between. He and Faraine left the four former prisoners there, with enough coin between them to pay for a night or two and a few meals at the local inn, and a bit left over to pay any passing caravan for passage to wherever they might want to go. Anything more, they'd have to manage on their own.

At least they were out of the reach of the Order for the moment, unless they were careless and put themselves into the crosshairs again. Of the four, Duncan was now in the least amount of danger, as without his magic, he could probably just disappear into any crowd of people with nothing to make him noticeable to the Order. If he could keep his mouth shut, that was. If he was too liberal with his tale of woe, the Order would manage to track him down again, just to shut him up.

By mutual unspoken agreement, Aeson and Faraine headed back out again at once, moving in the general direction from which they'd just come. They'd probably not find their way back into the Otherworld again, but they wanted to be somewhere in the general vicinity of the border, just in case Nym's mysterious would-be rescuer decided to honor his word and bring her back out to rejoin them. If not, then, well....

If not, he and Faraine would have to decide what to do about Grand Master Zebermar without her. Either way, the corruption within the order had to be stopped. Aeson had no idea how far it extended, but figuratively speaking, if he was going to cut the heads off a many-headed snake, he would have to start with the head that was closest.

TWENTY-ONE

ENTANGLED

Nym frowned at the spot where Tiri had last been standing. "Where did she go?" she asked, though the expression on Erevan's face and the abrupt, shocking absence of Tiriana told her she probably didn't really want to know the answer, even if he had one. Erevan looked...bereft. Bereft, angry, and a bit lost. It was an unguarded expression that Nym had never before seen from him, and she couldn't tell whether the sorrow and frustration she was feeling was his, or her own.

"I do not know," Erevan said after a moment. "But given her abrupt departure and the fact that we heard no commotion, there are only two possibilities, neither of them good. One is that she was somehow quietly incapacitated and spirited away, though the means would have to be akin to the way the two of you arrived here, and I do not find that particularly likely. The other is that she simply left, crept out of sight while we were distracted and traveled along one of the Trackways, quickly and silently. Even in Lyre, the Trackways are usually the fastest means of travel from one point to another, with just the right application of magic to help a traveler along."

"She told me her magic had been taken away," Nym said, completely bewildered. "I don't know what you mean by Trackways, but if she had to have magic to use one, then I don't see how she could have done that. But we'd have heard someone open a portal and come through if that was how she were taken, wouldn't we? We weren't *distracted* all that long. We'd have noticed. Unless they made her invisible."

"Invisible? Perhaps." Erevan's expression went blank for a moment, and Nym felt the shiver of *wyld* along her arms as he used it for some silent purpose.

"No. She is not invisible, or regardless of that, she is no longer here. I would sense her presence if she were close to us. When she told you her magic was gone, did she say so directly? This is important. The words matter."

Nym frowned, thinking back to that conversation. "Well, I guess she didn't actually say directly that her magic was gone. She spoke of what they had done to other magic users, and I assumed she included herself in that number. But no, she did not actually say in so many words that they had drained her magic."

"Then that, in itself, is a part of the answer," Erevan said. "We will speak further on this matter, but not here, and not now. We must be away from this place, quickly."

At that moment, Song trotted out of the trees toward them, the saddle and Nym's belongings still on her back. She came to a halt in front of Nym, snorted, then stuck her nose under Nym's hand. Nym petted her absently, still baffled. And worried, now, given that she saw no other horses besides Song.

Erevan seemed to have noticed her concern. "Your friends were here with people they had rescued from the goblins. I sent them all through the barrier to the mortal lands. To them, I appeared as a human wizard, traveling these wilds for purposes of my own. Though I am sure they suspected there was more to it than that, they were intelligent and spoke nothing of it. I assured them that I knew these lands well and would try to find you and send you back to them, but it seems that you have found me instead. Yet another thing we must discuss."

"I'm glad they're safe," Nym said, nodding. "It was kind of you to help them, when you didn't have to."

"Oh, I had to," Erevan said, mildly but with a hint of grimness behind the words. "They were traveling through wylden lands with escaped prisoners, which makes them fugitives here. Knowing they were friends of yours, I thought it best if they did not continue wandering near the border without knowing how to cross it."

"They are fugitives in the mortal lands, too. But yes, I also believe that was for the best." Nym retrieved her cloak, mounted Song and waited while Erevan mounted his dark horse. Not a white steed, but fae nonetheless, unless she missed her guess. Silently, she followed him as he led the way onto what at first appeared to be a deer track through the trees. But then he spoke one single, melodious word and the path lit up before her like a shining thread of light.

"Follow, and do not stray off the path. Give Song control, and she will keep you on the Trackway."

Nym tightened her calves against Song's sides, adjusted her grip on the reins and prepared for anything. Erevan's horse leapt forward and Song followed, and suddenly they were streaking along that straight path of light in a way that reminded Nym of skaters on a pond. It was so smooth as to feel nearly effortless, and the landscape slid by on either side of them at a speed that perhaps should have terrified Nym, but thrilled her instead.

What seemed like only moments later but—judging by the position of the sun in the sky—was probably an hour or more after they'd run onto the Trackway, they emerged into a clearing hidden in a low valley. The clearing was ringed with a mix of oak and ash, with a smattering of fir trees and gorse bushes, and here and there a bloom of color from some late-blooming flower or spray of berries. No obvious trails led into the valley, but as they hurtled off the Trackway, it seemed as though the trees and bushes parted to let them through, then shifted back into place without seeming as though they'd moved at all.

Instantly, Nym felt a calm stillness descend onto her, and she let out a breath she hadn't realized she'd been holding.

"This place is warded. None shall intrude here. No one can find it whom I do not invite in. You are the first elf—indeed, the first mortal of any kind—to have set foot on these grounds." Erevan seemed at once more relaxed than she'd ever seen him and also concerned, his mind still clearly on the problems they'd come to discuss.

"I'm...honored?" Nym said, unsure what the correct protocol should be for being the first of...well, anything...to intrude in this space that was obviously a refuge to her wylden acquaintance and mentor.

Blackberry bushes made a dense wall to one side of a tall, circular tower. A wild profusion of different food plants seemed to be taking up a great deal of space on the other side, though they were so randomly placed that *garden* didn't seem quite the right description for what that space was.

As they followed the footpath through the garden and around to the other side of the tower, Nym noticed some rather large animal tracks in the dirt, meandering off into the dense bushes toward the edge of the clearing. They looked feline in nature, but much larger than typical. Idly, she wondered whether creatures like lynx tended to live in Otherworld forests.

A sturdy shed nearby seemed to have been outfitted as a stable large enough to hold three horses. It was currently empty, but Erevan wasted no time in removing his horse's saddle and hackamore, so Nym did the same with Song. Song butted Nym with a nose to the midsection until she took up a wad of straw and gave her a good rubdown.

When she'd finished, she bowed to the horse. "Will that suffice, milady?"

Song whickered and turned regally to the rack of hay that Erevan was proceeding to fill for the two horses. The mare eyed Erevan's black stallion, who was already eating, and then the skin on her shoulders twitched in what seemed an equine semblance of a shrug. Song's coat rippled and flooded with that same dapple-grey color that Nym hadn't been sure she'd seen correctly the first time. A surprised giggle escaped Nym before she could clap a hand over her own mouth. Song looked over her shoulder, snorted, and turned back to the hay. All the while, Erevan's stallion continued eating, seemingly oblivious to Song's color-changing antics.

Erevan finished the chore of providing hay for the horses, dusting off his sleeves as he moved toward the entrance to the horse shelter. Nym, who had been gazing at the horses, did a double-take when the stack of bales he'd taken the hay from seemed to refill themselves as soon as they were emptied. Had she imagined it?

Erevan's chuckle told her she hadn't. "I see we have much to acquaint you with, though self-replenishing hay is by far the least important of subjects."

"It's important to the horses, one might argue," Nym said primly, earning another chuckle from Erevan.

"Come. They aren't the only beings who could use food, and we have things to discuss."

He shouldered his saddlebags, then led the way to the tower door and opened it, though Nym was sure she saw the flare of magic around the latch before he did so. *Warded, most probably.*

"Much the same kind of wards as I have shown you, though considerably more powerful," Erevan said, as though she'd spoken aloud.

Inside with the door closed behind them, he wasted no time in stowing his belongings and lighting a fire in the hearth. Then he set to preparing a meal from foodstuffs he took from the various cupboards and containers in what appeared to be a small food preparation area. Nym stood against a wall, laden with her own belongings, feeling awkward.

"Just put your things down anywhere that seems reasonable, and come help with this. Then we'll have food all the faster."

Suddenly shy, Nym did as he directed, trying to ignore the feelings that had begun to well up inside of her at the scene of domesticity that she hadn't expected. Well, yes, there had been the dream with the hut in the woods on the last new moon night, but this...this was clearly *his* place, a place he came often. And while this sense of shyness was new and uncomfortable, there was another part of her that felt more at home here than she'd felt anywhere else she'd ever been. It was a paradox, but just one of many, she supposed, since they'd met.

She hovered nearby until he handed her a carrot and a bronze knife, and left her to decide what to do with it. She took her cue from what he was doing to the onions and other vegetables, and before long, they had a pot of soup simmering on the fire and mugs of hot cider in their hands while they sat in chairs before the hearth.

Nym could have sworn there was only one chair before the hearth when they'd first entered, but by now, she was too lulled by the comfort of normal activities like preparing dinner and sipping mulled cider to worry over exactly how a second chair suddenly fit perfectly into a space she could have sworn only a short while ago had barely been spacious enough for one.

Erevan set down his mug on a small table by his armchair and stared into the flames for a few moments in silence. Then he sighed. "I suppose I should tell you about Tiriana, and why I wanted—needed—to make the bargain I made with you."

Nym waited, unsure whether to speak or not. Finally, she just nodded and took another sip of the cider, and waited for the master bard to begin a story she was fairly sure was going to be a painful one to tell.

"Tiriana, as you have just learned, is my sister. We wylden do not always hold to other people's definitions of good or evil, but in some cases, the choices some of our kind make can be deadly and dangerous for all of us as a whole. That, I would deem to be evil. My sister is not; or at least, she was not, before. Whether she fits such a definition now remains to be seen, but I cannot think her abrupt departure from us to be an indication of good intentions."

"She seemed nice enough, when we were trapped in the goblins' prison together," Nym ventured.

Erevan laughed, but it was a hollow, mirthless sound that made Nym's heart ache. "Well, she clearly wanted you for *something*. But I do not think that what she wanted was what she actually got from you. If I could judge by her face when the both of you came through, she seemed dismayed not so much by your portal, but by the fact that it brought you to me."

"But if she'd been missing for such a long time as

you say, then why wouldn't she want to be reunited with her brother?" Nym frowned into her cider. She didn't like the feeling of being duped by Tiriana. In fact, she was beginning to feel like a completely unwitting pawn in all of this. It wasn't a good feeling. And yet, her instints still screamed at her that she could trust Erevan.

"That is indeed a good question, and one that I do not have the answer to right now," Erevan said. "I do not know what she might have wanted with you, and why you found her supposedly in captivity with the goblins that also took *you* captive, but it all seems far too convenient to have been an accident."

"That's what I was thinking, too," Nym admitted. "How did she go missing in the first place? And how long had she been gone?"

Erevan looked pained. "She went missing when we were riding out in the woods one day, many seasons ago. She was always so full of life and curiosity. Precocious, always thinking of creative ways to use the *wyld*, or some sort of mischief to get up to. When she disappeared, it was as though some of the light and life had gone out of the world, both for myself and the rest of our kin. We all searched, of course, but as the days and mortal seasons went by, we began to despair, and one by one, the others left off their attempts to find her. Eventually, I continued alone.

"I have been searching for so long that I thought I might have to resign myself to her loss, for surely something terrible must have happened to her. Yet now I find her alive and well, and in the supposed captivity of goblins who just happened to be so close to the borderlands, and the very part of the borderlands through which you and your companions were traveling?" He shook his head. "I fear she is part of a larger problem that has now connected us both in ways that neither of us anticipated."

"You mean the problem of the missing mages, like the ones that Aeson and Faraine were tracking before they met me?"

"Exactly that. For what I have not told you is that mages from among the wylden have begun to go missing as well, Tiriana among them—or so I thought."

Nym considered. "So, what you are telling me is that someone or something is having all these mages kidnapped, and the ones taken may be from any group —human, elven, or wylden. But we don't yet know who is doing it, or why. Do we?" She shot Erevan a searching look.

"We don't. And that brings us to why I made the bargain with you. I have reached the end of my own resources in seeking the answer to this puzzle. Too many of my people are apathetic about what is happening, or blind to it. Some truly don't care, some do not realize, and others are so determined to pretend that there is no problem that by their inaction they are themselves contributing to the problem.

"I made the bargain with you in hopes that I might gain influence in the wylden courts, and thus gain the ears of the kings and queens, who have far more resources than I at this juncture. When it was just my own sister missing, I could understand everyone's reluctance to help, but since the numbers of missing mages of all races are beginning to swell, I fear there is a greater evil here than any one person alone can hope to deal with."

"I understand now," Nym said. "But why not just tell me this in the first place? Why make a bargain that sounded like it was all so both of us could seek our own sort of fame and glory? I would have helped anyway, had you asked me straight out at the beginning."

Erevan gazed at her for so long that Nym had to fight the urge to fidget.

"I begin to think that you would have, Nymariel Morren. At every turn you have proven yourself to be far more than what I first supposed you to be. Perhaps I should have asked for help. But given the cold war that yet divides our peoples, can you understand why I did not?"

After a few moments, Nym nodded. "Yes, I suppose I can. My people think that your people are only figures from nightmare, and that you all want us dead and buried, because we dared have relationships with humans."

Erevan sighed. "What else did your sages tell you? Did they put more to the tale?"

Nym shook her head. "Only that your people betrayed our people, and that you hate us for even speaking to humans, much less living alongside them or working with them."

"So they have either forgotten the original cause of this war, or they have chosen to bury it." He stood, stirred the soup, then returned to his chair.

"Long ago, well before either of us was born, our peoples were very closely entwined. Elves used to live easily as long as any fae, and many were the unions between us. But then some of the elves began to reach out to the humans they met, trade with them, teach them, learn from them in turn, and gradually even to live among them. Elven society changed, though whether for better or worse, no one person can truly say."

Nym put down her mug and leaned forward, elbows on her knees, listening intently. This was the part of history that her mother had never wanted to speak of, and none of her community's teachers or sages would speak of it either. It was not written in any books that Nym had ever had access to.

Erevan went on. "At first the fae, including the wylden, mostly ignored this new state of being that so many elves had embarked upon. But then eventually came a time when one of the elven monarch's daughters fell in love with a human man. That same human man killed a fae prince, and when asked to help mete out justice, the elves refused. Not just the girl, who might be forgiven for being blinded by love, but her parents and all of their people also refused to allow the wylden courts to have justice for the wrong done them. And it seems that this was not an isolated incident. There were other such happenings, though none quite as well-publicized as the one I have mentioned. Elves and fae are kin to one another, and the elves were siding with the humans. All the isolated similar incidents soon coalesced into an all-out war, and all the old allegiances and alliances were abandoned. Agreements broken or deliberately forgotten."

"I only have one question," Nym said, and Erevan's

eyebrows rose.

"And what is that?"

"Was the human who killed the fae prince justified in doing so? Was it justice, or jealousy? Does anyone even know?"

Erevan met her eyes, his own ice-blue gaze clear and steady. "I have no idea. And even if one such killing was somehow justified, what of all the other similar incidents? Perhaps some were justified, others not. Such conflicts can easily become muddied, lines blurred. Eventually, if a dispute goes on long enough, people can forget why it ever started in the first place, and yet they continue to give it new fuel so that it keeps burning nonetheless.

"What I do know is this. We must find a way to deal reasonably with one another, somehow. At the very least, the rift between elves and wylden must be healed, and if that could also result in better dealings between wylden and humans, so much the better. Not all wylden share my view. In fact, perhaps relatively few share it. But now an unseen evil arises that seems to threaten all of our peoples alike, and if a common enemy cannot unite even some of us, then I see very little hope for *any* of us."

"And if your sister has become part of that unseen evil, somehow? What then?" Nym waited, watching his eyes.

"Then we will find her and stop her, without question, even if that means taking her life. Though I love my sister, if she is bent on doing something that will result in disaster for our people, she must be stopped. Familial ties do not change that. Whoever is taking all these mages is building toward something, but what? Whatever it is, I cannot see how it could be good for any of the groups. I feel energies in the *wyld* that give me great pause, for they are chaotic in ways that fill me with dread I cannot even put a name to. Whatever this is, it must be brought to light, exposed, before it tries to destroy us all. And if those in power in all three realms cannot see it, we must find a way to make them see."

Nym blinked, shaken. "You think this enemy—whoever it is—is going to be that destructive? I mean, so far it has just been mages going missing. A *lot* of mages, admittedly, but...in the human realms, sometimes there are killers who go on a rampage and just kill a lot of people, one by one until they are caught. Mightn't this just be the work of a...serial mage kidnapper?" Even as she said it, it sounded ridiculous to her own ears.

Erevan considered. "I suppose anything is possible. But you still must ask yourself why it is mages being targeted in this way. What would a *serial mage kidnapper* possibly hope to gain by such actions?"

"Well, the Grand Master of the Order of Hawksfire who threw us into prison in Cambermere was planning to drain Aeson and me of our magic, so...maybe to increase his own power?"

Erevan took a slow breath. "Drain mages of their power? Is this a common practice among humans?"

"Well, it seems to be common among the Order of the Hawksfire." Nym told Erevan all that had happened since the last time they'd spoken, of their journey to Cambermere and their subsequent flight into the Otherworld to escape Zebermar and the Order. She told him, too, about Aeson and how his power was siphoned off continually, how he'd avoided having his memory removed, and how the Order seemed able to track him with means somewhat similar to their own link. When she'd finished, Erevan sat tapping his finger on the arm of his chair, considering.

At length he got up, ladled out two bowls of soup and handed one to Nym. They ate in thoughtful silence, but something had shifted in the energy between them. Erevan seemed troubled by something, and Nym had no idea what until they'd finished their dinner and were once more sitting before the fire, this time with mugs of tea in hand.

"I see now that our bargain has put you in great danger, Nymariel. That was not my intention. This situation seems to be multifaceted, and there are many more potential agents at work here than I had originally suspected, though there seems to be a common thread in all of it—a scheme to amass power, for reasons we have yet to uncover. I release you from your obligation. If you wish to go, I will remove our link and escort you from the Otherworld myself. You need not be entangled with me further. You owe me nothing. Perhaps this is not your fight."

Nym took a shuddering breath. Here was her chance to reconsider. If she voluntarily backed out of their original deal without any alterations on his part, then according to their agreement, she might not remember how to use the *wyld* anymore. But neither would she be in danger from whoever was kidnapping mages. She would no longer have to search out songs or stories for Erevan, or put herself at risk when she performed. Surely, she was a good enough bard to make her way without it now. But even as she considered it, she felt a certainty growing within her, one that said she was already too far in to back out now, if she even *wanted* to avoid any further *entanglement* with Erevan and his quest. Did she?

"No," she said, quietly but firmly.

"What do you mean? No, this is not your fight, or no, you do not want out of our bargain?" He sounded more vulnerable than she'd ever known him to be.

She reached out and put a hand on his arm, and to her surprise, he covered her hand with his own. "No, I do not want out of our bargain. But it would be nice if from here forward we could be...well...more like equals. I mean, I know that I only have the *wyld* because of you, but still—"

He shook his head, his expression bemused. "Were I you, I might well take me up on my offer of dissolution and be done with me. But Nymariel...Nym...I have told you before that I did not give you the use of the *wyld*, that it is and always has been a part of you. The fact that you opened a portal when you meant only to open the door to a cell makes that even more obvious. Leaving our bargain behind would not change that, whether I released you from it or whether you released yourself and then forgot how to use the *wyld*. It would still be there, burning beneath the surface, within you. But forgetting how to use it might at least allow you to hide among your people, seek safety among them. And perhaps warn them."

"I still don't see how the *wyld* could be part of *me*, but

I will find a way to accept that, and to learn to use it to help myself stay out of danger instead of lighting me up for any mage-hunter to see. But I won't be hiding among any people, elven or otherwise. I'll be helping my friends deal with this problem. *All* of my friends." She met his eyes as she said it, barely managing to ignore the rising flush in her cheeks.

He smiled finally, a warm smile that sent tingles through her. Not unpleasant ones, either.

"So, we are officially friends, at least. I will take that. But this is not an easy path we are on. The task at hand is a daunting one, to say the very least."

"My whole life has been a daunting task, but that's never stopped me before." The words sounded flippant even to herself. Perhaps she should be more worried about all that loomed ahead, but it was hard to feel too daunted with his hand still covering hers, and her awareness of their proximity still flooding her consciousness.

He laughed, and it sent her spirits soaring, sobering though their conversation had been.

"I have no doubt of that," he said.

TWENTY-TWO

REUNIONS

The night at Erevan's tower passed peacefully. Perhaps too peacefully, Nym thought when she woke the next morning. It was too easy to fall into a sense of ease and comfort here, where except for the movement of sun and moon to mark its passage in the mortal world, time might as well not exist, and there was only the now. At least, that was how it felt to her. She wasn't sure whether that was comforting or alarming.

They had talked late into the night—long enough for Nym to realize that too many of the things she had believed about the wylden were flawed and incomplete. She *did* have a lot to learn, and Erevan had been right; self-replenishing hay bales was the very least of it. She was well and truly in this now, for good or ill. Her learning from here forward would have to go far beyond just how to use the *wyld* to enhance her music or set a few protective wards.

To that end, Erevan had showed her some of the stronger defensive magic, as well as a few things that could be used as an attack against an enemy. She was nowhere near proficient with any of it, of course, but she thought she felt a little more prepared for whatever might happen next. She also had the feeling that they'd barely scratched the surface of what might be done with the *wyld*—another thought that both thrilled and terrified her, particularly since this time, he hadn't warned her against experimenting.

If anything, Erevan seemed resigned to the fact that unexpected things might happen when she used the *wyld* no matter what she intended, the portal being a case in point. He'd tried to help her work out how she'd opened the first one, but she hadn't been able to replicate it—not even a tiny little portal into a familiar and beloved place near her old village. Many tries later, it seemed apparent that she wouldn't be able to fall back on that as a surefire means to escape difficulty whenever she wanted to. Erevan hadn't chided her about it, but had only commented that perhaps it was just as well, because knowing she couldn't always summon a portal at will might mean she showed more restraint and less chaotic impulse when wielding the magic. That, and perhaps more caution against getting into situations that might *require* a portal in the first place.

Eventually, she'd fallen asleep in front of the fire, and though she hadn't remembered there being a rug of any kind on the floor beneath her, she definitely noticed one upon waking, because it was uncommonly thick, with wool tufts. There was another blanket draped over her—not one from her bedroll, although that was still rolled up and sitting with her other belongings against the wall where she'd left them.

Yawning, she sat up and tried to judge the angle of the sun through the small windows higher up in the tower wall, but it was the scent of onions and other vegetables cooking in a pan that fully made her brain come awake, even as her stomach insisted that it was time for breakfast.

He glanced at her as she got up and folded the blanket he'd draped over her, laying it across the arm of one of the chairs. "We've held back time long enough, I suppose. Unless I miss my guess, your friends will be searching for you on the mortal side of the border, and if they are going to do what I think they are going to do, they will need your help. In advance of our meeting, I give you leave to tell them my name and that we have an alliance between us. I leave it to you to give them whatever explanation you think would make the most sense to them, but be cautious. Trust is a rare commodity, and none of us can afford to either withhold it completely, nor squander it needlessly. Our arrangement still puts us in a great deal of danger; I would rather that danger did not come from your allies."

"I appreciate the permission very much, and I agree wholeheartedly about trust. I think you will find them to be worthy allies as well. But what are they planning to do?" she asked, a little alarmed. She wasn't the only one of the group who could be impulsive. At least, she didn't *think* she was.

"One of my ravens came to me as the sun rose, saying he had overheard them speaking of this Grand Master of the Hawksfire. Apparently, they mean to remove him from the gameboard, as it were. I cannot say that would be a bad thing. If he is as mired in this scheme as he seems to be, then taking one of the larger players off the board might stir things up enough for me to be able to determine from which direction this danger truly comes."

Nym blinked at that. "Can I take a raven with me, to bring you messages? It would be so much more reliable than trying to find my own way through a dreamwalk, or wait until the new moon each month to meet with you to update you on whatever is happening. Or even just to hope that you happen to have a raven spying on me in the right place at the right time."

Erevan wore an expression that seemed amused and dismayed, both at once. "A raven. You want to borrow a messenger raven. Of all that I just said, *that* is what you chose to focus on?"

"Well, if I have a raven sort of...assigned to me, I guess...then if something goes wrong, I can get a message to you. Not so that you can come and bail me out of trouble, but so that you'll be warned of what the cause of the trouble was, in case it's related to your own inquiries. And if Tiriana suddenly reappears near me for any reason, you'd know that, too."

"Now, *that* is a sound reasoning, and a good point. Tiriana is a wild card we may have to contend with, and I do not know what to expect from her now. Very well, I will send a raven with you. He will not be noticeably with you at all times, but I will give you a note of summoning for him. Now, what of your friends' plan?"

"Dealing with Zebermar?" Nym considered. "It

needs to be done. What he's done to all those young initiates to the Order, not to mention all of the older members as well—it's a travesty and a violation. And while some of them might truly agree with his philosophy, I know from meeting some of the children that most of them seem to dread and fear the memory removal process. And then, since he's also siphoning away part of their magic all the time into this Arboricanum, whatever that is..." She trailed off as a sudden thought struck her.

"What?" Erevan asked.

"I think I might know a way to stop him. Or at least, to even the odds a little if we're to fight him. You're right; I need to get back to Aeson and Faraine, before they give up and decide to do this without me."

Erevan handed her a plate. "Here. Eat, and then we'll go. I can manipulate time enough so that you will not be late. I have one small errand to complete first. I will return quickly, I promise."

"Where are you going?" Nym asked, but he only pointed meaningfully at her plate and left, latching the door behind him. She could tell that if she truly wanted to leave, she could get through those wards—he'd taught her how last night. He was trusting her to wait. Now she had to decide how much she trusted him.

It might be a test. It was unlikely to be a betrayal, though given Tiriana's actions, it was certainly possible. For a moment, Nym debated. But only for a moment. Shrugging, she set to the breakfast with a will. She either trusted Erevan fully, or she did not, and if not, then all of their dealings together thus far were moot.

But since she'd met him, he'd shown her only kindness. Well, perhaps a bit more than kindness.

She had finished the plate of food and washed it in a basin that seemed designed for the purpose when Erevan returned, a sturdy leather case slung over one shoulder. He handed it to Nym, then began to gather his own saddlebags.

"What is this?" she asked, though from the shape of the case, it could only be one thing.

"A bard shouldn't be without one of their most important weapons," he said mildly, and stopped to watch while she opened the clasps on the case and threw back the lid.

She gasped. "Oh...how did you...where.... This is completely stunning! It's more than I ever dreamed of. And it's my lute, but it's not. How?" Nym could barely frame a sentence.

Erevan was smiling at her reaction. "One of the ravens spotted it in the bushes and told me where to find it. Given your explanation of how you left Cambermere, where you'd found Song, and given your obvious lack of a lute, I surmised that it was yours. I had it remade from a combination of its own original wood and some from the forest here in Lyre. I think you'll find it to be rather more versatile now, and a bit less fragile. We'll leave the rest for you to discover."

Nym shook her head, still staring at the lute. It was an incredible mix of wood colors, polished and gleaming. "This is a gift fit for a queen, Erevan. I am humbled by it, and will strive to be worthy of it."

He made a gesture as if to brush off the praise. "You were already worthy of it. Now, let us go. Your friend

Wyldsong grows anxious to be away. She says she's had just about enough of Zephyr's arrogance, and finds the company of mortal horses to be refreshing."

That startled a laugh out of Nym, who snapped shut the lute case and began loading herself with her own belongings. "I really must learn to speak Horse one day."

"No doubt you'll speak that language and many others before this tale is told, Nymariel," Erevan said, and opened the door to the tower, waiting for Nym to precede him into the brightness of the Lyre morning.

Aeson looked up from putting out the morning campfire. The little copse where they'd camped was quiet, with a few birdcalls coming from various trees here and there. Overhead, a flock of migrating geese flew over, and for a moment, Aeson envied them their relative freedom. When one place grew too uncomfortable or unsustainable, they just flew on to another. Here in the world of scheming Grand Masters and duplicitous mage orders, nothing was that simple.

As autumn wore on, the nights grew colder, and it was harder and harder to go all night without a fire. He and Faraine could have stayed back at the village, but in truth, Aeson itched to *do* something. Anything to help him feel less ineffectual. He still battled with the shame of having been blind to Zebermar's duplicity for so long, and the worst of it was that he had no idea how much of the Order had been corrupted. Or—worse thought— had it been corrupted from the very outset, with every tenet, every standard just a smokescreen to disguise its true purpose? Surely, they'd done at least *some* good, hadn't they? Righted a few wrongs in the world, helped a few innocents?

More like, helped ourselves to a few innocents, he thought sourly, envisioning Zebermar siphoning off the Order members' collective magic to use for his own ends—whatever those might be—and outright draining the magic of people he claimed were criminals who had misused their abilities in some way. Some might indeed have *been* criminals, and Aeson knew that many of the outside contracts the Order took on to stop dangerous mages who harmed others with their magic were legitimate ones—particularly those where some local authority had hired the Order to track down someone already condemned by their own justice system for violent crimes against fellow citizens. But what of those who weren't? What of those like Nym who, through no fault of their own, had come to the Grand Master's notice and been falsely painted as a threat by him for whatever reason, when all they'd wanted was to be left alone?

"Zebermar is a hypocrite, and a dangerous one. We need to locate him, preferably before he locates us," Aeson announced to no one in particular, but Faraine made a noise of agreement. She'd already packed up their few belongings and saddled her horse. Aeson made haste to do the same; they'd waited for Nym too long already. If they were going to confront Zebermar, they needed to be on the move.

"What will we do when we find him?" Faraine asked, adjusting her saddle girth, which made Caeros snort and nudge her in the back. "I agree it is vital that we know where he is, but I'm not sure how just the two of us can stop him if he is really more powerful than you are and we have no magical backup. Also, he's probably already spread word that you've gone rogue, and then it won't be just one mage we have to fight, but several, if he's traveling with an entourage. Even if we find him while he's en route to his next stop, he could still overpower us, and then we'll be in a worse position than we're in right now. And they can still track you with the tattoo and warn him that we're coming. We don't have any advantage here that we can use."

"We don't yet, but I think we can make one," Nym said, appearing suddenly on the path ahead. She was riding a dapple-grey mare, but he recognized the saddle she'd used on Song. He'd felt a shift in the ambient magic just before they had appeared, but that had been his only warning. It was a bit unsettling, but he was glad to see her nonetheless. A stranger with wheat-colored hair and ice-blue eyes rode beside her on a dark horse.

The two dismounted and left their horses to their own devices. As they did so, a raven that Aeson only now realized had been perched on Nym's shoulder took wing, heading toward a nearby tree. The grey mare headed straight toward Seralo and Caeros, with a coquettish look over her shoulder at the stranger's horse, who snorted and followed, though he moved more slowly. In that one moment, Aeson thought he saw the mare's hide ripple from grey to white with red ears, then back to grey again. He blinked, but made no comment. Of course, it was Song. Had to be. What other faery horse would have decided to make itself a permanent travelling companion to Nym? It fit, somehow.

"Nym! What happened? We feared you were captured or worse when you didn't catch up to us. I wanted to look for you after we dropped off the captives we rescued, but we had no idea how to get back into the Otherworld, and...gods...it's a long story." Faraine fell silent, looking surprised at her own outburst.

Aeson settled for nodding at Nym, adding a respectful nod for her companion. "It's good to see you. The...ah...person who let us out of the Otherworld with the former prisoners promised that they'd look for you. It seems as though that promise has been kept."

The stranger beside Nym nodded, giving Aeson a level look. "It has indeed. You have proven yourselves to be good friends to Nymariel, and I wish to acknowledge that with a gift of assistance. She tells me that you contend with a mark that allows your enemies to track you. If you wish, I can remove it."

"Ah...I know I'm being obvious in my caution, but... to whom might we be speaking? I don't recognize you." Faraine's voice was very careful and measured, as though she feared to give offense but felt it vital to remain on her guard nevertheless.

To be fair, Nym's companion looked nothing like the wizard they'd met on the trail, but somehow, Aeson was sure it was the same person. It was something about the mannerisms, the way he held himself, the way he spoke. Or maybe it was just instinct. Either way, Aeson was fairly sure he surmised correctly.

The stranger smiled, and he and Nym exchanged a look. He nodded at her, in a way that made Aeson wonder about how the two had become acquainted, and what the stranger's role in all of this would prove to be. Nym, for her part, appeared to trust him, and that carried weight, as far as Aeson was concerned.

"This is Erevan," Nym said. "I've known him since not long before I met the two of you. He's wylden, and he's my...music teacher, so to speak."

The stranger—Erevan—burst into laughter at that, so infectious that it soon had everyone but Aeson giggling, including Faraine. Aeson stood watching, and shook his head, smiling bemusedly. Music teacher, indeed.

"It seems there was at least one remaining secret that you kept from us, Nym," Aeson commented as Erevan approached him slowly, giving him plenty of room and keeping his hands where Aeson could see them.

"It wasn't my secret to tell before," Nym said quietly. "I take promises seriously, and this one preceded any I made to you. But now that you know, it will make things a lot easier."

"I don't know exactly what sort of promise you made to one of the wylden, Nym," Aeson said. "But I know you well enough by now to trust that you had a good reason."

Nym nodded, but she didn't elaborate. "Well, good. That's sorted, then."

"One thing remains, before I leave you to your tasks while I go and tend to my own," Erevan said, gesturing to Aeson's arm. "If you would roll up your sleeve, so that

I can see exactly what it is they've done to you...."

Aeson hesitated only a moment, then did as he was asked. Only a fortnight ago, he'd have trusted any member of the Order immediately and without question. Now, all of his Hawksfire siblings were suspect, and he was about to trust a fae to remove what had once been a safeguard and which was now a danger and a liability.

How quickly the world could turn upside down.

TWENTY-THREE

DO THE UNEXPECTED

Nym tried to perceive the moment when Erevan stepped from the mortal world into the Otherworld, but she still wasn't sure exactly what to watch for. One moment he and Zephyr were cantering toward what she assumed was a trackway, and the next, they blurred and were gone. Yet another detail she needed to learn about how things worked for the fae in their realm.

As soon as he disappeared, she gathered up Song's reins and turned back to join Aeson and Faraine. They were also staring in the direction that Erevan had gone, as though they were each trying to work out exactly how he was to fit into their worldviews going forward. She could hardly fault them for that, and yet, watching their faces, she realized that she'd made her own decision almost from the first. In many ways, it felt as though she'd made the decision before she'd even met him, odd though that sounded.

"I appreciate your trust regarding Erevan," she said

when she reached the others, bracing for a barrage of questions. But it never came.

"Each of us came into this association of ours with a previously existing set of loyalties, priorities, and goals," Aeson said. "None more so than me. And none of those things just flies out the window when the three of us begin to work together as a group. As far as we are able, we'll try to help one another attain all our goals—mutual and individual—as long as none of them are detrimental to any of us or to others." Aeson had a resigned tone to his voice that bordered on defeated. Nym knew that the Order's betrayal and his own involvement in their practices weighed heavily on his mind.

"I am fairly certain that Erevan has no intention of harming any of us. It's time I told you about what happened after the goblins caught me," Nym said.

As the horses set a steady pace toward one of the smaller villages in the vicinity, where they hoped to resupply, Nym told her friends of the events that had transpired since the night they'd rescued the prisoners. She told them about meeting Tiriana, and included the fact that Tiri was Erevan's sister. That earned a scowl from Aeson and Faraine both.

"What if she's involved in this whole mage-kidnapping scheme, and then when it comes down to outright battle, Erevan takes her side because she is his sister? How do you know that you have his loyalty if it comes to a confrontation between them? I'm sorry to be blunt, but this Erevan sounds like he'd be a formidable enemy, and we don't need him on the opposing side." Aeson sounded more grim than usual, but that made sense; he'd had his share of betrayals lately.

Nym nodded, having anticipated the concern. "The truth is, I can't know with absolute certainty. But I saw his face when he realized that rather than being reunited with him after so long a time missing, she just left as soon as he wasn't looking. *Poof,* she was gone, with no warning other than a cryptic statement about how my portal taking us to him was an unexpected development. He tried to hide it to some degree, but I think he was devastated, after all the time he'd spent searching for her, thinking she was dead."

"What sort of a man...er, fae...person...is he? What's your read on him?" Faraine asked, sounding thoughtful.

Nym paused for a moment before answering, but she'd already put a lot of thought into this subject as well. "From what I know of him, he is honorable, and like most fae, he only speaks the truth. He seems very concerned with the safety of his people, and if Tiri really proves to be an enemy to that, then no, I don't think he'd hesitate to eliminate her. He told me as much when I asked him that question. He has a tendency to look a long way into the future and see a much bigger picture than most people want to bother with—even his own people. He's convinced that something really bad is coming in the wake of all this, and he's determined to save his people, even from his sister, if that's what it comes to."

"A noble fae? One with a conscience that extends to other races as well, and *he* happens to be the one you encounter and make a bargain with?" Aeson was shaking his head wryly, but he didn't sound entirely disbelieving. "And then there's Song. She seems attached to you for some reason, and she didn't have to be. She *chooses* to be with you and to carry you and your belongings. All the horses in that pasture, and you recruit the faery horse."

"What are you getting at?" Nym asked. "All that is true, of course, and I can see how it might look, like it's all too convenient or something. But it feels *right* to me. It feels like a blessing, not a trap. I can't describe it any other way."

Aeson sighed. "All right; I'm not about to question your instincts. I didn't get a bad read off Erevan myself, just for the record. I think there's more to this than we're seeing right now, Nym, but I don't necessarily think that's a bad thing. It's an unusual thing. Maybe a rare thing. But not a bad thing. Makes sense to wait and let it all play out, and see where that takes you. Just... warn us if you have any sense that things are going wrong with your...ah...fae allies. All right, Nym? I just like to be able to anticipate what I might be letting myself in for."

"Will do," Nym said. She glanced toward Faraine, but the other woman only nodded her agreement and made no comment.

They rode in companionable silence for a while, but it wasn't long before Faraine brought up the question of just what their plan was for dealing with Zebermar. It was the question they'd all been dreading, probably more than the question of how much they could trust Erevan.

Aeson's scowl returned, and it seemed to be etched into his face. Nym noticed that he kept touching his sleeve above the spot where the Order's tattoo had been, now completely gone, leaving only unmarked skin beneath.

"At least they can't track you now," she offered, and he gave a start as though he hadn't realized that he'd been touching the absent symbol of his Order that had once embodied his connection to his fellow mage-knights.

"That is good, though it also means that I cannot track them, either." Aeson said.

"We will find another way," Faraine said. "Does Zebermar have a specific itinerary and route that he follows on his journeys from one chapter house to another?"

"He does. It is not something he ever announces, however, as each Chapter is supposed to be ready for a visit at any time. Usually, he follows a set path and schedule, but he has been known to make random, unannounced visits on occasion, just to ensure that every Chapter house is ready to receive any of the Grand Masters at any time. I could see him deciding to randomize his stops this time, given our recent escape —just in case we went to one of the other Chapters for help."

"But would he assume we'd do that, though? Weren't you declared a renegade by the Order?" Faraine sounded confused.

"Zebermar could do one of two things, as I see it," Aeson said grimly. "He could announce me as rogue to all of the chapters so that everyone will be on the hunt for us. Or he could decide to tell all the witnesses to our escape to keep it quiet so that none of them will suspect what went on, and assume we'll be more likely to turn to one of them for succor or shelter."

"Well, since we can't know which course of action he's decided on, we probably need to avoid the Chapters altogether. Much safer to ambush him on the road in between them, if we're able to determine his movements somehow. He'll have fewer resources at hand when he's travelling," Faraine said.

Nym had been looking from one to the other as they hashed it all out, but now she spoke up. "I think we need to take care of a different problem first, before we do more than think about confronting Zebermar himself."

"And what problem is that?" Aeson asked, glancing over at Nym, a confused frown furrowing his brow.

"This Arboricanum thing. The container for all of the power he steals. Where is it?" Nym asked. "And for that matter, *what* is it?"

"It's...you know, I'm not sure," Aeson said, his frown deepening. "Why? What are you thinking?"

"I'm thinking that instead of confronting Zebermar right away, we first try to even the playing field a bit. If we find this Arboricanum and, well, *break* it—what would happen to the magic stored there?"

Aeson seemed to consider for a moment before answering. "I can't be completely sure, but...I think it would likely release all of the stored magic, and then that magic would either be flung out into the world in a general sense, or it would return to the people from whom it was stolen."

"Meaning that if we find this thing and destroy it, then not only might you get your magic back, but it's possible that all of the other mage-knights would get their magic back as well."

"Possibly," Aeson admitted. "In theory."

Faraine went still. "But that could be bad! If it happens as you hope, Aeson would have full access to all of his magic again, but so would the knights who are in support of Zebermar. That increased magic could be used against us." As she finished speaking, Caeros gave a shake of his mane as though to emphasize her point.

"But would it, though? What if breaking the Arboricanum gave them back not just their magic, but their stolen memories, too? And what if it broke any ties to Zebermar that might be on them? How do we know that when he has their memories removed, he doesn't also implant a sort of suggestion of loyalty at the same time, so they won't question him?" Nym asked. "It's just a guess, but I think it fits what we've seen from the man thus far. And it also explains why he might want everyone's memories gone, so they'd remember no loyalties that predated him."

Faraine's eyes gleamed, and for a moment the irises seemed to narrow, reminding Nym of the cat she could become. "Aeson, how common is it for anyone at the Order to question Zebermar? Has anyone ever done so, even the other Grand Masters, that you know of?"

"Hmm. Not that I can recall, though I never thought much about it before. But wait! Nym, if that's something he actually does, then it means that the moment I questioned him in his office...." He trailed off.

"Yes. If he was expecting complete agreement and obedience from all of the Order members, then when you questioned him, it would have tipped him off immediately that you had no compulsion in place to prevent you from disagreeing with him. He'd have surmised that you had intact memories also. It seems likely that he'll have declared you rogue just because what you know and remember would be dangerous and potentially damaging to him."

Aeson groaned. "I played right into his hands. I knew that already, but knowing how easily I tipped our hand to him is appalling. This just keeps getting worse and worse."

"Well, we have a chance to potentially introduce some chaos into his Order," Nym said, earning a small salute from Aeson at her pun. "If taking out the Arboricanum happens to return everyone else's memories of their personal pasts, then it means all of them will know that he did more than just siphon off their magic and remove a few childhood memories, and that he's been lying to them about it all. Any unnatural, implanted impulse to obey him will disappear as well. He could have a full insurrection on his hands, which would make it far easier for us to find potential allies even within the ranks of the Order, some of whom might be more powerful than Zebermar if their missing power were returned."

"That could be a mixed blessing, but given the alternative—to leave Zebermar alone to keep doing whatever it is he's doing, and keep us on the run as fugitives for the rest of our lives—I don't see that we have much of choice," Aeson said, patting Seralo in a gesture that Nym now recognized as a means of self-comfort.

"It might make things better for us. It will definitely

make things *different*—but it's unlikely to make things worse," Nym said encouragingly.

After a moment, Aeson nodded. "All right. Let's do it. Let's find the Arboricanum, blow it to bits, and let the magical fallout land where it may."

"I'm in," Faraine said, her teeth bared in a fierce smile.

Nym nodded, satisfied. "Good. At least we have a plan. Now, how will we locate this thing? Aeson, maybe we can start by having you tell us everything you know about Zebermar."

"Well, at this point, I feel I really don't know him at all. What did you want to know about him?" Aeson asked.

"Just...all of what you've heard of his preferences, his habits, descriptions of paintings he placed on the office walls...anything that might give us a clue as to how he thinks, and what is important to him. It all could help give us clues to where he's storing the magic."

"What if it's in an item that he carries on his person?" Faraine asked suddenly, looking aghast at the thought. "That could be a huge problem."

But Aeson was shaking his head. "The Arboricanum? Not likely, I'd say. There is no small object he might carry that would be capable of retaining *all* of that magic—there's just too much of it, and more going into it all the time. Objects—particularly human-made ones —can only absorb so much magical energy, though they can function like a conductor of sorts when linked to a larger object. Too much energy stored in a small object can tend to break it or warp it so that it's no longer functional. Something about the limitations of physical forms versus the capacity that form has to hold whatever is put into it, be that magic or...rice." He shrugged. "At least, according to my old magical theory teacher at the Order. I don't know if that's still true of objects of elven or fae make, though. There may be different rules at play there."

Nym nodded; it made sense, to a point. All physical forms in the mortal realms had some sort of limitation, so for a physical world object to hold power, it had to have sufficient capacity and affinity for the power it was mean to contain. An object that could hold the combined power bled from hundreds if not thousands of mages? It would have to be a very unusual sort of item indeed, and it seemed as though that might be horribly uncomfortable for anyone to keep on their person, even if it were possible to do so.

"Is there anyone who wouldn't be under his control who might know for sure? What about the other Grand Masters?" Nym asked.

"Don't be too sure that the other Grand Masters aren't in on this scheme to gain power. I wouldn't be too quick to trust them just because they aren't likely to have had their memories blocked. But there may still be one person who might be able to tell us where or what the Arboricanum is," Aeson said. He lost his frown; Nym hoped that was a good sign.

"There was one Grand Master who was a part of the Order long ago, when it was founded. But they retired well before my time, and were subsequently replaced. They went into seclusion, supposedly to study. No one has heard from them since, but I happen to know where they live. I only know because they were a particular friend of Melly's, and Melly used to speak of them from time to time. Less so in recent years, but I think they kept in touch. The last I heard of them from Melly, they were living just outside Trovale, somewhere in the hills above the city. If anyone we might be able to trust actually knows anything about the Arboricanum, it would be them."

"Outside Trovale? That's what...about two-and-a-half days' ride from here? We could make it there in just over two if we hurry," Faraine said.

"Then that's where we go. Hopefully, Zebermar won't think to look for us anywhere near there. But if he does, well then at least we can warn them. What is their name, Aeson?" Nym asked.

"Jarrah," Aeson said. "Formerly Grandmaster Jarrah. They used to carry the Standard of Earth, before they stepped down."

Nym nodded. "Well, we have a plan, at least. Let's pray we're not too late."

"We were too late from the beginning," Aeson grumbled. "But maybe we can avoid falling any further behind."

The trio urged their horses to a steady, ground-eating canter, and the distance between them and the mysterious Jarrah began to fall away.

TWENTY-FOUR

JARRAH

The human-built town of Trovale was of middling size, and Nym noted that nothing about it seemed likely to draw attention. The market square was modest, and most of the local businesses seemed to stock staple food and other everyday items, with nothing too pricey or out of the ordinary, and nothing that looked as though it had been imported from father away than the next closest village. On the surface, there was nothing to distinguish this town from any other, and Nym suspected that if former Grandmaster Jarrah had intended to retire in a place no one would feel inclined to bother with, they'd chosen very well indeed.

Aeson stopped to ask directions of the local grocer, who vaguely waved a hand in a northerly direction. Aeson nodded affably, shrugged, and bought some ears of late-season corn, some carrots and onions, and a largish pumpkin, which seemed to make the grocer a bit more talkative after he took out his lockbox and stashed the silver Aeson handed him.

"Old Jarrah doesn't come down much these days. Not much at all. In fact, they usually lay in a decent stock of root vegetables and gourds for winter, and visit the miller for grain, but they haven't been down so far this year. Hope nothing's happened to them. For all that they're a recluse, they're pleasant enough, and their coin is good. I've always wondered whether they had any friends, but it seems that they must, after all, if you lot are asking after them. Well, that's good. Good. Give them my regards, will you?"

"Will do, and our thanks for the vegetables," Aeson said. "We may stop by again on our way out of town."

"Well, that's fine! Just fine!" The grocer beamed, and waved after them as they rode away.

"Why did you tell him that we'd be back through here?" Faraine asked once they were out of earshot. "We probably shouldn't risk it, even for more pumpkin soup."

Aeson shook his head. "I have no intention of returning there. But if the townsfolk think we will be, then it might just make any pursuers more likely to wait in town in comfort rather than chase us through the countryside. If there are any pursuers, that is."

"Oh, right. Good thinking," Faraine said. When Aeson smiled at the praise, she shot him a quick smile and then busied herself adjusting her reins. Nym pretended not to see. Whatever was going on between them, they'd sort it out eventually.

"You know, I've been thinking about how we might be able to tell whether we have anyone on our trail, and I have an idea." Nym gave the low call that Erevan had taught her to summon Kierok, the raven who'd agreed to shadow her and relay messages. He arrived more quickly than she'd expected, so he must not have been far away. In low tones, she asked him to scout their backtrail for any pursuers, and if there were none, to see whether he could see Grandmaster Zebermar's caravan, and which way they were headed. After listening carefully, Kierok gave a low caw and flew away in the direction from which they'd come.

Faraine looked impressed. "That's amazing. Another new fae-adjacent companion, huh?

Nym laughed. "Fae-adjacent? I've never heard something put quite that way before. But yes, Kierok is one of Erevan's messenger ravens. He does the job for treats and protective wards and friendship. I hope he'll be my friend, too, before long. Ravens are extremely intelligent, you know. He'll check our back trail for us, and he'll let us know where Zebermar is currently."

"How will he recognize him, though? Don't all humans look pretty much alike to birds?" Faraine sounded mystified. And perhaps a bit hungry—thought that might just have been Nym's imagination at work.

Nym shook her head. "Ravens and crows both can tell if a person has wronged them, and what one knows, their entire community will soon know as well. It took me several tries to fix a good enough image of Zebermar in my mind, but once I did, Kierok was able to project the image back to me. I'm not used to speaking either mentally or otherwise with ravens yet, but the more I do it, the more I'll get the knack of it, I think. Mental communication with him at this point is mostly just images, not words, but he understands common speech quite well, as well as elven and fae languages."

"Not so very unusual, really," Aeson said. "We mages sometimes use birds as messengers, though there are other methods we can use. I was going to suggest scrying to try to find Zebermar, but this method seems a lot less likely to alert him, since it won't involve magic being directed at him."

"Well, I hope Kierok finds that he's far away from here, and won't have thought anyone might go looking for a Grand Master who left the Order so long ago. Zebermar's been a step ahead of us all this time; it would be nice if we could have some kind of advantage for once—other than the obvious one of having a fae on our side," Faraine said.

"It would also be nice if we weren't scrambling for any little tidbit of information that we can use against Zebermar," Aeson said in a sour tone. But he looked resolute as they kept moving at a steady pace, alternating a fast walk with an easy canter. Nym suspected that the fact that they were actually doing something to counter Zebermar's efforts was beginning to help pull the mage-knight out of the state of betrayed fury and self-deprecation he'd been in over the past several days. Acting always seemed to feel better than *re*acting, no matter what action one took.

They were traveling into scattered woodlands—here and there a small copse of trees in between open fields of grain, pumpkins, and other vegetables either ready to harvest or just completed. Most of the houses here were made of stone quarried from the nearby hills, and Nym found herself looking longingly at the smoke rising from chimneys. It would not be pleasant to be on the road like this once winter came, and while it was still possible to pass a night on the road in decent comfort, both days and nights were growing colder.

After a while, they turned off the main road onto a smaller track, one of many like it along the road that led to individual farmsteads and small holdings. This track seemed far less used than the others, and Nym wasn't sure whether to feel relief at the lack of evidence that Zebermar had come here before them or worry that the grocer in town hadn't seen Jarrah in months, despite them being a regular customer.

"I hope Jarrah is still there, and can give us some insight," Aeson commented, having apparently had the same thought as Nym. "If not, then we can at least search their place for any information they may have hidden about the Arboricanum. I don't mean to sound pessimistic; it's just that if they were very old, then they might be...well...gone by now. I'm always on the lookout for a backup plan."

"We won't need one this time," Nym said suddenly. Kierok had returned from scouting their backtrail over the course of their ride, and without being asked, he'd scouted ahead in the direction they were going, and sent Nym a mental image of a stooped, older mage dressed in a stained blue tunic, using a walking stick while gathering firewood near a very small round cottage. The cottage looked like...Nym frowned. She'd seen it before. She knew she had. But where?

Then she remembered. Her second meeting with Erevan had taken place in the dreamspace, in just such a cottage as the one she was seeing now through

Kierok's eyes. Shaking her head, she groaned aloud. Every step she took all seemed to lead her back in the same figurative direction.

"What? What's wrong?" Faraine asked, concern in her voice.

"Kierok sees Jarrah, and their house. And it's...well, it's one I've seen before. Erevan took me there in a dreamwalk, or maybe it was a copy of this one, but...it all looks familiar to me. And that leads me to think that maybe there's more to Jarrah than we expected. Just in case I'm right, make sure you do not thank Jarrah directly for anything, just like you would not for Erevan. Do not thank directly, do not apologize, be polite and honest, and we'll be okay. I think."

"Jarrah's fae?" Faraine squeaked. Aeson mumbled a curse word under his breath.

"Maybe. But that might not be a bad thing, right?" Nym asked with a shrug, though it wasn't really a question.

Regardless of whether she was correct, she had to work with what was in front of her. Where one decent fae could be found, others might be found also. No one intelligent race or species were all one thing or another; different people had different motives and goals, varied ways of looking at the world. She'd deal with one problem, one meeting, one solution at a time. It wasn't as though she could snap her fingers and find herself back in a cozy tavern with her lute in her lap, so she might as well be pragmatic.

After realizing that Jarrah might be fae, Nym had half expected to have difficulty in finding the cottage. But the farther along the path she traveled, the more the overgrown brush, vegetation, and even the deadfall seemed to move out of their way, almost as if they'd been expected guests.

When she glanced over her shoulder, however, she noticed that the brambles seemed to be moving back into the trail behind them, thicker and higher than before. Maybe getting in was going to prove easier than getting out again. But she'd worry about that later, after they met Jarrah.

Before long, the cottage that Kierok had mentally shown her came into view. It was as she remembered, both from the raven's sending and from her dream meeting with Erevan on the last dark moon. Round, made of stone, and topped with a domed, thatched roof, it had two small windows to let in light, and she could see a chimney on one side, suggesting that it probably had a proper fireplace rather than just a fire pit in the center like similar round huts sometimes did. The door looked to be of stout oak, and despite the chill in the air, it stood ajar.

Uncertainly, Nym and her two companions dismounted and Aeson moved to hobble the two mortal horses. Song snorted and tossed her head as she watched, then fixed Nym with a glare that spoke volumes.

"Uh, Aeson…Song seems to be trying to tell me that you should leave the other two unhobbled. I don't know whether she knows something we don't, or if she just considers it an indignity, but I think we should trust her on this."

"Hmm. I'm not sure I'm entirely comfortable with that, but maybe, given that leaving this clearing looks a bit difficult at the moment anyway...." Aeson shrugged and replaced the hobbles in one of his saddlebags. Song snorted again in a satisfied way, and she and the other two horses set to cropping the grass—uncommonly green for the time of year—in the clearing around the hut.

Nym approached the door first, peering into the dim interior. "Hello? Is anyone home?"

"Who's asking?" came a querulous voice from inside the hut.

"Nymariel Morren, bard. And also two companions, Aeson and Faraine."

"A bard, is it? What need do you think I might have for a bard?" But the voice grew louder as its owner came closer, and as they moved into the open doorway, Nym recognized the stooped old mage from the raven-vision.

"I did not presume that you had need of a bard, but I am glad to offer up a tale or a song in exchange for a bit of information," she said, trying on a smile. "That is, if you are the Jarrah who was once Grandmaster of the Order of Hawksfire."

"Hsst! Do not speak the name of that ruinous organization! You are not agents of theirs, are you? Roll up your sleeves!" Jarrah rapped the staff they were holding on the ground, and Nym sensed wards placed around the perimeter of the clearing respond in some way.

Hastily, she rolled up her sleeves. Aeson and Faraine did the same. Jarrah peered closely at all of their arms in turn, looking quickly up into her face when they saw the faint purple mark on Nym's arm that embodied her agreement with Erevan.

"You walk in interesting circles, young bard," they said quietly, but she noted that the tense set of Jarrah's shoulders relaxed slightly when they released her arm. Jarrah's eyebrows raised nearly to their hairline when they saw the bare patch of skin on Aeson's arm where the Order tattoo used to be.

"Interesting indeed. You, young man, were once of that Order we shall not name, but you are no longer. Yet your magic is still bound and out of your reach. I see now that we have much to discuss, you three and I. And to answer your question, yes, I am Jarrah, once a Grandmaster, but no longer. Come. Come inside. We will speak of the things that I had hoped never to speak of again. Do not worry for your horses; they will be safe here. Especially with *that* one guarding them." They nodded in Song's direction.

Jarrah ushered them into the hut, closing the door behind Nym, who was the last to enter. The hut was clean and orderly, and Nym recognized the interior as being the same as the one from the dark moon dreamwalk. Not for the first time, she wondered whether Erevan and Jarrah knew one another, and what their exact relationship was. But to find that out, she'd have to speak of Erevan to Jarrah, and that, she would not do.

When the three travelers were all seated on the large rug before the fire, and Jarrah in the one armchair, Jarrah nodded as though a meeting had been convened.

"I would know more of what brings you here, young mage, and how you managed to remove a mark that you should not have been able to remove, among other things. More importantly, I would know *why* you chose to remove it. But you will begin your tale first, madame bard, starting with how you happened to make a bargain with one of the wylden, and why you are under his protection."

They gestured to Nym to begin.

She refused to tell them any details about Erevan, saying only that she intended to hold to her agreement, and that it was one of mutual respect, a bargain struck, a favor for a favor, and no names mentioned. Jarrah's gaze went to the lute case on her back, and they nodded, a sage, crafty look coming into their eyes. "You are prudent, and loyal, I see. Very well, I will not ask the name of your fae benefactor, nor the details of your arrangement. I think I know of whom you will not speak, and I must assume you made an astute deal indeed. Be sure that you honor it well."

Nym nodded. "Always."

Jarrah chuckled. "Always is a long time, little bard. One can hope you do better with your always than most humans or elves might. But then, you're not entirely elven, either, are you?"

"What do you mean by that?" Nym was startled into asking.

Jarrah shook their head and waved the question away. "That is not a question for this moment, little bard. In this moment, you must tell me the rest of the tale that brought the three of you here, with the name of the Order-that-shall-not-be-named upon your lips."

Nym wanted to insist that Jarrah tell her what they'd meant by their comment, but they were correct; now was the time to speak of Zebermar and the Order, and the danger it posed. It was not the time to demand clarifications of randomly-offered, oblique comments from reclusive mages who lived in huts in bramble-filled woods while pretending to be human when they were, in fact, as fae as Erevan.

She told the tale up to the point at which the three of them had come to Cambermere, and then yielded the story to Aeson. As he took up the tale of how he had parted from the order and what he'd learned about them, Jarrah nodded, eyes intent on Aeson's face.

When Aeson finished, ending the recounting with their quest to find Jarrah, the former grandmaster sighed, a sad, faraway look on their face.

"You have spoken truth here this day, and so truth I will speak to you, mage Aeson of Valterra. The Arboricanum is indeed a thing capable of sequestering and retaining great power, and of directing that power steadily toward the purpose for which it is needed. It was originally intended to store power in reserve to guard against great evil, should such a need arise, but it was never intended for the use of the Order, nor yet for humanity at all. I am the bearer of a great shame, and as you have all been touched by that legacy, I will speak it to you now, truly. And you will see me now as I truly am."

Jarrah's elderly visage blurred and changed, revealing slightly less lined features, though the hair was still white. Gone were the stained robes, replaced with plain, serviceable robes of pale blue wool with extremely understated embroidery about the neckline and sleeves. The rheumy eyes were now a sharp, clear amber, and their gaze pierced Nym and the others every bit as intensely as Erevan's ice-blue. Jarrah's skin seemed to glow with a faint inner luminescence. Some of the fae might look mostly human, but there was always an otherworldliness about them, and that was strongly apparent now that Jarrah had dropped the fae glamour with which they'd been disguising themself.

Nym held her breath, waiting for whatever they would say next. Aeson had reached for his sword, then apparently remembered that it was propped against the wall near the door. He dropped his hand back to the floor, his cheeks turning ruddy with color.

"You'd think I'd be used to that sort of thing by now," he mumbled. Nym was just glad he hadn't offered an apology.

But Jarrah seemed to ignore Aeson's moment of panic. "The Arboricanum was built to sequester power taken from humans in the Order, it is true. When I designed it, I deemed that if all human and elven mages were to have their power decreased to some degree, the world would be much safer for all, both mortal and Other. We were at war, you see. I thought that if we could form an order whose members were all equals in power and whose very purpose was to police those who would abuse their magic, then perhaps all races would have the time and ability to learn how to better govern themselves and live in mutual cooperation. But if they would not, then the fae would have at their disposal the means with which to ensure our safety, to protect ourselves against those who would make war upon us simply for what we are."

"You designed the Arboricanum? To take humans' power for the fae?" Aeson's face was pale, shocked.

But Jarrah only nodded. "I reiterate; we were at war. The Betrayal was close in everyone's minds. The humans were bent on wiping my people out, and the elves appeared to side with the humans in the initial dispute. The fae were outnumbered, as humans breed rather rapidly, and now they had elven magic adding to their own magical bloodlines. The Arboricanum was to help safeguard the fae, not create a genocide of humans or any other race. But any weapon used as defense can also be used as offence, and I had forgotten that for a moment.

"I had worked on a prototype only, a smaller version of the Arboricanum that would allow magic to be siphoned from multiple sources and stored until the fae had need of it. But then Grandmaster Zebermar found out about my design and convinced me that if my aim was to make all mages equal and to police the use of magic, then we needed a much larger version of the original design, one that was not subject to the limitations of the mortal world and the magical objects in it."

"But how did he even think to ask you for something like that?" Nym asked.

Jarrah sighed. "He knew I was fae. I trusted him with the knowledge because I thought we had become friends and had common goals. He, too, thought human mages were all too apt to abuse their power, and he suggested that a way to redress the wrongs done to my people would be for willing humans to bolster the power of the Arboricanum with the excess power of their own that they were too unprincipled to use wisely. In my arrogance and at the peak of my ire for the injustices against my people, I believed him. I thought he must surely be different than most of humanity, that he really wanted a more equitable world. I was wrong."

Aeson barked a laugh, though there was no amusement on his face. "That must have been a great day, when you found out what he was really like. I know it was for me."

"I found out the hard way, indeed. After the work was completed, I agreed to be one of the mages whose magic was siphoned and stored, though we did not remove memories in those days. That, apparently, was a later invention that Zebermar came up with after my departure from the Order. I allowed much of my magic to be siphoned into the Arboricanum, thinking that a show of good faith was needed.

"In those days, I still hoped for a way for the war between species to be contained. If my giving my own power to the Arboricanum was a way to help protect my people, I was willing to do it. I did not know that Zebermar would not undergo the same procedure. I still do not know how he managed to mute his magic so it appeared that he had. But mine is a greater shame. I, who had attempted to use humanity's magic as a weapon to hold in reserve against them, only succeeded in putting all of that power into an enemy's hands." Jarrah's tone was matter-of-fact, but their expression spoke of a deeply-rooted sorrow and no small amount of anger.

"I can't speak for humans, and I don't have the authority to speak on behalf of all elves either, but I think the most important thing we all need to know now is how to stop it," Nym said. "We have all pledged to put an end to Zebermar, as well as uncover any other related plots that may be underway. But without the knowledge of what the Arboricanum is or how to destroy it, we have lost the battle before we even begin fighting."

"It is true you are a very small force with which to battle the likes of Zebermar and his followers. But you are exactly the right size party to infiltrate and destroy the Arboricanum." Jarrah considered for several long moments, and Nym had the uncomfortable feeling that they were sizing up the strengths and weaknesses of her entire group.

Finally, Jarrah nodded, as if deciding something, and said, "Very well. If you swear to me that you will destroy the Arboricanum, then I will tell you what you need to know. It will require a Song of Unmaking, just as the original creation required a Song of Making. It must be tuned precisely, and all steps must be carried out exactly as I tell you. Bear in mind that this Song will not work for any other purpose, so do not suppose you can use it to unmake your enemies, young bard. It requires not only your own musical talent, but several keys to which I will attune you personally. Once the job is done, I will know. The keys will unmake themselves once sung to carry out their purpose, after which, they will cease to exist. It would be easier with two voices to call the wyld, but you can probably do this with just one."

"Probably? We're risking a lot on just *probably*," Nym said.

Jarrah shrugged. "Well, then, ask yourself this one question; what other choice have you got?"

Reluctantly, Nym nodded. "You're right. I don't like it, but you're right. I presume that for teaching me how to unmake the Arboricanum, you are getting something out of the bargain."

Jarrah smiled, and for a moment, that smile seemed to have fangs. "I am indeed, young bard, but it is a personal matter only, and nothing that need concern you. I am sending you to do work that I am unable to do myself, and thus you will remain under no obligation to me for my small instruction. I only wish I could do more. If I were able, I would undertake this task myself. But I cannot, and so you must, if Zebermar is to be stopped and all his plans brought to ruin."

"Better Zebermar and his plans to face ruin than everyone else, no matter their origin," Nym said grimly. "We all need to work together if we're to first break things that need breaking, and then mend things that need mending."

Jarrah smiled, rather sadly, Nym thought. "You sound so young and idealistic. Much like someone I once knew well. I wish you success. Now, all of you may sleep here this night, and during the hours of darkness, young bard, you and I will dreamwalk together so that I may teach you how to sunder that which I was fool enough to build."

Nym nodded, glancing at Aeson and Faraine, who also nodded their agreement. Nym would have thought there wasn't much more to say, but Aeson cleared his throat.

"I know that I can't help much with any magical

singing," he began. "But there must be something for Faraine and myself to do. I had a part in this madness too, even if it was just by believing the lies I was told and allowing my own guilt to lead me down a path that I shouldn't have taken. I want—no, I *need*—to do something."

Jarrah smiled again, and there was a sharpness in that smile that reminded Nym of predators that stalked in the night. "Ah, young mage, did you think you would sit idly by while your friend did all the work? No. You wish to atone, to avenge, to right wrongs in the world? Then sharpen your blade, and be prepared for what you will do once your magic is returned to you, as it surely must be when your friend finishes her Song. Do not let it overwhelm you, for it will be more than you are used to. But even before you face Zebermar—and you will eventually, though that time is not yet upon us—you must embrace all that you are, embrace your power fully. If you fear it, it will destroy you."

"That is anything but reassuring," Aeson said. "But I meant, what should Faraine and I do when we get to the Arboricanum?"

Jarrah chuckled. "Why, watch your friend's back, of course. And be prepared to unleash your power upon any foe that attempts to disrupt the Song. That is more important than you know, mage knight. Once begun, the Song must not be interrupted, and you and your valiant shapechanger are all that stand between this young elven bard and whatever will seek to prevent her from carrying out her task."

"Still not reassuring, but better," Aeson said, earning an outright laugh from Jarrah.

TWENTY-FIVE

THE ARBORICANUM

After making a meal from the pumpkin and other vegetables that Aeson had bought, they spent most of the evening discussing plans and contingencies. The Arboricanum, it seemed, was located in the Otherworld. *Of course it is,* Nym thought. For some reason, she seemed to be forever on a collision course with the *wyld,* in one way or another. And if it somehow really was a part of her, then there would be no escaping it, regardless of whether she actually wanted to.

She'd wanted to become a bard. That had been her dream. Perhaps the notion of fame had once colored her vision to some extent, but all she'd really ever been after was the chance to make her own way in the world. To sleep in a warm bed with a roof over her head—preferably a roof she could easily afford to pay for—eat regular meals, wear clothes that weren't mostly worn through and mended several times over. And most of all, even before all of that, she'd wanted to sing songs and tell stories to people who wanted to hear them. To express her true self in music and words, and have people see it for the labor of love that it truly was, and appreciate it just for the beauty and the joy in it—that had always been her notion of happiness.

But fate, it seemed, had other plans for her. She'd used her music to bring joy, amusement, entertainment, solace, comfort, and even to express sorrow. She'd always believed that music could heal, and recently, she had used it as a defense. But until that night in the forest with the goblins, she hadn't ever thought to use it as a weapon. And now, it was the only weapon that could unmake something that should never have been created. It was daunting. So much so that when Jarrah asked her to sing and play the lute after dinner so that they could determine her strengths and what approach might work best against the Arboricanum, she hadn't been sure how to begin.

"Just play whatever is on your heart and mind, and don't worry about the rest," Jarrah advised.

And so Nym did. She began with the lullaby that her mother had once sung for her as a young child, and moved on to songs that she'd found especially powerful or moving—mental armor against the slurs and insults of the townsfolk at being an unacknowledged, fatherless blot on Wimble's otherwise spotless reputation. And then she sang for herself alone, songs that she'd only heard in dreams or tunes half made up during times when she needed to remind herself that no matter what happened, she always had the music.

Through it all, the voice of her new-yet-old lute

blended with her own like a duet with an old friend, and its sweetness and resonance made her want to laugh and cry at the same time. How she'd missed it. And yet, it was a new thing entirely, born of two worlds, its tone richer and fuller than it had been before. She could feel Erevan's magic in it, and, oddly, her own, reflected back to her in its clear tones as her fingers reverently touched the strings.

It was only a few songs in reality, though it felt like many more. Jarrah didn't want her to wear out her voice. But when she was finished she felt wrung out, empty but clean, absolved of whatever had happened before now. Aeson and Faraine were looking at her as though seeing her for the first time, Aeson's mouth actually agape until Faraine leaned over and put a hand gently under his chin to close it.

"It was just a few songs," Nym said, waving a hand as if she could brush away the awkwardness of the moment. But Jarrah was nodding, and she thought she saw something very like respect in those amber eyes.

"You will do, young bard," was all Jarrah would say.

Nym nodded uncertainly, an odd sense of urgency stealing over her, as though this evening had been a respite, and that respite was drawing rapidly to a close.

When Nym inquired about the horses, Faraine reassured her that at some point, Aeson had gone out to unsaddle them, but the saddles and bags had all been gathered close to the hut in case they were needed. It did something to ease Nym's mind, but she was having a hard time shaking the feeling of a steady, impending... *something*. The music had drowned it out for a time, but as soon as she stopped singing, it had returned. Regardless, they'd go nowhere without the knowledge that Jarrah needed to impart to her, so her impatience and apprehension had no say in the matter.

The three travelers slept that night in bedrolls on the floor in front of Jarrah's fire. Jarrah had a bed in a small loft up under the eaves, close to where the chimney rose through the roof. Despite the fact that they didn't know their host well, it was nice to sleep inside a house, with a fire to keep off the chill.

At first, Nym wasn't sure she'd be able to sleep due to sheer nervousness, but her doubt didn't seem to matter to her body. Consciousness slipped away. She dreamed, and in that dream she met Jarrah, out walking in the riot of plants that passed for a garden. Jarrah spoke, and the words dropped into Nym's mind like rain onto parched earth, filling in gaps in her knowledge of the *wyld* that she hadn't known were there. She gave up trying to grasp every word and just let them wash over her, sensing that if she tried too hard to remember, all might slip away.

It wasn't like the dreamwalk with Erevan, where Nym was able to remember with reasonable clarity what had happened. This dream was more surreal, moments of clarity and sharp memory punctuated with moments of haziness and the sense of knowledge more sensed and felt than observed. It perfectly mirrored the impression she received of the Arboricanum—an odd merging of tree, vines and crystal, but with parts that kept moving in and out of focus, as though it existed in physical form and did not exist that way, both at once.

Huge roots grasped and split the dirt of the forest

glade in which it stood, but no other trees grew near it. It was tall and wide of girth, but situated down in a bowl-shaped valley, so far as Nym could tell. In the center, right at the point where trunk became crown, a mass of crystal seemed to have been enveloped by or merged into the tree itself, and it pulsed with multicolored light, some of which Nym instinctively realized was not within the visual spectrum of most species.

She sensed its purpose almost at the same time she sensed its wrongness. Many of the branches were twisted and misshapen, and some looked to be rotting, though others were bright and beautiful with new growth. Dimly, she wondered whether the limbs were more a representation of individual strands of magic than real branches on a real tree. If that were true, then what did those dead or rotting branches mean for the mages whose magic they seemed to represent? Out of hundreds of branches on the massive tree, only a few still looked reasonably healthy.

Nym had barely begun to understand what she was seeing and sensing when a loud noise jolted her awake. Heart thudding, she sat up, staring wildly around the dim predawn interior of Jarrah's small hut.

Aeson and Faraine were awake, grimly rolling bedrolls and pulling on boots. Jarrah came down from their sleeping loft, alarm and fury written plainly on their face.

"What is it? What's happening?" Nym asked while reaching for her own boots.

"Zebermar is what's happening," Jarrah grumbled.

"Your raven alerted me in the dreamspace while you were getting a look at the Arboricanum, and if that wasn't enough, they're making quite a racket trying to break through my thorn wall and wards. I fear our instruction is at an end. You must go, and go quickly."

"I thought they were some distance away," Nym said, finishing with the boots and reaching for the bedroll.

"They were, but *someone*—and I think we can all guess who—has apparently remembered me, and has been lending speed to their horses. They were probably nearing the town as we were listening to your music after dinner."

"But I'm not ready! How will I...how can I...?" Nym trailed off. There were no words, and there was no time. She'd go, and she'd do whatever she could do, but if what she'd sensed just before the dream had ended was true, it was going to be more difficult than she had originally feared it would be.

Jarrah looked at her kindly, even as they were handing her the lute case and urging her toward the door with a hand at her back. "You will do as you must, young bard. Your heart will guide you, and you will listen to that, I think, much better than most. It is in all of your music, and is vital for this task. Now, go. I will hold them off as long as I can. Song will take you to the pocket dimension that I created, and the rest will be up to you and your friends. Luck be with you."

"Will you be all right?" Nym couldn't help asking. She knew what was at stake, but the idea of leaving Jarrah behind and perhaps in danger bothered her.

"In truth, I will be somewhat safer once you have

gone, but there are no guarantees. Do not fret, young bard. I may be without a great deal of my magic, but this old wylden still has a few tricks up my sleeves."

"Nym! Hurry! We've got the horses saddled, but it won't be long before the Order breaks through!" Aeson beckoned to her from just outside the door.

Nym hurried through it and made straight for Song, trying to ignore the crashes, screams and explosions that came from the surrounding forest beyond the thick wall of thorns that had sprung up between the intruders and Jarrah's clearing.

As Nym mounted Song and they started toward a bank of mist that was suddenly in front of the mare's nose, she glanced over her shoulder to see Jarrah striding purposefully toward the closest-sounding of the explosions. There was nothing old or weak in their appearance or expression, only the energy of grim resignation and more than a hint of controlled anger. As Song moved through the fog and everything else around her and her companions fell away, Nym found herself wondering who would come out the sorrier that day—Jarrah, or Zebermar. She hoped it was the latter.

If Nymariel Morren had anything to say about it, Zebermar would be extremely sorry when the job was done, no matter how grim the task looming before her. With that thought in mind, she felt the moment they cleared the barrier between the mortal lands and the Otherworld.

This part of the Otherworld, however, was unlike anything she had yet experienced, being a much smaller, adjacent part created just by Jarrah for the purpose of housing the living receptacle for far too many disparate energies.

The space was at once smaller and larger than Nym remembered from the dreamwalk. It felt oddly stretchy and flexible, and she had the sense that the Arboricanum as well as the pocket dimension that held it would stretch to make room for the growing number of magical energies that it had to contain. But despite that innate malleability, the whole place also felt somehow unstable.

Concern became near-certainty, and she held up a hand to the others, whose horses halted beside Song. Song, it seemed, shared her feeling that the place was not safe, but she hadn't shown any inclination to retreat, which was good. At least, Nym *thought* it was good, since she needed to be here, now, in this place that felt as though it must be slowly tearing itself apart.

"The Arboricanum is down in that hollow," she said, pointing ahead. "I have to be close to the tree as I work, but you and Song should be ready to get out of this place at the very earliest opportunity. I can't be sure that when I destroy the tree, this whole place won't start falling apart. I don't want you getting caught in it if it does." She dismounted Song calmly, and draped the tied-together reins over the mare's neck where they wouldn't drag on the ground.

"But what about you?" Faraine asked. Aeson had opened his mouth, then shut it again as Faraine spoke, apparently having been about to ask the same question.

"I don't know. I'll get out if I can," she said. "But *you* have to get out regardless, both of you. Aeson, you heard what Jarrah said about you facing Zebermar in the future. You have to be in the world to do that, and Faraine needs to be there to watch your back. The Order will need you, too, with all the fallout from this and what Zebermar's done, especially if all of the initiates and knights get their memories back. It's vital that you be there to deal with that. So, if it looks like things are getting unstable and the place won't hold," she turned to the mare, "then Song, I need you to get the others out of here. Please?"

"We can't just leave you here!" Faraine insisted hotly. Aeson just stood there looking stricken until Nym forced a smile and shook her head.

"You have to. Your jobs are as important as mine. There's no other choice."

"Jarrah might handle Zebermar, and then he won't be an issue," Aeson said, sounding torn.

"Jarrah might succeed, or they might not. Jarrah might die today. I hope not, despite the fact that they were hugely responsible for this situation we're all in. But you two must be able to go back and find out for sure. We can't just leave Zebermar to chance, and everyone else at his dubious mercy. Remember, he's a lot more powerful right now than Jarrah is, and we don't know what might be happening back there. All we can do is move forward, and before I go down into the hollow to do this job, I need to know that the two of you will follow Song out of here when the time comes."

"All right. We hear you," Faraine said. Aeson nodded.

Nym nodded at them once, kissed Song on the nose,

and headed down the slope ahead of her, lute case slung over her shoulder. There was no time to rethink anything or change course now, even if the task ahead was monstrous and daunting in ways that she'd never anticipated.

Today she faced the biggest performance of her life, and it was all for the purpose of killing a being who'd done nothing wrong, whose life had been co-opted and re-shaped to a singular purpose. She wasn't just going to be unmaking a tool or a weapon. She was going to be taking an innocent life in the process. The closer she got to the tree, the more certain she was that it was sentient and fully conscious despite the rot and corruption.

The tree waited in the hollow below, and as Nym made her way down the slope, she felt a wave of magic envelop her, as if the tree were reaching out to determine what sort of being she was, and what her intent might be. She got a sense of immense power, but power that was increasingly unstable. Rather than the beautiful harmonies and waveforms that made up most of the wyld, this magic was all hard angles and sharp edges, some of the more harmonious melodies seemingly snared and tangled in a web of crystalline strands. There was something about it that felt harsh, alien.

The tree had become a misshapen blend of mineral and plant and etheric energies that were neither, but it wasn't the inherent shape of it that had so warped it, Nym realized. In part, the warping had come about due to the discordant energies it was trying to contain, for the magic taken from so many different species vied for some semblance of harmony. Yet it wasn't even just that variance of magical energies, signatures and other beings' soul and memory fragments that was causing the worst damage. The worst of it was something else entirely, and as Nym focused her senses and opened to let the *wyld* tell her more, she stiffened with shock.

There was something else attached to the tree, some energy tendril that was slowly sucking on the magic the tree held, sapping the borrowed energies and also the tree's own life force. The energy preying on the tree was twisted, wrong, and—from what Nym could tell—ancient. It glowed with a whirl of colors, but all of them muddled and clouded. Olive greens, muddy purples, colors of blood and bile. She'd expected to find some sort of evidence of Zebermar drawing on the energy here, and when she looked for it, she saw it—a smaller tendril that pulsed with a sickening, olive-green light. It was also feeding on the energies of the tree, but in a much, much smaller way. The other parasite, whatever it might be, was so much larger and stronger than Zebermar that it made him seem an insect by comparison.

Nym shuddered. Whatever else was feeding on the tree, it didn't change what she was here to do. Grimly, she took out her lute and began to play, softly at first and then with more volume and resonance. She felt the tree turn its consciousness toward her and focus on the sound, and in that moment, she was reminded of Dannel when he'd asked for the lullaby his mother used to sing to him. Frightened and alone, facing a future he wasn't even sure he wanted, he'd yearned for some small bit of comfort in the hours before his childhood memories—all the things that had made him who he was up to that point—were to be lost forever.

This great misshapen tree felt like that. As the energy of her song took hold and wove itself into the air around the tree, beginning to sink into the bark and roots, Nym could feel its pain and loneliness, the sense of great age and weariness, the longing to rest. It didn't speak, but she could feel a sense of anger, too, and despair. She fought against slipping too far into its dark dreams—fever dreams they seemed, in some way—and remained on task as best she could, putting more volume into her song.

Volume isn't what it needs, though, Nym realized. What was it that Tiri had said, back in the goblins' prison cell? *A whisper may carry more power than a shout; it is how you interact with the wyld—how you flow with it and allow it to flow through you—that determines the strength of a Song or any other working.*

She felt for the tree's great core, the heartwood, and allowed the wyld to carry her song on the wind that sprang up from nowhere and caressed its leaves, letting her heart lead the notes wherever it would, from the quietest note to the most resonant and back again. A sun that had never been a part of the hollow between realms shone down on its crown, sung into being in that moment. She felt the tree respond slowly, reaching upward to the light. Something grasped her about the waist, and then she was up in its branches, surrounded by all those pulsing, twined, stolen energies.

Somewhere down toward the roots, she heard and felt the shock of anger that came from the larger of the two attached tendrils. Whoever it was on the other end, they did not like what she was doing. She felt as though the grotesque tendril had *seen* her, though of course it had no eyes. But somehow the Presence behind the tendril saw her nonetheless, and the hatred and fury she felt from it nearly made her fumble her notes. Resolutely, she firmed her grip on the lute and kept playing, forcing the intrusion to the periphery of her mental shields.

Partly subsumed by the music, Nym looked down on the hollow from the great height as the moving branches brought her closer to the crystal heart. It pulsed rhythmically, so much like a heartbeat that it brought tears to her eyes. And still she Sang, solidifying her connection to the life force of the tree itself. It was slow going, and more than once Nym nearly lost her connection with the *wyld*, but once she began to get the sense of the tree's underlying energy separate from all the other energies twined through it, the *wyld* and the song gradually began to meld and flow.

Somewhere on the ground below, Aeson and Faraine were fighting; she could hear the clash of swords and the sound of arrows shot at a number of misshapen beasts that she could just glimpse on the ground beneath the tree, some of them trying to gain purchase on the bark to climb up after her. It all seemed so very, very distant, like the news of a battle in a far-off land she'd never heard of.

She Sang of sorrow, of loss, and the tree wept, leaves falling like rain. She Sang again. Songs to comfort, songs to soothe, songs to heal. The tree shuddered and went still, its pain beginning to lessen, even as the drain on its energies from the parasites seemed to intensify. And then Nym began to Sing the melodies and harmonies that Jarrah had taught her—the ones that would pull apart all the other weavings. The words of the Unmaking sprang to her lips as though she'd always known them, even though until that moment, she had been unable to summon them to memory.

Cracks began to appear in the crystal, small splinters at first, then wider ones, until light began to spill from between them. The dark hollow began to glow, and the earth beneath the tree bucked as if from an earthquake. The tree groaned and shook, but Nym could feel its consciousness reach out to hers, even through the Song of Unmaking that poured from her like water through a sieve.

Thank you.

She heard the words more as a concept or feeling deep in her mind, and tears flowed from her eyes and down her cheeks as she felt the tree embrace the Song, reveling in its dying as it had not been able to revel in its life.

Wyldsong! Get them out of here! The mental request was all she could manage as the earth bucked beneath her, heaving like a wild animal caught in its death throes. The tree shuddered again and was still, as the last notes of the Unmaking began to take hold.

Nym sensed more than saw Song, leading the other horses, come tearing down into the hollow. She caught a glimpse of Aeson and Faraine vaulting into their saddles, then one last glimpse of Song, mane and tail streaming out behind her as she ran, leading them all toward the now-familiar wall of mist, even as the ground gave way behind them.

All around Nym, the shimmering branches of the tree were unraveling, all of the energy shooting back along the limbs, racing toward the crystal heart, branch-forms melting into nothing as they came. They raced past Nym, and somehow between one moment and the next, she found herself perched on one of the very few branches that remained—one that had been part of the tree originally, but which was hoary with age and felt none too stable beneath her. A single twining branch touched her, and what looked like a seed broke loose and fell into her lap. Absently, she reached down between chords and tucked it into her pocket.

The smaller of the two sickly parasite tendrils tore free and whipped back in whatever direction it had come from, and through the *wyld*, Nym heard a wordless shriek, though from pain or rage, she could not tell. There was a sickening crack like that of breaking bone, and a fissure began to open in the center of the tree.

She had a distinct feeling that when all of that energy hit the crystal heart, everything would explode, which meant that she had only moments to get herself out of here, if she could. She thought of trying to climb down and wait for Song, but that seemed a futile hope, as there was hardly any ground left beneath the tree. As she'd feared, the pocket dimension was being unmade along with the Arboricanum; of course, Jarrah had neglected to tell her that part. But to be honest, she didn't blame them—not for that, at least. She might have neglected that detail too, were she in their place.

Trying to remember what she had done before, when she'd gotten herself and Tiriana out of the goblin prison, she began the words to a song that she thought might create a portal, but after all the singing she'd already done, her voice faltered and she couldn't seem to hold the *wyld* long enough to give herself to the process. The sorrow nearly overwhelmed her as the tree's great spirit tore loose of all moorings and began to dissipate, becoming motes on the wind that also didn't exist.

If she was going to die with the tree, then so be it, she decided. She'd done what she could. But as the many-colored energies hit the Heart and began to coalesce and pulse in an increasingly insistent countdown, she found her thoughts and her attempts at Singing turn to Erevan, who'd been the first to teach her about her own power. She felt the mark on her wrist pulse in time to her heartbeat, though she might be imagining it as she clung to the side of the tree that was being Unmade all around her. Tears still leaking from her eyes, she Sang. She'd go out Singing. It seemed right, somehow, and as true to herself as she'd ever been.

Next to her, the Heart began to shudder, and the shriek of hatred and anger that echoed through the large parasitic tendril nearly deafened her. The creatures below, whatever they'd been, seemed to have been Unmade as well. She could feel herself also being Unmade, becoming transparent, though somehow her grip on the lute remained steady, and her voice continued, growing stronger even as she felt her life force begin to ebb. Then another voice sounded nearby, taking up her melody and building upon it, adding complexity and stability to the notes. A shimmering oval opened next to her, right in front of her branch.

Come away. It's time you left this place. The disembodied voice broke through Nym's reverie, and she reached instinctively for a hand that wasn't there. But the oval was there, and without hesitation, she leapt for it, right off the branch that disappeared from underneath her. Off to her right, the Heart pulsed, then shattered, crystal shards and tendrils of energy shooting off in all directions. Something grabbed her leg, and she felt a moment of intense pain. Then everything went white, an explosion of sound-without-sound and all colors at once. And Nym tumbled through energy, spiraling down and down, drifting on a sea of *wyld*, letting it take her where it would.

TWENTY-SIX

SOULHALLOW REVERIE

Nym blinked, slowly coming awake. She was lying on something soft—most probably someone's bed, from the feel of it—and a gentle, warm light was coming from somewhere below, as well as the sound of quiet conversation and the aroma of baked bread and mulled cider. For a moment she was disoriented, but as she sat up slowly, she gradually began to recognize voices.

The light was coming from the stairwell that she could see nearby, and as all of her senses began to reorient themselves, she made out Aeson's distinctive laugh as well as Faraine's low, husky voice. Something was lying on top of her feet at the end of the bed, and she was surprised to find a large black cat with a white spot on its chest and tufts of fur on its ears, much larger than a normal housecat, purring and gazing at her with glowing yellow eyes.

As soon as it saw she was awake, the cat leapt off the bed and trotted down the stairs, as though it had assigned itself to watch her while she was...asleep?

Unconscious? Nym wasn't sure which. Her memories of what had happened just before she'd fallen though the portal were hazy. There had been a tendril of something, whipping through the air to wrap around her leg at the last moment, and she had a vague sense of some kind of tug-a-war that resulted, but somewhere in that struggle and the explosion of white sight and sound, she'd lost her grip on consciousness. And now she was here. Wherever *here* was—though she had a good suspicion, and desperately hoped it was true.

Her leg hurt where the tendril had wrapped around it, but a quick inspection revealed that the limb seemed intact, with a bandage over a rather large wound that she assumed had come from a thorn. Moving the leg experimentally, flexing her ankle and toes, she presumed she'd be able to walk on it, though it was likely to be painful. But still she hesitated in getting up. If Jarrah was down there, she wasn't sure she felt up to facing them right now—not after seeing the atrocity they'd committed and having to put it to rights by taking the life of a tortured being that in itself had never done any wrong.

If she had to speak to Jarrah—at least, before she'd had some time to fully process all that had happened— she wasn't sure she could manage to be civil, no matter who and what they were and what they could do. That was *if* they'd survived the battle with Zebermar. And if this was their house, regardless of whether Jarrah was alive or dead, then...she needed some time still, before she could bring herself to deal with either eventuality.

A few moments after the cat went down the stairs, Nym heard footsteps on their way up. She sighed, hope lodging in her chest and making her throat feel tight—though that might just be residual soreness in the aftermath of all the Singing.

Please, let it not be Jarrah. Please, by all the gods, let it be... The thought trailed off as the figure reached the top of the stairs.

"Erevan!" The name burst from her lips in a rush of relief, before she could think further, before she could stop herself. "I'm so glad it's you!"

The wylden in question met her gaze with a quizzical look, lips quirking upward in the version of lightly teasing humor that just skirted the edge of affectionate mockery. It was familiar, and despite the relatively short length of time of their acquaintance, she felt immediately as though she were back on solid ground after a long time adrift. He seemed to have that effect on her.

"You were expecting it to be someone else?" he asked lightly, but she had the feeling he'd caught the drift of her thought and understood her reaction.

"I was afraid it might be," she admitted.

Erevan nodded. He sat carefully on the edge of the bed, which reminded Nym rather abruptly that it was his bed she must be in, and examined the leg she'd bared for her own examination.

"This will heal, but it is taking longer than I'd hoped. The wound was poisoned, and it took some... cooperative magic...to eradicate it and start the healing process. I won't speak of who else might have been involved in the healing if you'd rather not hear about it."

Nym swallowed. Avoidance wasn't going to serve

her, she realized. Truth was better, even if it felt like putting salt in a wound just now. "Jarrah. So they survived Zebermar's attack, then. Are they here now?" She couldn't help the reluctance in her voice.

Erevan's gaze narrowed, and Nym definitely felt the edge of anger in his energy. "Jarrah has much to answer for, but no, they are not here. They have gone back to their own abode to salvage whatever could be saved from the wreckage of their battle with Zebermar, who is still alive and at large, by the way. The return of Jarrah's magic resulted in something of a stalemate at first, followed by a hasty retreat by Zebermar as he felt his magic begin to dwindle."

"I see," Nym said. "I was hoping they'd kill Zebermar outright, but I suppose even that was too much to ask. I don't mean to be uncharitable, but Jarrah is not high on my list of trusted allies right now. Not after what I saw they'd done to others, and what they made me have to do."

Erevan nodded. "Do not worry; Jarrah knows they are not welcome here unless called for. I would relay their apologies, but I don't think even the highest rank of master bards could render the words properly. Forgiveness, if you wish to entertain it, will take time. They realize that, and respect it. I, too, will have to work on the concept of forgiveness, and I may be the slower of us to arrive at that destination. The danger they thrust you into without proper preparation was inexcusable. Had they called me, we might have gone together, and I know time was short in your realm, but...."

Erevan sighed, then shrugged, the gesture so eloquent that Nym found a hesitant smile coming on. Greatly daring, though the gesture made her cheeks flush with heat, Nym reached out and laid a hand on Erevan's knee.

"You were angry with them? Over me?"

Erevan looked down at her hand, then covered it with his own. "Should that be so very surprising, given all that we have experienced together over the past several weeks?"

Nym's smile grew until the hesitancy was gone altogether. "Not so very surprising, no. I appreciate your coming to pull me out of there, your healing, and just...you. How did that happen, anyway? Not the healing; the portal. I was trying to open one, but everything was happening at once, and I couldn't hold onto the *wyld*. I didn't know if my attempt at a message got through, and there just was no time."

"Song brought Aeson and Faraine straight to me," Erevan said. "I plucked the images and location from her mind and theirs, then honed in on your sending, which did, in fact, get through. You created the portal, but it was unstable; I merely merged with it and opened it further. When you came through, part of you solidified, and Aeson and Faraine grabbed your arms and pulled you the rest of the way. I think you left a piece of your flesh back there, though that's now unmade along with everything else in that now-nonexistent pocket dimension. You're lucky you didn't emerge with only your torso intact."

Alarmed, Nym made to look at her leg again, but Erevan caught her hand halfway to the bandage and raised it to his lips instead. "It will be fine. Flesh and muscle we can regrow, especially if you stay here in the Otherworld with access to the *wyld* and allow that to happen. We can continue your musical training while you heal. Unless, of course, you'd rather do that elsewhere. I understand your elven healers are quite good; I'm sure something could be arranged to suit you. Either way, you will be well, and whole again."

The touch of his lips on her hand sent tingles throughout her body, but it was the look in his eyes that decided her. "I think I'd like to stay here with you at least for the length of the human-realm winter, if that's all right. I do need more musical training, it's true. Someone's got to teach me how to play that flute I bought."

Erevan smiled then, a genuine, joyous smile that made Nym's toes curl and warmth suffuse her body. "Well, in that case, I'm sure *someone* can be found to teach you."

"Someone would be lucky to have me as a student, much less a roommate," Nym said, then blushed at her own daring. At the look in Erevan's eyes, she burst out laughing, followed a moment later by his own laughter as he shook his head.

"Someone might think you incorrigible, albeit correct, dear bard," he said, still holding her hand in his. "And that person would count himself lucky indeed to have you around, even if it is just for one mortal winter."

Nym couldn't help herself. She leaned forward until their foreheads nearly touched. "Maybe the winter will be a very long one." Then, making a decision that seemed to acknowledge a truth that had existed long before they'd met, she kissed him.

His hand rested on her neck as he returned the kiss, only pulling away when they heard Aeson's booming voice from below.

"Well? Is she alive or dead?"

Nym looked around at her small circle of friends gathered in Erevan's tower on Soulhallow Eve, the day that marked the death of autumn and the beginning of winter. It was a time of transition, when spirits freely walked the planes of existence and the year's triumphs and regrets were acknowledged. The tower had been decorated for Soulhallow and harvest season; a great wreath of autumn leaves and vines hung on the door, and autumn leaves with dried berry sprigs framed the windows.

In one of the windows was a small pot of dirt that now held the seed the dying Arboricanum had gifted to Nym. Erevan had found it in her pocket and planted it. It seemed such a small thing to be all that was left of the great tree being the Arboricanum had originally been. But the seed, free of any of the parent tree's corruption, gave Nym hope, which she suspected had been the tree's intention—a reminder that life was a cycle, always.

Faraine and Aeson had their travel packs ready to go, but Nym's few belongings were now stored upstairs in a chest that Erevan had provided for the purpose. In some ways, it felt like the ending to a fireside tale, but Nym knew that it was merely a prelude to whatever would come next.

It seemed almost surreal to be talking, laughing and feasting when they'd all been through so much over the last few weeks. The celebratory bonfire that Erevan had allowed them to build in his clearing added to the odd contrast, bringing with it echoes of home and community, family and bonds of memory. It hardly seemed possible that Soulhallow could be upon them already; revelry and merriment had seemed far out of their grasp only days before. But even such a small hint of normalcy was perhaps more important precisely *because* of what they'd been through.

"Nym! You need more wine! Or ale. Or mead. I can't be the only one drinking!" Aeson gestured with his mug, nearly sloshing some out onto the floor.

"Just mulled cider, please. And you'll have to bring it to me," Nym said, pointing meaningfully to her injured leg, propped up on a low stool in front of the cushioned armchair in which she sat, and raising an eyebrow. Aeson saluted her and turned toward the pitcher of cider, but not before Nym caught the flash of sorrow in his face that he couldn't quite hide.

Aeson's face wore a haunted look all too often these days, even when semi-hidden underneath the appearance of merriment. Nym knew he'd be dealing with his own personal aftermath of Zebermar and the Order's duplicity for a long while to come. But he was dealing with it. Slowly, one tentative smile and quiet confidence at a time. So far as she knew, though, he hadn't used his magic, even though he said he'd felt it come back fully when the Arboricanum shattered. If fear was the cause of his reticence, he hadn't seen fit to admit to it, yet.

Faraine, in contrast, seemed cheerful. So cheerful, in fact, that Nym suspected it of being more bravado and defiance than anything else, or perhaps an attempt to will herself to happiness by acting as if she really felt it. By spring, her brother would have been missing for well over a year. Nym knew that Faraine was beginning to have a harder and harder time holding out hope for Jerric's eventual safe return. But she seemed determined to persevere as best she could, and it was clear that she was firmly committed to doing whatever it took to locate the other missing mages at the very least, whether or not her search led to her brother.

Nym's heart ached for both of her friends, but at the same time, it was good to see the calm, supportive way they looked at one another, each ready to back up the other no matter what might happen next.

Smiling, she accepted the mug of mulled cider that Aeson handed her and took a sip, careful not to spill it on the blanket that covered her lap.

"What are your plans for the winter?" she asked when Faraine came to sit by the fire beside her.

"We decided that we'll winter in various small villages just across the border between Valterra and Cymbrona, so we can avoid the Order finding us. We need to regroup and prepare for whatever comes next with Zebermar. And you need to heal fully, so you can help us," Faraine said, her gaze resting on Aeson as he leaned against a wall and focused studiously on his ale. "I won't let him rush off unprepared, whatever else I do."

"That is smart. Do you think you might pass through

Wimble at some point?" Nym tried to keep her voice nonchalant, but Faraine turned to look at her, her gaze sharp on Nym's face.

"Wimble is where your mother lives, right? It's an elvish town? In Cymbrona?"

"Yes, it is." Nym squirmed a little under Faraine's scrutiny. "I was hoping you could perhaps drop off a letter to her if you were going that way."

The letter already existed. It now resided in Nym's travel satchel. She'd spent quite some time on it, writing carefully and—she thought—tactfully, asking one last time for more details about her father.

She knew better than to expect an answer, but some small voice deep within told her that she needed to try, at least. She had the sense that the more she knew about herself, the safer she would be, especially when dealing with wild, untamed magic she should probably not be able to wield in the first place.

"I think we can manage that," Faraine said quietly. "And don't worry about Aeson making any judgments. He knows that no matter how hard we may try to outrun our pasts, they catch up to all of us eventually."

Nym nodded, grateful for the understanding. The two sat in companionable silence, listening to Erevan play music that somehow didn't contain even a hint of wyld but made her feel better all the same. She just wished Aeson could absorb some of the calm she felt, rather than imbibing articifial calm via a mug of ale.

Unlike Aeson, Nym realized she didn't *fear* her magic—not exactly. The magic was part of her music, and her music was part of her magic, and the two were so inextricably melded that even had she been able to separate them, she had no desire to do so. If anything, she would have to pay attention to Erevan's instruction and learn all the control she could so that she didn't find herself unthinkingly succumbing to the lure of the *wyld* without consciously intending to. Instinctual magic might sound wonderful, even enviable, but without control, it was often as much a danger as a blessing. In that, she could understand Aeson's caution, even if she couldn't fully relate to his fear of embracing the power he had at his disposal.

Erevan joked that Nym sometimes approached the wyld the way she might approach a feral cat, desperately wanting to make friends but mindful of the teeth and claws even while the fluffy fur was an irresistible draw. She had to admit that it was apt, and the analogy still made her chuckle now and then. Especially when she petted Moonshadow, the big black faery cat whom Erevan told her was a regular winter tenant.

"It isn't a person's magic itself that causes most problems, nor yet the magnitude of their power," Erevan had advised her and Aeson. "Magic is neither good nor evil, right nor wrong; it simply is. It is what the wielder chooses to do with it that matters most. You have seen what happens when power is wielded to selfish purposes—greed, fear, anger, the desire to dominate. But when that same power is wielded with compassion and empathy, the outcome can be very different."

Aeson had shaken his head and muttered something about good intentions often being for naught, but Nym had caught him later deep in thought, staring out into the peaceful Otherworld forest that surrounded Erevan's home.

Just at the moment, mug full of mulled cider in hand and her beautiful new lute by her side, Nym found it hard to believe that so much had happened all in the space of a few weeks. She'd gone from being an aspiring bard seeking gigs with merchant caravans to a...well... she wasn't quite sure exactly what she was now. A bard, certainly, but one with friends and allies, and no small amount of power, not that she'd set out looking for those things to begin with. Who could say where this new path might lead her?

She hoped for more audiences, sure, and she still wanted to help people and let her music chase the shadows from their hearts, if only for the length of a song. But the path Fate and the *wyld* seemed to have set her on might produce music of a different sort altogether, altering in whatever way it most needed to along the way. All she could do was keep the brightest notes in mind, be they songs of mirth or mayhem, and follow the melody wherever it might lead.

ABOUT THE AUTHOR

Kathy Hurley writes epic and urban fantasy with a dash of romance. She is an avid gamer and crafter, and is rarely found far from a book. Somehow, the fae always seem to make their way into her work, so if she ever disappears, you'll have a pretty good idea where she might have gone.

If you enjoyed *Song of Mirth and Mayhem*, be sure to watch for the forthcoming next book in the Wyld Harmony series, *Dance of Fear and Fancy!*

In the meantime, urban fantasy lovers can pick up *Morrigan's Exile*, available from Amazon, Barnes and Noble Online, and many other online booksellers.